SHATTERED SILENCE

SHATTERED SILENCE

Book 2 of Men of the Texas Rangers Series

Margaret Daley

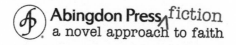
Abingdon Press fiction
a novel approach to faith

Nashville, Tennessee

Shattered Silence

Copyright © 2012 by Margaret Daley

ISBN: 978-1-62490-224-6

Published by Abingdon Press, P.O. Box 801, Nashville, TN 37202

Published in association with the Steve Laube Agency.

Printed in the United States of America

Acknowledgments

I want to thank my family (Mike, Shaun, Kim, Ashley, Alexa, Abbey, Aubrey, and Marcella) for their support. I also want to thank Steven Hunt, Jan Warren, and Texas Ranger Ron Pettigrew for their help in research and brainstorming ideas for this book. Finally, I want to thank Ramona Richards, my editor, and Steve Laube, my agent, for believing in me.

1

No one sees me. They walk right by me and don't even know I am here. I'm invisible.

But that's all going to change today. The woman who has agreed to marry me will be here soon. The world will finally know someone cares about me. It was worth all my savings to bring her across the border. I'm tired of being alone. Being nobody.

I'm getting married. I won't be invisible anymore—at least she'll see me.

☙

Maria Martinez lay flat on the dust-covered wooden planks, her right eye pressed against the hole in the floor of the abandoned house. *Pedro won't find me here. I'll win this time.*

A sneeze welled up in Maria, and she fought to stop it. She couldn't. Quickly she looked through the small opening to make sure Pedro hadn't come and heard her. Her older brother always thought he could do everything better than her. Not this time. He'd never think to look here. He'd think she was too afraid to hide here. A rattling behind her sent a shot of fear through her. She went still. Her lungs held her breath and wouldn't let go.

There's no such thing as ghosts. He just told me that to scare me. I'm not a baby. I'm eight.

Her words fueled her courage, and she popped up to look over her shoulder. Nothing. Just the wind blowing through the broken window. Maria sank to the floor in relief and took up her post again. Watching through the hole. If Pedro came into the house, she'd be ready to hide. He was not going to find her. For once, she would have the last laugh. He was just two years older, but the way he acted, you'd think he was Papa.

Another sound caught her attention. Down below. Footsteps. She started to hop up and scramble to her hiding place nearby, but a gruff, deep male voice stopped her. Not Pedro. Who?

With her eye glued to the hole again, she waited to see who it was. Another voice—a woman's—answered the man, then she laughed. A funny laugh—like Pedro when he made fun of her.

"Dumb. Evil eye," the woman taunted in Spanish.

The man raised his voice, speaking in the same language so fast Maria had a hard time keeping up. Mama insisted on only speaking English at home. Now she wished she was better at Spanish. But she heard some words—the ones he slowed and emphasized, repeating several times in a louder voice a few cuss words that got Papa in trouble if he said them at home. The deep gruff voice ended with, "You will pay."

The woman laughed again, but the sound died suddenly. "What are you doing?" she said in Spanish.

Maria strained to see the two people. The lady moved into her line of sight as she stepped back, shaking her head, her long brown hair swirling in the air. Maria glimpsed the top of a tan cowboy hat that hid the man's face from her.

The beautiful lady held up her hands. "No!"

The fear in that one word chilled Maria.

Before she could think of what to do, a gunshot, like she'd heard on TV, blasted the quiet. The lady jerked back. She glanced down at her chest, then up, remaining upright for a few heartbeats before crumbling to the floor.

Maria froze. Her mind blanked.

The man came closer to the still lady on the floor, her unseeing dark eyes staring right at Maria, pinning her against the wooden planks. She saw the gun as he lifted his arm and aimed it at the woman. He shot her in the stomach then the forehead.

Maria gasped.

The man must have whirled away. Suddenly he wasn't in her line of vision. She bolted to her feet as the sound of heavy footsteps coming up the stairs echoed down the hallway.

Terror locked a vise about Maria and held her in place.

Then her gaze latched onto her hiding place—one she'd found when she'd first come to the house. She'd laughed out loud that her brother would never find her there. Now she wasn't so sure it was perfect.

But the approaching footfalls prodded her into action. She had no other choice. She clambered toward the couch as quietly as she could. She ripped the seat cushion off and squeezed herself into the small place someone must have used before. The pounding of her heartbeat in her ears drowned out the sound of his footsteps.

The man threw open a door at the end of the hall. The slam of it against the wall startled Maria as she set the cushion over her like a shield a knight used in a movie she'd seen. When he'd stormed a castle, hundreds of arrows rained down on him. He had survived. Could she?

The scent of mold and dust threatened to set off her sneezing. She held her hand over her mouth and nose praying that would stop her from making any sound.

As the man's footsteps came nearer, her heartbeat reverberated against her skull, again overriding all other sounds. Surely he could hear it. Find her.

Please, Lord, help me. Mama said You protect children.

But not her prayers or her fear calmed her thundering heartbeats. The racket grew louder inside her chest and clamored in her ears. Her head spun. She uncovered her mouth to try and breathe deeply. She couldn't get enough air.

The door opened, crashing against the wall.

She flinched, hoping the seat cushion hadn't moved.

Please. Please, Lord. I'll be good.

The footsteps approached the center of the room.

Lightheaded, Maria closed her eyes as if that would hide her from the bad man. Something scurried over her leg. Something big. A rat? The urge to flee her hiding place robbed her of any thoughts. She curled herself into the tightest ball she could and prayed, her chest rising and falling so rapidly. The darkness continued to swirl behind her closed eyelids.

An eternity passed. A brush of whiskers reinforced her fright. She tensed, expecting any second the cushion being plucked off her hiding place or sharp teeth sinking into her. A warm gush between her legs and the odor of pee heightened her terror. He would smell it and . . .

I'm going to die. Mama . . .

❧

Liliana Rodriguez sat across from her older sister at the Bluebonnet Cafe in Durango, Texas, waiting for the waitress to bring their sandwiches. She leaned across the table and lowered her voice to a fierce whisper. "I don't want to hear those bruises are from an accident, Elena. We both know who did that to you. Samuel, your low-down excuse for a husband."

Her sister's dark eyes clouded, her brow knitted. "Oh, no, I really did get up in the middle of the night and run into the wall."

"Yeah, after he tripped you." Liliana lifted her iced tea, hoping the cold drink would cool the fire in her belly.

"No. No, don't say that. He's a good husband and father. Like Papa."

Liliana choked on the swallow of liquid sliding down her throat. Coughing, she nearly dropped her glass as her eyes watered.

"Are you okay?" Elena started to stand.

Liliana waved her down. "Fine," she managed to get out while sucking in deep breaths of air that didn't fill her lungs. When she could talk, she caught her sister's attention and added, "But you aren't. Your husband is an abuser just like—"

"Don't. Papa disciplined us when we needed it."

When it rained, Liliana's left arm still ached from her father's form of discipline that ended in a broken bone.

The middle-aged waitress set their lunch plates in front of them and asked, "Anything else?"

Liliana shook her head.

After the waitress left, Liliana fastened her gaze on Elena. "If you don't do something about him, I will."

Her sister's eyes widened. "What?"

Liliana brushed the top of her gun in her side holster, running her finger over the handle. The action held her immobile for a second. The realization of what she was automatically doing shook her. She immediately brought her hand up to clasp her iced tea. No matter what she thought of her brother-in-law, she would not overstep that line. "Have a little talk with Samuel."

"No!" Her tone raised, Elena gripped the edge of the table and half rose. "Don't you dare. This is none of your business." She glanced from side to side, noticed people around them staring at her and sank back into her chair, lowering her voice. "I'll never forgive you if you interfere. Samuel is a good husband. He gets angry sometimes, but so do I."

"As a police officer, I can't ignore his behavior, but even more so as your sister. I love you. I can't sit by and let him hurt you."

Tears shone in Elena's eyes. "Don't do this. I love Samuel. You'll ruin my life. My children's."

Liliana reached out and covered her sister's hand on the table. "You're family. You mean everything to me. I don't want to see your children go through what we did."

"Oh, Samuel never disciplines them. He loves them. He . . ." A tear rolled down her cheek.

"He takes his frustration out on you instead?"

"No, it's not like that. I mess up sometimes and make him angry, but . . ." Elena snapped her mouth closed, wiped her napkin across her face, then stood. "I need to go. I have errands. Remember, this is none of your business. I meant what I said, Liliana. I won't forgive you if you interfere."

Her sister started for the exit. Liliana clasped her arm to stop her escape. Elena winced.

Liliana dropped her hand into her lap but pinned her full attention on her sister. "I love you. I am always here for you. If you need anything at any time day or night, call. I'll be there immediately."

Elena's eyes filled with moisture again. "I know you would be." She bent down and hugged her. "But I can take care of myself. The bank has had some problems, and he's upset right now. That's all."

"That's an excuse. We all have to deal with problems."

"He told me there were signs of an improving economy in the area. He feels directly responsible when the bank doesn't do as well as he thinks it should. You know men and their egos. He's not responsible for what's been going on with the financial market, but he thinks he is. Things will be like they used to be when the economy in Durango picks up." Elena continued her trek toward the front door.

I bet they will. Liliana wasn't convinced Samuel would change. She'd seen too many abusers in her line of work to believe that. Even bank presidents weren't protected by the façade of their jobs when the truth about abuse came out. It would take all her discipline and willpower not to say anything to her brother-in-law, but that didn't mean she wouldn't keep watch over the situation and continue to talk to Elena about getting help. While they had been growing up, Elena had stepped in and protected Liliana from their father. The least she could do was return the favor. Her big sister needed her whether she would admit it or not.

She'd never liked how Samuel Thomas had treated Elena in front of others—belittling her and blaming her for anything that went wrong. Now it appeared as though he had turned physical. Liliana sighed and stared at her untouched turkey and Swiss sandwich. Her stomach knotted. The thought of food didn't appeal to her, but she was on duty this afternoon and evening, so she needed to eat.

❧

"Don't ya think you should go look for your sister now?" Brady asked Pedro.

He looked up from playing war with his best friend. "Nah, I'll let her think a little while longer that she's fooled me. I know where she's hiding."

Brady moved one of his soldiers. "The abandoned house in the field?"

"Yep. I've been talking about it and telling her it's haunted. Not a safe place to go. She acted all scared." Pedro laughed. "But for the past hour she hasn't been bothering us. She thinks if she wins I'll do her chores for the next week."

"When is your time up?"

"Soon. I wish she'd stop pestering me all the time." Pedro studied the layout of his soldiers on the battlefield, facing Brady's.

"Pedro," his mama called as she stepped out onto the porch of their house.

He swung around toward her. "Yes?"

"Lunch is ready. Go get your sister, and come in and wash up. Brady, can you stay for lunch?"

His best friend grinned. "Yes, ma'am."

"Then I'll set a place for you." Pedro's mother turned back into the one-story adobe house, the screen door banging close.

"Guess we gotta get Maria now." Brady hopped to his feet.

"Yeah, we'll leave this set up and finish later. Maybe I can think of another way to get rid of her for the afternoon." Pedro stood and looked toward the field at the end of the street. "I'm gonna hate it when they start building houses in that field."

"Mom said it's gonna be a big subdivision with a pond and everything. I hope there's fish in the pond. Then we can at least go fishin'."

Brady traipsed next to Pedro across the mounds of dirt in the field where they rode their bikes. They jumped over the small stream and plowed through the tall weeds until they came to the two-story wooden house nestled among a grove of trees. He and Brady had played numerous times in the place since the owners left last year. Pedro chuckled to himself. Maria didn't know that.

"It does look spooky. I never saw the door open like that." Brady approached the steps that led up to the front door.

Pedro leaned close to him, put his finger to his mouth, then whispered, "I told you she would be here. She didn't even close the door. Let's scare her."

A giggle came from Brady before he clasped his hand over his mouth and tiptoed forward. He squeezed through the foot-wide opening because the door creaked. Halfway inside he stopped.

Pedro frowned and shoved him so he could come into the place. *What's wrong with him?* Brady wouldn't budge. Then his best friend swiveled toward him with terror in his eyes and lifted his hand to point into the room. His fingers shook, and his face went so white that Pedro feared something had happened to his sister. He thrust the door open and stared at the bloody scene. His stomach roiled. He pivoted away and threw up all over the porch.

❧

Hauling in their last load of possessions from the SUV, Cody Jackson followed his son, Kyle, into their new apartment, bumping the front door closed with his hip. Kyle trudged toward the hallway that led to the two bedrooms.

"What am I supposed to do while you're gone?" Kyle asked as he dropped the box he'd carried onto the floor next to the bed—fortunately a box full of linens.

Cody bit back the words he wanted to say to his teenage son. He'd known this move to Durango would be tough for

Kyle, especially after the recent death of his mother, but Cody hadn't really had a choice, not if he were going to protect his son. "I shouldn't be gone too long," he replied in the calm voice he'd been using a lot lately. "You could start putting away some of our things."

"So you get to run off and leave me with all this work." Kyle swept his arm wide to indicate the box-filled room.

"We were supposed to be here yesterday. This meeting at the police station has been set up for a while."

"It's not my fault you had to stay to finish up a case." His son's blue eyes—so like his mother's—pierced right through Cody.

"Look, son," he clasped Kyle's shoulder, "I know this is hard for you, but give this new place a chance. You'll make friends in no time. You've never had a problem with that."

Kyle shrugged away from him. "I don't want to make new friends. I wanna keep the ones I had in Houston. I don't wanna live in this pathetic town out in the middle of nowhere. What am I supposed to do?"

Deal with the changes like I have to. Cody clamped his teeth down and fought to control all the emotions bombarding him since his ex-wife died three months ago and Kyle came to live with him full time after years of wanting to have little to do with his father. He was quickly discovering loving his son and relating to him were two very different things.

"That will change when you enroll in Durango High School on Monday."

Kyle turned away. "Sure. That'll solve everything."

Cody plowed both his hands through his hair. *Lord, please give me the patience I need with Kyle.* "Durango isn't that small. There are thirty thousand here."

"Yeah and most of them are Spics."

Cody stiffened. "What did you say?"

"You heard me. Mexicans don't belong here. This is our country."

Cody had heard Kyle's stepfather say that on a few occasions—almost word for word. "The United States was settled by many different nationalities. Didn't you learn in history class that America is called the melting pot?"

"They're taking jobs away from hard-working Americans. They aren't paying taxes. They're overrunning Texas."

"Nate has a narrow view of this world."

"Wake up, Dad. A lot of people are saying those things, not just Nate."

"Who? Your friends in Houston?"

"Yeah and Mom—" Kyle snapped his mouth closed and charged toward the doorway.

Cody stood in the middle of his son's bedroom, trying to fortify himself with deep breaths. But his constricted chest burned. He hated hearing his son parroting his stepfather's words. Every other weekend for the past ten years hadn't been enough for Cody to shape Kyle into the young man he'd hoped he would be. Frustration churned his gut as he scanned the boxes stacked around him—a picture of chaos like his life of late.

Checking his watch, Cody strode into the hallway and toward the kitchen where he found Kyle standing in front of the near-empty refrigerator, studying its meager contents. "I'll pick up some food on the way back here."

"Don't forget PowerUp Bars." Kyle shut the fridge's door and left Cody in the middle of the kitchen, wondering how he was going to get through to his son, a fifteen-year-old who resented Cody for taking him away from Nate when his mother died.

Then on top of everything, he had made the hard decision to take the Company D's position in the Durango area. Ranger Al Garcia, his mentor when he had joined the Texas

Rangers seven years ago, had been shot and forced to retire due to medical reasons. The case of his attempted murder was still unsolved. He owed Al and planned to figure out who shot him.

That coupled with Kyle needing to get away from Nate and his influence had convinced Cody coming to Durango would be the best thing for his son. He needed a new set of friends. He was afraid if he had stayed in Houston, his son would have ended up in trouble—with the law. His son's friends weren't in a gang—at least he had not found them to be, but the peers Kyle hung with were the closest thing to a gang without being called a white supremacist group.

Cody snatched up his keys and left his new apartment. It was situated in a complex of well-tended units with landscaped terrain, a pool being cleaned to open April 1st, and a fresh coat of tan paint and dark green trim on the buildings.

Hopping into his navy blue SUV, Cody surveyed his surroundings, something he did everywhere he went even when he was off duty, a habit that had saved his life once when he had gone into a Quick and Go in the middle of a robbery. He slid a glance at his tan hat on the seat where he'd left it, then started his vehicle.

His gaze fell onto the apartment complex's main building where the office was, and he remembered something he'd wanted to tell Kyle. He withdrew his cell and called his son. Kyle answered on the second ring.

"I forgot to tell you there's a great exercise room off the pool area. I know it'll take a while to set up your home gym. Until then, use their equipment. It's top-notch."

"That's okay. I'm searching for my stuff and putting it together first."

Click.

Cody stared at the silent phone, punched the off button and slipped it back into his pocket. The counselor had said it would take time to reach his son, that he had suffered a devastating loss. He'd had ten years to get over the fact he and Paula wouldn't stay together, that she would move on with another man. When he allowed himself to think about it, it still hurt, and if he were honest with himself, he missed seeing Paula even if it was only occasionally and solely because they shared custody of Kyle.

Cody backed out of his parking space and headed toward the Durango Police Station on Alamo Boulevard, the main thoroughfare through the town. If he continued on that street to the highway, he would be at the Highway Patrol building where he would have his office.

Halfway there, he heard a call come over the radio concerning a body found in a vacant house adjacent to the Rancho Estates, south of town. He programmed the address into his GPS, made a U-turn, and headed toward the crime scene. Most likely, he would be called in to assist in the investigation. He'd call the police chief and let him know where he was going. He might as well see the crime scene fresh.

⬡

As I pace my living room, the adrenaline pulsing through my body finally subsides. I drop onto my couch, my hands trembling. Staring at the gun lying on the table a few feet from me, it finally sinks in. I killed her, that lying whore. She deserved it, using me like that. She laughed at me. Me! After I paid her way here.

I hardly remember coming from the coyote's drop-off site, listening to Anna tell me she hated the sight of me. How dare she say I was dumb and had an evil eye. I'm not even sure how I ended up at the abandoned house with my gun in my hand.

I surge to my feet. Anger festers in my belly, as if eating holes into its lining. We were to be married next week. Now . . .

I scan the room I painstakingly prepared for her arrival. No dust on any of the furniture. The hardwood floors swept. A new television set. Sitting on the coffee table in front of me is a glass vase with fresh flowers I bought at a florist.

The sight of the bright red roses shoves the rage into my throat, clogging it. I inhale over and over, but the tightness in my chest threatens to send the fury to every part of me again. Consuming me. Changing me.

Empowering me.

For the first time in a long while, I controlled a situation. I took charge earlier. Me! She will no longer laugh at me. I pound my chest and the tightness breaks up, freeing me to be who I am.

2

"It's been quiet the past few months. Is it too much to ask for that to continue?" Brock Patterson, Liliana's partner and the only other detective on the Durango Police force, asked.

Liliana released a long breath and turned onto the dirt road that led to the vacant house. "I like quiet. Less paperwork. But I guess that's over."

"I'm just glad you're the lead on this one. I've got my vacation planned. Two days, three hours," Brock glanced at his watch, "and thirty-eight minutes I'll be boarding a plane for my camping trip in Colorado."

"Thanks for reminding me. It's not like I haven't heard all the details for the past month. What I don't understand is how you and your wife can consider camping in a tent in the middle of nowhere a vacation."

He laughed. "Jealousy doesn't become you."

The jostle of the ride and the potholes created by the spring rains forced her to concentrate on driving rather than her partner's humor at her being stuck in Durango working on a murder case. Maybe they would catch a break and solve it in two days.

Three minutes later, Liliana sighted the vacant house—a patrol car and a dark blue SUV parked out front. The uniformed officer who was the first responder was talking to a man by the SUV.

Liliana climbed from her car and covered the short distance to them while her partner walked toward the back of the house to check it out. Liliana tried to place the man angled away from her. Why was he here? A witness? Two children found the body and ran home. The six-foot stranger, dressed in dark brown slacks, white long sleeve shirt, yellow-and-tan striped tie, brown boots, and a tan cowboy hat, shifted toward her. She caught sight of the silver star over his heart. The new Texas Ranger assigned to the Durango area. Oh, great!

She didn't like change, and Al Garcia, the last ranger who served in Durango, had to retire due to a shooting. He would be missed—at least by her. In the cases they had worked together, they had fallen into a good rhythm and routine. She'd always felt she'd complimented him. He'd never tried to showboat her or keep her out of the loop. This new ranger could be entirely different, and she didn't have the time or patience to break in a new one.

"I'm lead on this case, Officer Vega." Liliana said to the uniformed officer standing next to the ranger.

"Good to see you. I figured you would be since Patterson is leaving on vacation."

Her partnership with Brock had fallen into a good pattern after working together for three years. She usually took the lead on cases involving the Hispanic population of Durango since that community could be closed mouth with a *gringo*. Swinging her gaze to the ranger standing next to her, she held out her hand. "I'm Detective Liliana Rodriguez. Are you Al Garcia's replacement?"

He shook her hand. "Yes. I'm Cody Jackson. I was on my way to the station to meet with your police chief when a call came over the radio about the body found here."

Tension gripped her neck and spread down her back. She knew that the Texas Rangers often worked murder cases in Durango, but she had never felt Garcia had been heavy-handed. What was this man's intention? He didn't even know the town or its people yet. Probably hadn't been here a day.

"Nice to meet you. If I can help you, please let me know." Hoping that would be all, at least for the time being, she returned her attention to Officer Vega. "Have you checked the premises?" Liliana moved toward the porch, taking out her notepad while the Texas Ranger hung back for a minute speaking to Brock, who had joined him and introduced himself. She'd find out later what the man said to her partner, but for now she had a job to do.

"Not thoroughly yet. The ranger pulled up before I got the chance to complete my search."

On the porch, Liliana stepped around some vomit, throwing a questioning look at the patrol officer.

"According to what his mother said, Pedro Martinez did that. His friend, Brady Roberts, made it to the bushes over there. At least that's what she rambled off to the dispatcher when she called this in." Officer Vega pointed toward some foliage growing wild against the house. "I haven't had a chance to interview her yet about the boys."

"Did she come to the crime scene?"

"No, she only relayed what her son told her. He and his friend ran home right after they found the body. They were hysterical and she was trying to calm them down."

"So the two boys are at the Martinez's house?"

The officer bobbed his head once. "But Brady's parents were on their way home."

She glanced back at Ranger Jackson and Brock striding toward them. "I'll take care of interviewing the boys. The chief said there was a possibility a little girl could be here. Pedro was looking for his sister. She still hasn't come home. Her mom and some of the neighbors are out looking for the child. The chief is sending some officers to help while we check here." She pivoted toward Brock. "Cordon off the area around the house and check the rest of the grounds. I'm going to search the house. Officer Vega hasn't had a chance yet."

Ranger Jackson removed his gun from his holster. "I can help with that."

"Fine." As she entered the place with the ranger, two other vehicles pulled up to the scene and parked behind the ranger's SUV. The scent of blood hung in the air, vying with a moldy, musky odor. Her attention riveted to the body lying in a pool of blood about ten feet inside the entrance.

The woman, approximately twenty to twenty-five, stared up at the ceiling with vacant eyes. Inching closer, Liliana swept her gaze down the victim's body, noting the bullet hole in her forehead and chest as well as her rounded stomach. Pregnant? If she was, she was probably about six months, at most.

The ranger panned the living room. "Tell me what you know. The radio didn't mention anything about a little girl. Do you think she was taken?"

Liliana continued her visual inspection of the woman, dressed in a loose, full blouse over brown pants and tennis shoes, muddied. Bits of green foliage stuck to the bottom of her slacks. "Pedro Martinez, age ten, came looking for his eight-year-old sister, Maria. He was sure she was hiding in this house. They were playing hide and seek, and he saw her going this way. He had a friend with him named Brady Roberts. Instead of finding Pedro's sister, they found this woman. When he saw her, he ran home and told his mother."

"So it's possible the killer kidnapped Pedro's sister."

"Yes or worse, but I'm hoping she's somewhere in the neighborhood waiting for her older brother to find her." Liliana drew her weapon and looked over her shoulder at the patrol officer standing in the entrance to the house. "How far did the two boys come into the house?"

"Brady, according to Mrs. Martinez, went in a few feet while her son only came about this far." Officer Vega, who had been on the police force for a year, gestured to the spot where he stood in the doorway.

"You said you didn't get a chance to thoroughly check the house. How much did you do?"

"I went as far as the dining room. That's when I saw his SUV pull up." The officer nodded his head toward Ranger Jackson.

"Okay. Let's do a room-by-room search to rule out the possibility she's here, maybe hurt . . ."

"Or dead." The ranger started toward the hallway leading to the back part of the house. "For that matter, the killer could still be here."

"Officer Vega, keep everyone outside until we're through and know the house is safe for them to come in and process the crime scene." Liliana inhaled a deep breath and peered toward the Texas Ranger. "I'll take the upstairs."

Liliana ascended the stairs, alert for anything unusual. When she moved into the first bedroom, she surveyed the empty area, not one stick of furniture present. Crossing to the closet, the door open, she peered into it. Empty. She shone her flashlight into the dimness, checking for an entry to a crawlspace or storage area. Again, nothing.

Back in the hallway, she repeated her inspection of the bedroom next to the first one. Discovering no evidence anyone had been up here recently, she backed out into the corridor and headed to the last door upstairs, like the others, it was open wide into its room.

Stepping into it, she immediately noticed the few pieces of furniture—a couch along the north wall, an end table next to it, and a cabinet, the doors open to reveal its empty contents. Funny, how all the doors were open as though someone had searched what lay behind them. What was he looking for? The girl? Something else? Had the girl even been here? Mrs. Martinez had told the dispatcher her husband was on his way home to search Maria's favorite places in the field while she stayed with Pedro, who still shook.

"I wish the walls could talk," she murmured.

Out of the corner of her eye, she glimpsed the middle cushion on the old couch move. With her weapon still drawn, Liliana crept toward the sofa, aimed her gun, and quickly yanked up the cushion in question. Wide, terrified eyes stared back at her.

Liliana holstered her gun immediately and knelt next to the couch. This was the part of the job she hated, seeing a child hurting and afraid. "Maria?"

The child sat up and hugged her arms to her, then rocked back and forth.

The scent of urine wafting to her, Liliana unclipped her badge from her belt and held it up. "I'm a police officer. Are you all right?" she asked in Spanish in a calm, soothing voice. When the girl didn't respond, Liliana switched to English. "Are you Maria?" When the child nodded, Liliana added. "You're safe now. We've been looking for you."

Out of the corner of her eye, she spied a gray mouse scurry out from under the couch and race toward the hallway. The little girl stopped rocking. Her dark brown eyes, shiny with tears, grew even rounder as the mouse disappeared out into the corridor. A tear rolled down her plump cheeks. "Did he get him?"

"Who?"

"Did the bad guy get Pedro?"

"Your brother is fine at home with your mama." She offered the little girl her hand. "C'mon. I'll help you out of there."

"Are ya taking me home?" Putting her hand in Liliana's, the child started to rise.

"Down to the police station first."

Maria yanked away and sank back into her hole in the couch. "I want my mama and papa."

Liliana smiled. "I know and they'll meet us down at the station. You'll see them real soon."

She lifted her gaze, her big, brown eyes glistening with tears. "Promise."

"Yes, sweetheart." Liliana offered her hand again.

The child averted her head. "I wet my pants. Mama is gonna be mad."

"She'll be happy you're all right. I'll have her bring a change of clothing."

"Is the mouse gone?"

"Yes."

The child peered at Liliana for a long moment then fit her fist into Liliana's palm. She helped the little girl rise then climb out of the hole she'd buried herself in—a hole that probably saved Maria's life. Liliana stooped in front of her, still clasping one hand.

"Did the mouse bother you?" Liliana couldn't see any bite marks, but the child wore jeans, wet down the legs, and a long sleeve shirt.

"Scared me, but I stayed real still."

"He didn't bite you?"

Several tears coursed down her face. "No."

"You're safe now. I won't let anyone—"

Maria glanced toward the door, her eyes growing round and huge again. The child threw her arms around Liliana, hugging her so tightly she nearly cut off her breath. "Don't let him get me."

Grasping the girl with one hand and groping for her weapon with the other, Liliana swiveled on the balls of her feet toward the door. Ranger Jackson stood a few feet inside the entrance into the room. Her tensed muscles relaxed. "He's one of the good guys, Maria. He's a Texas Ranger helping me. You're still safe."

Slowly the little girl released her tight grip on Liliana and raised her head to look at her. Tears continued to spill from the child's eyes. "He's wearing a tan cowboy hat."

"Yes. A lot of people wear them."

"Bad man did." Maria backed away until she bumped into the couch.

"But Ranger Jackson isn't the bad man. He's here to help." Liliana said in her calm, controlled voice she used on Elena's children when they were frightened of something.

"A Texas Ranger? Really?"

"Yes, really."

"My brother's always talking about being one when he grows up. Him and his best friend. They play war a lot."

The ranger closed the distance between them in a slow gait. "Your brother did a good job today reporting the crime downstairs." He squatted a few feet from Maria, a smile crinkling the corners of his gray eyes. "But you did, too."

"I did?" Maria stared at the silver star he wore.

"Yes, you protected yourself by hiding. Some wouldn't think to do that."

"That woman . . ." Maria chewed on her lower lip, tears welling into her eyes again. "I couldn't do . . ." Her voice broke as she cried.

Liliana gathered the child against her, wishing she could take away the images that probably would haunt her dreams for a long time. "But you can help us now." She brushed some spiderwebs from the girl's long brown hair.

Sniffling, Maria leaned back. "How?"

"You can tell us what you saw."

"No, no. I don't remember anything. I can't." She pulled away and started for the door.

When Liliana saw the Texas Ranger reach out to clasp the child before she darted away, she quickly shook her head. "I'll take care of this."

He dropped his arm to the side and rose.

Liliana was on her feet and racing after the girl before she ran downstairs and saw the woman's body. In the hallway, a few steps behind Maria, Liliana called out, "You don't have to tell me anything you don't want to."

The child slowed and then halted, her gaze fixed on the stairs that led to the ground floor. Suddenly she began backing away. "I can't go downstairs. I can't."

Before Maria collided with Liliana, she settled her hands on the girl's shoulders. "I won't let anyone hurt you. I'll carry you and find another way out of the house." She didn't know for sure, but she hoped there was a back door in the kitchen.

The child turned toward her and wound her arms around Liliana's neck. As she lifted Maria and stood, she sensed Ranger Jackson coming up behind them.

"Do you need any help?" he asked in his Texan drawl.

Pressing Maria against her, Liliana locked gazes with the ranger. "I've got this."

"There's a back door. I'll show you."

She smiled. "Thanks." Maria was small for her age, probably no more than fifty pounds, but Liliana had been so busy lately with family and her job that she hadn't worked out with her weights as she should have.

By the time Liliana reached the bottom of the stairs, Ranger Jackson appeared in the doorway down a short hallway and signaled that she follow him. Half a minute later, she and Maria exited the house through the kitchen.

Bright sunlight beamed down on her, but a cool breeze made the day feel perfect. The sound of birds chirping in the trees surrounding the vacant house mocked the tragedy that had occurred inside.

As Liliana started for the front of the place, Maria clung to her and buried her face even more against Liliana. She hurried her steps while the ranger slowed his until she caught up to him.

"We can take my car to the station."

She opened her mouth to tell him she would take hers then remembered her partner had come with her. "Fine."

When she rounded the side of the house, everyone shifted to watch her stride toward the SUV with Maria safe in her arms. A few spectators, a hundred yards away, cheered. Her partner broke free from the cluster of officers waiting for the go-ahead to process the crime scene and bridged the short distance to her.

Ranger Jackson had the back door open to his SUV. She tried to set Maria on the leather seat, but the child wouldn't let go of Liliana.

"It's okay, Maria. I'm going to get into the car, too. I just need to talk to my partner for a moment."

A minute passed before the child unlocked her arms and slid them away from Liliana. "Promise?"

"Yes. I'll be right here where you can see me." She settled the child on the seat then turned toward Brock.

"Process the crime scene. I'm taking Maria to the police station to interview her once her parents arrive. She may have seen the guy who did this. She was hiding in a couch upstairs and terrified when I found her."

"We'll get on it. Let you know later what, if anything, we find. Is the Texas Ranger taking over the case?"

Liliana glanced at the man in question. He had stopped to talk with Officer Vega. Ranger Jackson looked up and snagged her gaze. Although the brim of his cowboy hat shaded his eyes, she could feel their scorch like the sun in the middle of a Texan summer. "Probably. We need to ID the woman. Is she from around here? She looks Hispanic, but from what I saw of her face, I've never seen her in the area."

"Durango has about thirty thousand, so I'm sure there are a few you don't know."

"Not that many in the Hispanic community. I've lived here all my life and know most of the locals."

"It's possible she's in this country illegally. Maybe she angered the coyote who brought her over the border. Most of the time they're interested in one thing—money. But you and I know occasionally one will have something else on his mind before he lets his merchandise go. Maybe she wasn't cooperative." Her partner fished into his pocket for his Latex gloves.

"I think she might have been pregnant."

"It won't be the first time someone wants to come here and have her child so the kid will be a citizen."

Liliana glanced toward the backseat to check on Maria, who sat with her shoulders slumped and her chin touching her chest. "If we can't ID our Jane Doe through our normal channels, I'll have ICE contact the Mexican authorities about her." Immigration and Customs Enforcement would have better connections in Mexico to run down her identity, if she was Mexican.

"If she's an illegal alien, they may know something we don't about a smuggling ring currently working in this part of the state. I've heard rumblings since we shut down the last one."

It was an ongoing problem the Durango Police dealt with—like other communities along the border. "I'll see you when you get back to the station. I'm going to have Maria's parents bring Pedro down to the station while everything is fresh in his mind. He might have seen something important and not realize it. I'll have Brady Roberts come down with his parents, too."

Ranger Jackson disengaged himself from talking with Officer Vega and sauntered toward them. "Ready to go?" He paused next to Liliana.

"Yes, I'm sitting in back with Maria."

"I figured as much. I don't mind being a chauffeur." He tipped his hat, opened the door for Liliana, and then rounded the front of his SUV to slide in behind the steering wheel.

After Liliana climbed into the vehicle, she helped the child fasten her seatbelt. For a few minutes she put her arm around the little girl as she sniffled, keeping her head down.

"Okay, Maria?"

The child nodded, wiping her hand under her nose.

"I'm going to make some calls before we get to the police station, but if you need me, let me know." Liliana pulled out her cell phone and called the police chief, then Maria's parents. "Mrs. Martinez, this is Detective Liliana Rodriguez. I found Maria and she's all right."

"Praise God. Can you bring her home?"

"We need to talk with Maria and Pedro. I'm taking Maria down to the police station and would like for you or your husband to come down with Pedro and bring a change of clothing for Maria."

"Why?" Mrs. Martinez's voice rose.

"I found Maria upstairs in the abandoned house, hiding. She wet herself."

"Oh, my poor baby. *Sí, sí,* we both will be down there."

Maria tugged on Liliana's arm. "Can I talk with Mama?"

Liliana nodded. "She wants to speak with you."

The second Maria took the cell she burst into tears. "Mama, I'm scared," she said between sobs.

Liliana's heart twisted at the sound of anguish in the child's voice. She was so young to see this kind of cruelty in the world. Where was the Lord when this little girl was frightened that the killer would find her? Where was He when that woman was facing that man with the gun? There were days this job made her question her childhood faith. As a kid, she'd clung to it when her father had gone on his rampages. That had been the beginning of her doubts, and the past eight years on the police force had only increased them.

3

*F*orty minutes later, after Detective Rodriguez interviewed Brady Roberts and Mrs. Martinez and got nothing useful, Cody stood in front of the mirror that afforded him a view into the interrogation room. Detective Liliana Rodriguez was questioning the little girl found at the crime scene. Her clothes changed, Maria sat in a chair so close to her mother's that she was plastered against Mrs. Martinez's side while Mr. Martinez was outside with Pedro.

Liliana, seated across from Maria, waited until the child, sucking in her tears, calmed down. Quiet reigned for a few seconds before the Durango detective cleared her throat and looked up from her notepad. "Thank you for coming down here, Mrs. Martinez. I just have a few questions for Maria, then Pedro. After that, you can take them home. It shouldn't take too long." The corners of her mouth tilted upward while a serious look remained in her dark brown eyes. "I imagine Maria is exhausted after the day she's had."

"How could this happen in our neighborhood? We only live a few houses from that field. My children play there all the time. I have forbidden them to go into the abandoned house. She shouldn't have been in there. You gave me such a fright."

"I'm sorry. I wanted to win. I . . ." Maria's voice faded under her mother's stern expression directed at her.

"We will talk about that at home."

The child dropped her head and stared at her lap.

"Maria, can you tell me what you did from when you entered the house until I found you?"

"I went inside and decided to hide upstairs if Pedro came to the house. At first I was gonna hide in a closet." Maria peered up at Liliana. "But I thought he might find me there, so I looked for the best place. I was gonna hide in the cabinet until I sat on the couch. It sank in the middle. I lifted up the cushion and saw the hole. I knew then I would win. He'd never find me even if he came to the house."

"How long were you waiting?"

Maria shrugged. "Don't know. I was checking for Pedro through a hole in the floor. I noticed the sun was starting to come into the window when that . . ." she gulped and looked toward her mother, "he came into the house with that—lady."

"Did you see the bad man?"

Maria nodded.

Liliana leaned forward. "Do you know him?"

"No," the child mumbled and hung her head again.

"What does he looks like?"

Maria didn't say anything. Cody studied the Durango detective. Her composed expression suggested she wasn't in any hurry. He knew from experience that with a child it was difficult to press for information. You could press an adult but with most children you lose them. He liked how Liliana Rodriguez handled herself.

"Baby, you need to answer the police lady."

"I can't."

～35～

Before Maria's mother responded to her, Liliana said in an even voice, not a trace of anxiety on her face, "What do you mean by 'I can't'?"

"I can't remember." Sobs tore from the child.

Her mother hugged Maria against her. "She's too upset right now."

"I understand." The detective gave Mrs. Martinez a reassuring smile. "I just have one more question for the time being."

Maria's mother rubbed the girl's back, mumbling soothing words to her daughter. "Maria, the nice lady has one other thing to ask you. If you don't know the answer, it's okay, baby."

Finally, the child lifted her head, swiping the tears away and peering at Liliana. The girl's bottom lip trembled. Her eyes still held unreleased tears.

"You have been a big help. I know this isn't easy for you. Just a little bit more, then you can go home. Did they speak Spanish, English, or both?"

Maria thought for a long moment. "Spanish."

"Do you remember what they said?"

The child stared straight into the mirror behind Liliana. Cody felt as though the girl could see him standing in the viewing room watching them. He stuck his hands into his pockets and shifted from one foot to the other.

"They were talking very fast. Sometimes too low. I couldn't catch everything, but she said to him something about an evil eye. The lady laughed and the man got real mad."

"Anything else?"

Maria shook her head slowly.

Liliana grinned. "That was great. You have been a big help. If you think of anything else, please tell your mother. She can let me know. Okay?"

The child nodded, then buried her face against her mother's chest.

Liliana rose, withdrawing a card from her pocket. "Thank you. If you or Maria remember anything, you can call me anytime."

Mrs. Martinez scooted her chair back and stood, holding her daughter against her. "Are you going to talk to Pedro now?"

"Yes, then you all can leave. If I have any more questions, I'll contact you." She walked the woman and girl to the door and opened it for them.

Cody exited the viewing room and met Liliana in the hallway. She hung back while Mrs. Martinez and Maria headed into the main area where Pedro and his father were waiting.

"I wasn't expecting a full description of the killer, but it would have been nice if we knew more than we do."

For the first time, Cody glimpsed disappointment in Liliana's expression. Not once had she exhibited it to the mother or daughter. "She may remember more later. She has been traumatized. A lot of people forget details until they've had a chance to distance themselves from the situation."

"True. That's why I'll pay them a visit in a few days as a follow-up. I'm not sure how helpful a tan cowboy hat or an evil eye will be."

"A gang tattoo?"

"Maybe or just a tattoo."

"It could be a look the woman saw right before she was going to be killed."

"But the woman laughed after she said it, according to Maria."

"A nervous laugh?"

"It could be nothing. Whatever it was, though, her comment made the man mad." Liliana strolled toward the main room. "I'm hoping Brock finds something at the crime scene because right now we don't have much except that the pair spoke rapid Spanish."

"A lot of people in this area speak Spanish fluently. Including me."

"I know. It doesn't narrow down the search field by much. Maybe Maria's brother will have something to help with the investigation." Liliana came to a halt at the end of the hallway. Beyond her was the large room where there were several desks, all empty at the moment. The chief's secretary/dispatcher was at the counter facing the front door. Liliana glanced at the Martinez family sitting in a group of chairs along the opposite wall.

"I'd like to be the one to do Pedro's interview. I remember Maria talking about how her brother would like to be a Texas Ranger one day. I can use that to our advantage. If he knows anything, he should be willing to talk to me—want to talk to me."

"Fine," she said, then crossed the room to the Martinez family.

He was the new kid on the block and still had to prove himself to the others. One of the aspects of his job was to establish a good relationship with the local police. It made his job a lot easier. Al had told him a little about the different officers and the two detectives. But his friend had forgotten to mention how attractive Detective Rodriguez was.

Pedro and his father accompanied the pretty detective, her long, dark brown hair pulled back in a ponytail that swung slightly as she walked toward him. Dressed in black slacks, white shirt, and comfortable-looking shoes, she appeared professional and capable. When she passed him in the hallway, he caught a whiff of lilacs. According to Al, she was a very capable investigator.

He followed the lilac scent to the interview room and entered last, shutting the door. "Mr. Martinez, I'm Ranger Jackson." He shook hands with Pedro's father then took a seat across from the boy. "I don't want to keep you long, but I do have a few questions for you, Pedro. Actually I need your help. Do you think you can help me?"

The young boy's eyes grew round, and he straightened in his chair, his shoulders thrust back. "Yes, sir. I'll try."

"Tell me what you did, what you saw right before you found the woman. Why did you think your sister was in that house?"

Pedro grinned for a second before he realized his father was frowning at him. He sobered and cleared his throat, slanting a glance at his dad next to him. "I peeked and saw her going that way when she was hiding."

"But there are a lot of places she could hide near the house. Why did you think she was inside?"

With another look at his father, Pedro squirmed in the chair. "Lately I've been . . ." He fell silent.

"What? It's okay. You can tell me anything. I have a son not too much older than you."

"I've been teasing Maria about how scared she is of everything, especially the abandoned house." Pedro stared at a spot halfway between him and Cody. "I told her I don't play with babies. I knew she would go hide in the house." The boy angled toward his father. "I didn't know anything bad was gonna happen. I would never have let her go there."

"Of course, you wouldn't have. Big brothers protect their little sisters," Cody said to ease the tension that was building between father and son without a word being spoken.

Pedro returned his attention to Cody. "Yeah."

"When you went looking for Maria, did you see anyone or anything out of the ordinary? Think carefully about it. Sometimes a seemingly small detail can lead us to the killer."

"Really?" Pedro tilted his head to the side, squinting, his gaze directed to an area behind Cody. "There was some dust stirred up near the road. I glanced toward the area, and I think I saw the back of a black pickup."

"Still in the field?"

He nodded his head, his brow furrowed.

Cody caught Liliana's gaze. He could see her taking that bit of information and running through the trucks she'd seen in town lately. "Are you sure?"

"I think so. Ask Brady. He was with me. He's my best friend. He lives two streets over from me. We play all the time in that field."

"Not anymore," Mr. Martinez said, his frown permanently carved into his features.

"But, Papa, we have a fort out there."

"We'll talk later about this."

Although earlier in his interview Brady didn't say anything about a black truck, Cody said, "I'll talk with your friend again. See if he saw that, too." He would speak with the child in a couple of days. He might remember something else by then. "Pedro, do you know the kind of truck it was?"

"No, but it looked old, a smaller one. My uncle has a big Ford 150."

"Did you see anything else?"

"No—except that lady." Pedro's eyes glazed over as if he were revisiting the scene in his mind. He shivered and folded his arms over his chest. "I—I didn't get a good look. I saw her and ran. I thought someone could still be in the house. I've seen TV."

"Did you see anything as you were leaving?"

"Nope. I was running too fast. I beat Brady back to my house. I was way ahead of him."

"If you think of anything else, please let me know." He slid his card across the table toward the pair. "That has my cell number on it. Remember in police work even the smallest detail may be important."

Before his father could snatch the card, Pedro pocketed it. "I'll remember. Can I ask you a question?"

"Sure."

"How long have you been a Texas Ranger?"

"Seven years."

"Do you ever ride horses?"

"Sometimes when we're after a criminal and the terrain is too rough for a vehicle."

"I want to learn to ride."

"Son, I think we've taken up enough of this man's time. Let the police do their job. I want to take Maria home." Mr. Martinez pushed to his feet, his shoulders drooping.

Pedro left the room with Liliana. Mr. Martinez swung around in the entrance and blocked Cody's exit. "My children have cooperated with you, but they don't know anything. I want that to be made clear so nobody comes after them. Don't expect anything else. They have told you all they can." He pivoted and strode away from Cody.

He caught up with the man. "I can have a patrol car—"

Scowling, Mr. Martinez halted. "No. I protect my own. Having the police around only tells the world my kids know something about the killer."

He continued his quick pace toward his family, brushed past Liliana, and herded his wife and children out the door. Liliana watched them leave, then covered the distance between them.

"Mr. Martinez was upset. Did you say something to him?"

"You don't think it's enough that both of his children are involved in a murder case?"

"Yes, but—"

Cody's cell rang, the sound cutting off her words. He took it out of his pocket and saw it was his home number. "I have to take this. Excuse me." He turned his back on the detective and moved a few feet away from her. "Yes, Kyle."

"Where are you? I thought you would be back by now. I'm starved."

"I'm at the Durango Police Station."

"How long does it take to introduce yourself?"

"There has been a murder."

"Just great. I don't know anyone here, and you're gonna be gone a lot now."

Patience. I've taken him away from all he's known. I hope for a fresh start. "You'll be enrolling in school soon. You'll have plenty to do after that."

"I can't wait. You could have said no to the assignment, then I wouldn't be stuck out in the middle of nowhere."

Cody gripped his cell until his hand ached. He'd asked for the position, much to the surprise of his captain. "We'll talk about this later."

"Yeah, sure."

Click.

Inhaling a calming breath did nothing to relieve the tension coursing through him. He needed to remember his son had lost his mother recently and been uprooted from the only home he'd known. He hadn't shared with Kyle his own part in the transfer. But after a police officer had brought Kyle home one evening, he'd known he needed to do something. Kyle had been riding around with a group of "friends" from high school—there was some drinking. Kyle had been one of the teens drinking.

Cody stuffed his cell into his pocket and took his time facing Liliana, schooling his expression into a neutral one. "Sorry about that."

"Everything all right?"

"Just my son wondering where I am."

"A move can be hard on a family."

"Yeah. He especially isn't thrilled that he's stuck at home unpacking by himself."

Liliana chuckled. "I don't blame him. I wouldn't be either. If you need to leave, I'm perfectly capable of taking things from here."

"I'm sure you are." Irritated that he was being dismissed so casually, he strode toward the police chief's office and knocked.

As the man called came in, Cody peered over his shoulder and caught the detective drilling him with an intense look. He was determined he would do his job to the best of his ability, and if it meant upsetting a certain young detective, so be it. He pushed open the door.

Police Chief Don Winters rose and shook Cody's hand. "Welcome to Durango. I just returned from trying to soothe our mayor. What is your assessment of the murder today?" He gestured toward a chair in front of his desk.

Cody sat. "I think it's likely the killer knew his victim. It's possible she's an illegal alien. For that matter, the man who murdered her could be a coyote responsible for bringing her into this country. He may not even live around here. Maria Martinez, the little girl found in the house, said something about an evil eye, that he wore a tan cowboy hat and spoke rapid Spanish. Detective Rodriguez wasn't aware of any gangs in this area with a tattoo similar to an eye."

"So you think it's a tattoo?"

"Maybe."

"This isn't even your official first day and you're knee-deep in murder. I hope you'll help us. We'll be a man short in two days."

"I'll help any way I can. I've got a feeling there's more to this murder. It's possible it's connected to a smuggling ring so we may be coordinating with ICE. Have there been any illegal aliens recently found dead anywhere in the area?"

"No. For the past few months, things have been quiet. I should have realized it wouldn't last. My other detective is going on vacation Monday for two weeks. We can use all the help we can get."

But will Liliana Rodriguez feel that way? "How long has Detective Rodriguez been a detective?"

"Three years. She had a good working relationship with Ranger Garcia."

Cody came to his feet. "I'll be heading back out to the crime scene to do a walk-through before going home."

Chief Winters rose and followed him to the door. Out in the main room he waved his hand toward the detective. Liliana said something to a man dressed in blue coveralls, then sauntered toward them.

"Juan was telling me about his nephew. He's on the high school baseball team. Made a home run last night at the game. My brother is on that team. I'm glad to hear they finally won."

"My grandson says it's just a streak of bad luck that's broken now." The chief pointed to Liliana then Cody. "You two will be working together on the murder case. We need to get that woman identified. If you can't find anything in our database, turn it over to ICE."

"Will do, Chief." After he left, Liliana asked, "How do you want to handle this?"

He knew exactly what she was getting at, but he needed to establish a good working relationship with her. "As a partner. I understand yours is leaving on vacation soon. I'm new in town and will have to learn the area. I hope I can count on you."

The corners of her mouth stretched into a smile, but he saw strain in the facial gesture. "Sure," she mumbled in a tone that implied as long as he behaved himself and didn't butt in where he shouldn't.

"I'm going back to the scene for a walk-through. The last time my attention was focused on finding either the little girl or the killer."

"My partner is still out there. He called to tell me they are almost through processing the scene. He has taken a ton of photos and notes for us to review. The body has been transported to the ME. They're going to canvas the neighborhood near the field to see if anyone saw something. Can I hitch a ride? My car is at the house."

"Sure," he repeated her word with confidence from years of working with local law enforcement in a compatible relationship. "Let's go." As he headed toward his SUV in the parking lot, he asked, "Do you think they'll turn up anything from canvassing the neighborhood?"

"It's standard procedure that needs to be done, but no, I don't think they will. I believe the black pickup Pedro saw was the getaway car. That dirt road doesn't run close to the neighborhood."

"And it's a bumpy one."

She looked at him and genuinely smiled. "Yes. It has been raining this past month for a change. The ruts were small ditches. We might be better forging our own path off-road."

"I might take you up on that."

"I'm flattered you're going to listen to me." She opened his passenger door and climbed inside.

After he settled behind the steering wheel, he shot her a long, assessing look. "When I said we'll be partners, I meant it. I don't know Durango and especially the Hispanic population. I'll need your help."

"May I remind you of that when we disagree?"

"What if we don't?"

"My experience tells me we will, Ranger Jackson." She flashed him another smile that reached deep into her dark brown eyes framed with long black eyelashes.

"Please, call me Cody, Liliana." Her name rolled off his tongue with ease as if he'd been saying it for years. That surprised him. After his divorce, he'd poured what life he had into his job.

When he reached the turnoff to the vacant house, he started down the dirt road, jostling him and Liliana as though they were on the back of a bull in a rodeo. He turned his four-wheel drive SUV off the path that looked as if it had been bombed repeatedly and headed across the field toward the crime scene.

Liliana held onto the vehicle as they bounced over the terrain. "I don't know which is worse, the road or this."

"The grass and weeds are deceptive. I think it's a toss-up."

She laughed, the sound easing some of his tensed muscles that gripped the steering wheel. "A lot of things in this life are deceptive."

He brought the SUV to a stop behind the house and to the left of it. He threw her a look that remained fastened on her olive complected face, those dark eyes snaring him. "A cynic at the age of what? Twenty-six?"

"I'll have you know I am twenty-eight and those two extra years have given me a world of insight into the human psyche."

"Wait until you're thirty-eight then tell me that."

"Age has nothing to do with cynicism."

"I agree. I think it's the kind of profession we are in." He opened his car door.

"We do see the dark side of human nature."

He glanced back as she exited his SUV. "Which makes it even more important to balance seeing that dark side with light."

"Not alcohol?"

"I know some cops who do. It doesn't solve the problem, just masks it and makes it worse." He thought of his dad, then his son caught drinking with his friends. Only because the officer had known Cody had he brought his son home instead of to jail.

"We do have something we agree on." She strode toward the front of the house.

He fixed his gaze on the yellow crime scene tape flapping in the wind. Maybe Durango would be more interesting than he'd originally thought. The first day certainly had proven to be.

෬෬

I look through the binoculars at the medium-size man strolling up to his house. There's a swagger to his walk. Like he is the king of the hill or at least the territory between Durango and the border. No one is going to touch him.

But I can. I control if he lives or dies.

I'll wait until dark then make my move. No mistakes from now on.

An hour later as I creep toward the house with several cars parked out front in various stages of repair, my hands sweat. I wipe them on my pants then tighten my grip on my gun. I peer into the dirty window and see the coyote lounging in a chair with a beer in his hand, watching TV. A couple more beer cans litter the table next to him and spill over onto the floor around him. The man's head lolls to the side and the can slips from his fingers. It drops to the carpet, liquid gushing from the container. Perfect.

I make my way to the back door and jimmy it open, then sneak inside, treading lightly toward the living room where the man still sleeps in his lounger. I take my gun and turn it so I can use the handle as a weapon. Nearing the chair, I feel a surge of adrenaline calm any anxiety I have about carrying out my plan. I control this.

I bring the handle of the gun down on the coyote's head. Just one strike. Enough to knock him out until I subdue him.

Within a few minutes, I have checked to make sure he is alive and tied him to the chair. Then I wait. I have time. He doesn't.

I walk to the blinds and draw them. Outside, darkness has started to fall. Before the man regains consciousness, I start my search of his house. I want my money back, and I want information. I will have answers to who the coyote told about me, who Anna might have told about me. But mostly who was the father of Anna's child. He will tell me. The only thing he controls now is how much pain I inflict on him before I kill him.

❧

Sweat pouring off him, Kyle plopped down on his bare mattress in his new bedroom. He wiped the towel down his face, then tossed it to the floor. His sore muscles screamed their protest at the grueling workout he'd just completed. Even though he had pushed himself until he couldn't lift another weight, anger still banded his chest and contracted it, causing each breath he took in to hurt.

I hate Durango. I don't wanna be here.

He clenched his hands into fists and pounded his mattress in frustration. Still the fury gripped him. No control over his life. He had to do what his dad wanted him to do.

Dad doesn't care what I want. It's all about what he wants. I hate him.

Kyle bolted to his feet and searched the stack of boxes still packed in his room. Finally, he saw the cell he'd left on the top of one of the cartons.

Maybe I can do something about that. He punched in his stepfather's number in Houston and waited.

"Kyle, how are you doing? Are you in Durango now?" Nate asked when he answered the phone.

"I want to come home." His words barely made it past the lump in his throat. Men did not cry. Nate would be disappointed if he did.

A heavy sigh sounded, followed by Nate saying, "I wish you could, but your father has total custody of you now. I tried to keep you with me, but he wouldn't let me. You're his son."

"No, I'm not. I'm your son. He doesn't love me. He doesn't understand me."

"I miss seeing you. Maybe this summer you'll be able to come visit."

"I hope so."

"Starting school on Monday?"

"Yeah?"

"Then you can meet some friends. That'll make it better."

"I doubt it. Too many of *them* are here."

"Being so near the border, that's what I was afraid of. Houston isn't much better. Remember it's not much longer until you'll be able to do what you want. You'll be sixteen soon, and before you know it, you'll become a young man living on your own. Hang in there and call when you need a friend to listen."

The lump in Kyle's throat swelled. He swallowed several times but couldn't dislodge it. "Thanks," he finally murmured, his voice wavering. He winced and coughed. "On top of everything else, my allergies are worse with all this dust around here. It's so dry."

"We'll make June work. You can go camping with me and the boys. Practice target shooting some more."

"I'd like that."

When Kyle disconnected, he placed the cell on the box and began tearing into the cartons, searching for his punching bag. He needed it before he destroyed something.

⤫

Standing in the field behind the coyote's house, I watch as it burns, the dead man sitting in the lounger where I left him tied up. He didn't last as long as I thought he would for such a tough macho man. The shock on the coyote's face was priceless, especially in the end when I finished him off. But not before I got my money and the names I wanted.

In the early morning dawn, the sound of sirens in the distance signal that it's time to leave. With one last glance at the flames consuming any evidence of my presence in the house, I walk away, my steps light for the first time in years, my spirit full of hope. I'll be able to contain the mistake from my earlier moment of passion yesterday morning with Anna.

4

*A*ll around Liliana, darkness let go of its hold on the day. She lengthened her strides, the sound of her running shoes hitting the pavement almost soothing—until the blare of sirens disturbed the rhythm of her jogging pace. She slowed her gait and scanned the sky. In the distance, she spied the plume of dark gray smoke mushroom into the air, threatening to return the sky to predawn dimness.

Liliana reached her turnaround point and started toward her house, the murder case yesterday hounding each step. Who was Jane Doe? Why was she killed? About all they had was: an old black truck leaving the field, the killer wore a tan cowboy hat and spoke Spanish, the gun was a .38 and something about an evil eye. What, she wasn't sure.

When she reached her front yard, she paced while downing half a bottle of water. The first rays of the sun peeked over the horizon. She turned in the direction of the fire and found the smoke in the air diminished although its scent lingered on the breeze. Durango didn't need a brush fire. It might have rained some this month, but it was still too dry. It wouldn't take much to have a real problem with a wildfire getting completely out of control.

Inside, she quickly took a shower and headed for her kitchen and her usual breakfast of peanut butter on a banana with a cup of strong black coffee. As she ate, she thought of what she needed to get done that day. She wanted to revisit the crime scene. Although she and Cody had gone through it again yesterday, she couldn't accept there wasn't a piece of evidence somewhere. Maria's description of the murder reinforced her feeling the crime was a spur-of-the-moment decision, one of passion. The way he'd shot Jane Doe supported that—overkill.

Liliana rose to refill her mug, but the ringing phone detoured her steps to the stove. She snatched her cell from her purse on the desk and said, "Yes, Chief?"

"The fire captain called me a few minutes ago and reported a dead body in a chair in the living room. It's still too hot to go into the house, but he thinks it's murder."

"Why?"

"Because the man in the chair was bound with barbwire. Someone wanted our victim to suffer." The chief gave her the address.

"When can I get into the house?"

"Not until the fire department gives me the go-ahead, but you might go to the site and see what you can find until then."

When she clicked off, she thought of calling the new Texas Ranger but decided not to. She didn't know what was going on yet. Let him sleep in, and she'd call him later.

⨮⨭

"Two murders in two days?" Half an hour later, Cody stopped next to Liliana outside the charred ruins of a one-story house.

"Who called you?"

"Not you."

She slanted a look at him. "Sorry. I thought you might need your beauty sleep."

He grinned. "I'm touched you would think of my well-being. We only met yesterday."

"At the first murder scene. We need to stop meeting like this."

"As the scene goes, there isn't much we can do until the house is declared safe."

"But we can start talking to the neighbors." Liliana scanned the few homes on the street at the edge of town, conveniently isolated for the killer.

Although the places on Javelin Road sat on half-acre lots, they all needed a coat of paint, massive cleanup in the yards, and rotten boards replaced in their wooden houses—except the one directly across the street from the victim's.

"And find out all we can about Victor Ruiz." Cody took several steps closer to the smoldering structure, small wisps of smoke trailing upward from the charred pieces of the house. "Someone wanted to make sure *Señor* Ruiz died this morning." He rotated toward Liliana. "Do you know anyone who lives on this street?"

She gestured toward the house directly across from the burned one. "Yes, *Señora* Emilia. She is a friend of my mother's. I think we should start with her."

As Liliana approached *Señora* Emilia's, the living room curtains moved as though someone had been looking outside and stepped away. Liliana smiled, picturing her mother's friend avidly following the commotion across the street. She was the poster person for the Neighborhood Watch.

Before Liliana had a chance to knock on the front door, it swung open about a foot and *Señora* Emilia poked her head through the gap. "Liliana, I was expecting you . . ." The older woman's voice faded into the silence of an unspoken "but" as she studied Cody behind Liliana.

He leaned toward her. "I'm going to interview some of the other neighbors. I'll see you in a while at the crime scene."

Liliana nodded, his departure another reason she was beginning to like the man. He knew when to disappear and let someone else do the job. *Señora* Emilia opened the door wider and moved to the side to allow Liliana into the house while Cody descended the porch steps and strolled toward the place next door.

"He's taken over for *Señor* Garcia, yes?"

"*Sí.*" Liliana trailed the family friend into her living room and took a chair across from the couch where *Señora* Emilia sat. The smells of baking bread and cinnamon teased her senses. Her mouth watered. "Did you make your cinnamon rolls?"

"*Sí.* I can get you one if you're hungry."

"No, I had breakfast, but I wish I could bottle that scent." For a moment, the aroma masked the odor of the fire, the stench of death.

"How is it going? Your mama didn't tell me about this new ranger."

"That's because I haven't said anything to her. He wasn't supposed to be starting till Monday."

"But the murder yesterday changed everything, yes?"

"Can you tell me anything about your neighbor, Victor Ruiz?"

Dressed in a flowered smock, *Señora* Emilia smoothed her hand over her perfectly styled black hair, her forehead creased. "*El bandido.*"

Liliana waited a moment for her to elaborate on her comment, but when all she did was deepen her frown, Liliana asked, "Why do you say that?"

"When he looked at me, I saw evil." The older woman shivered and folded her arms across her chest.

Evil eye? "Has he done anything bad you know about?" *Señora* Emilia liked to gossip with Mama, but she didn't spread unfounded rumors. Liliana had come to respect her keen observation of people.

"*Mal hombre* coming all the time to his casa." *Señora* Emilia's eyes fastened onto Liliana's, fear reflected in the dark depths. "I know I shouldn't feel this way. Our Father wouldn't approve, but I am glad *Señor* Ruiz is gone. It doesn't surprise me he was murdered with the kind of company he kept."

Liliana scooted to the edge of her chair. "Murdered? I didn't say he was. Why did you say that?"

"Because Carla called me and told me. Her son overheard the firemen talking about finding a dead man tied up in the house."

"Carla lives on Javelin Road?"

"*Sí*, her son was leaving for work and saw the fire. He called it in. I'm glad he did. My house could have caught fire, too. Fire department got here fast, yes?"

"I agree. I've seen a fire like that spread to other houses because of the winds."

"Too dry here. I still remember my cousin in Fort Davis almost getting caught in that wildfire a while back. Burned his place down. Nothing left."

"*Señora* Emilia, what is Carla's son's name?"

"Luis Morales. A good son. A bit shy. But he did good today."

"Where does he work?"

"The hospital. He's an orderly."

Liliana rose, went to the closed curtains, and pulled them open. "Do you see him out in the crowd?"

Señora Emilia pushed herself to her feet and covered the distance between them. Squinting, she studied the people from the neighborhood milling around, several small clusters huddled together, arms gesturing as they talked. "*Espere un momento.*"

Her mother's friend scurried toward a cabinet and retrieved a pair of binoculars. At the window she used them to survey the crowd. "No. He's not there."

Liliana imagined *Señora* Emilia doing that often, at least according to her mother. "Which one is Carla's house?"

"Luis wouldn't have gone home. He would have gone on to work. He is very good worker. When I was in the hospital for a couple of days last fall, he took great care of me. It's just such a shame others don't see how special he is."

"I'd like to talk to Carla, too."

"Oh. It's at the end of the block. The brown one without rusted cars or junk stacked in the yard. I will not be sorry to see *Señor* Ruiz's cleaned up. He'd only lived here four months and look at the trash." The older woman shook her head, tsking.

That explained why she didn't know much about Victor Ruiz. He was relatively new to town. "Does he have family?"

"A lot of people came and went from his place at all hours of the day and night, but I don't think so. At least not here. He came from Brownsville."

Liliana removed a business card from her pocket and fit it into the woman's palm. "In case you don't have my number at the police station. If you remember anything about Victor Ruiz, *Señora* Emilia, please call me."

"We have been fortunate to avoid the violence other communities in the area have experienced. We are in for trouble, yes? I live alone and—"

Liliana clasped *Señora* Emilia's arms. "Not if I have anything to do about it. If you get worried or see anything that concerns you, call me. I'll be over."

Her mother's friend patted Liliana's hand. "You are a good daughter for your mama." A twinkle sparkled in her dark eyes. "Carla has been looking for a young woman for her son. You could do worse. Any man who loves his mama like he does would make a good husband."

"I'm past the prime age to marry."

Señora Emilia giggled. "I've heard it all. Who told you that?"

"Mama, just this week—*again*."

"I will deny I said this, but don't listen to your mama. You have a few good years left to marry and have *bebes*. You are twenty-five or six, yes?"

Liliana started for the hallway. "No, twenty-eight."

"Well, in that case, when you talk with Luis, keep in mind he has plans besides being an orderly all his life."

"I will, *Señora* Emilia. *Gracias*."

When she left the house, Liliana stood on the porch for a moment and scoured the area for anything or anyone out of place. Nothing, other than the torched house and the partially burnt detached garage. Even the people were returning to their homes as the sun climbed higher on the eastern horizon.

She started toward Carla Morales's house at the end of the block, spying Cody standing on a porch talking to a man who was shaking his head. Cody gave the neighbor a card right before he slammed the door in Cody's face. He pivoted, a glimpse of a grimace beneath the shadow of his cowboy hat. He spied her and came toward her.

"I've struck out. No one saw a thing. That one," he tossed his head toward the last house he'd been at, "doesn't even admit to seeing the fire. How about you?"

"Not much better. *Señora* Emilia did share with me that Victor Ruiz was a 'bad man.' Lowlifes visited the victim at all times of the day. Ruiz hadn't been in Durango long and was from Brownsville. He wasn't on the police radar yet." She resumed her strides toward Carla's house. "She did say one thing that was interesting. That when Victor looks at you, it's evil. That made me think of what Maria said about the evil eye. You think these murders are connected? What if Victor killed our Jane Doe?"

"Then who killed him?"

"The father of her baby?" The ME had confirmed Jane Doe had been pregnant.

"Maybe. Where are you going?"

"*Señora* Emilia told me that the man who called in the fire was Luis Morales. She knew about the murdered man without me saying anything because Luis told his mother about the dead body in the house. Luis is at the hospital. He's an orderly, but I thought I would talk to his mother before seeing him." Liliana stopped in front of Carla's neatly tended place. "This is where she lives."

"I'll go to the hospital and talk with the son while you interview Mrs. Morales. When I'm through, I'll be back. Hopefully by then the fire department will let us go into the crime scene."

"Our fire investigator has been busy in the past year with all the wildfires around here."

"Arson?" asked Cody.

"Most have started from carelessness. He says arson is the cause of one of the fires he's looking into."

"I'll be back after I speak with Luis Morales."

Liliana hadn't intended to turn and watch Cody walk toward his SUV, but something drew her. His strides were long, nothing wasted about his movements. Wearing the ranger's usual attire of slacks, dress shirt, and tie, coupled with his cowboy boots and hat, the man looked impressive. Strong features with gray eyes the color of a brewing storm. Solidly built, not an ounce of fat on him. His tan and crinkles at the corners of his eyes attested to his time spent outdoors. She couldn't imagine a man like Cody Jackson lying in a tanning bed.

As his vehicle pulled away from the curb near the crime scene, Liliana swept around and strolled toward Carla Morales's house. But after she took a couple of steps, her cell rang. She smiled as she answered the call from the very man she'd been admiring.

"I forgot to ask you. Have you had breakfast yet?"

His husky Texan drawl sent a flash of warmth through Liliana. "Yes, but not enough coffee yet. Only one cup. The things I do for my job."

He chuckled. "You need to let Chief Winters know about these sacrifices you make for the job. I'll vouch for you."

"He already knows. This is a small town. We almost don't need the *Durango Daily*."

"Almost?"

"I love the funnies, the food section, and the puzzles."

"Interesting picture that draws of you."

His voice held a teasing, light tone that sent her pulse rate up. "I'm not even going to ask what."

"On the way back from the hospital, I thought I'd stop and pick up something to eat and drink. Do you want me to get you some coffee?"

"Where are you going?" Liliana continued toward the front door.

"I could stop at our friendly fast-food restaurant or do you have a suggestion that's better?"

"Mom's Cafe on Alamo Boulevard. It isn't too far from the police station or the hospital. About halfway between them."

"What's the specialty?"

"Everything. I'll take the largest cup of coffee they have."

"Will you be okay until I get back? I wouldn't want you to fall asleep on the job."

She looked toward the burnt house. "I'll manage. I want to talk with the firefighters after I speak with Mrs. Morales."

"See you in about an hour."

By the time she reached the porch, she received another call and half expected it to be Cody again. But when she glanced at the number, she closed her eyes for a few seconds then answered. "Hi, Mama."

"Are you coming by for lunch today?"

Most Saturdays she had lunch with her mother. "Sorry. I'm at a crime scene and will probably be tied up for most of the day."

"What happened?"

"Arson and a dead body."

"Another murder?" Her mother spoke in a high-pitched voice.

Liliana heard the concern and hurriedly said, "But you don't need to worry. We'll find out who did this." *I hope.*

"Weren't you supposed to have this weekend off?"

Liliana pressed the doorbell. "Criminals don't care what day it is and with Brock leaving early tomorrow I'm the only one responsible." She would explain about the new Texas Ranger later. Knowing her mother, she'd get the drill. She didn't have time now for it. Liliana checked her watch that read eight twenty. Surely, the woman was awake since she'd called to tell *Señora* Emilia about the fire. The lock clicked, and the door started swinging open. "Gotta go, Mama. I have people I need to interview. Sorry about lunch. I'll take you next week."

As the woman peeked outside, Liliana plastered a smile on her face and held up her badge. "*Señora* Morales, I'm Detective

Rodriguez and I have some questions I need to ask you about the fire."

The petite lady gripped the wooden frame and frowned. "I don't know nothing. I was asleep when it happened." Then she slammed the door.

∽᷎᷎

Kyle stood in the entrance to the gym at the apartment complex and took in all the weight equipment. For once, his dad had been right. Much better than what he had.

"Hi, are you new here?" a soft feminine voice said behind him.

"Yeah," he replied, glancing over his shoulder to see who it was. His gaze locked with the darkest brown eyes, large and round, with long, long black eyelashes. Beautiful eyes.

Then she smiled and transformed her average features into a look of radiance. "I'm Serena. I live in 156."

He wrenched his attention from her face, and it fell onto the wheelchair she sat in, one hand on the wheel. "I'm Kyle," he managed to get out, his words thready. Questions scrambled his thoughts until he couldn't think of anything to say.

Serena cleared her throat, peering around him, her long ponytail swinging with her movement. "You're blocking my way."

He blinked. "You want to come in here?" He jerked his thumb toward the room behind him with all the exercise equipment.

Her gaze fell to her lap, drawing his focus to the fact she was dressed in workout clothes with sweatbands around her wrists. "I use the gym every day, trying to get into shape to race."

"Race? How? You are . . ." Heat blazed a path across his face, and before he made a total fool of himself, he stepped out of the doorway to let her pass him.

She rolled herself into the room then looked back at him with that dazzling smile on her face. "I've challenged myself to participate in a wheelchair race in San Antonio in April. I intend to win."

The two women and three men in the room greeted Serena as she planted her chair in front of a rack of weights. Serena struggled to pick up a twenty-pound one. Kyle hurried to her and grabbed it before she dropped it into her lap.

"How long have you've been lifting weights?" Kyle placed the barbell back on the rack.

"This is my fourth time. I did five pounds the first day then added five every day after that."

"It's better to build up to a higher weight gradually. I'd work with fifteen again."

"Do you lift weights?"

"Yes, for the past two years."

"Good, then you can help me. Give me some pointers. I only have two weeks till the race. I need to build up more strength in my puny arms." She raised one to show him her biceps. When she squeezed her upper arm, she laughed. "See? Flab."

Kyle thought about the apartment, boxes still cluttering much of the space in the living and dining rooms, then he stared down at Serena, her grin fading at his prolonged silence. "Sure. I can help you." If his dad could be working today instead of unpacking, then he could teach Serena how to lift weights correctly.

"*Señor* Morales?" Cody asked when a medium-size man with a patch over one eye and a clubfoot limped down the hall toward the nurses' station on the second floor at the hospital.

The orderly slowed and surveyed Cody. Wariness entered the man's eyes. "*Sí.* I'm busy. I can't talk right now. I have another patient to see to."

"You have the time. A nurse is taking care of it." Cody waved his arm toward an empty office behind the counter. "Let's talk in here." After he trailed Luis Morales into the room, Cody said, "Tell me about what happened earlier this morning."

"I smelled the smoke when I left for work. As I neared Ruiz's house, I saw the smoke. That's when I called 9-1-1. That's all," Luis said as though he'd rehearsed it over and over.

"Nothing else? No one else?"

"*Sí. No es cosa de mi incumbencia.*"

"What happens where you live is your business. A neighbor is dead."

"*Sí,* he's a criminal. So why are the police trying to find his killer? *Loco,* if you ask me."

"How do you know he's a criminal?"

"By the company he kept. Ruiz terrorized the neighborhood. Good riddance."

"So there were many people who wanted him dead?"

"The whole neighborhood, but none of us would have killed him."

"Why not?"

"Most of the people who live on Javelin Road are older. Women."

"You live there."

"We know how to mind our own business. Safer for us." His dark eyes narrowed. His jaw clenched. "As much as I'm glad he's gone, I didn't do it."

"But you're holding something back. What?"

"I have nothing to tell you. I know nothing." He pivoted and limped away.

Frustrated, Cody started to go after the orderly but stopped. He wasn't going to say anything else and Cody didn't have a lot to go on in order to ask the right questions, at least not now. After going through the crime scene, Cody intended to look into Luis Morales. It wouldn't be the first time a criminal called in his own crime.

He headed for the stairs, trying to call the landline in his apartment for the third time. No answer. Then he called Kyle's cell. Still no answer. Worry knotted the muscles along his neck and shoulders. With two murders in two days, he didn't care to have his son walking around an unfamiliar town, especially without letting Cody know where he was going. Kyle knew that, but probably didn't care his father would be concerned.

❧

Cody put pieces of evidence in a lock box in his SUV. "Maybe what we found in the house will lead us somewhere. Certainly my conversation with Luis Morales didn't produce anything of value other than that the neighbors, including Morales, hated Ruiz."

"There isn't much here either. Most of the evidence went up in flames," Liliana said.

"Which was probably the reason for the fire. I won't be surprised if the autopsy shows the man was dead before the fire. We have the barbwire and metal gasoline can."

"Minus any fingerprints."

"We still need to see if we can find where these are sold around here."

"I can tell you. The Super Store, where everyone shops in Durango."

"Then that's where we'll start. Are there any hardware or feed stores in town?"

"Yes, two feed and one hardware store. But barbwire is common around here as well as gasoline cans."

Cody shut the back of his SUV and leaned against it, his arms folded over his chest while he studied the remains of the house. "At least we know who was murdered. This doesn't feel random. According to your mother's friend, Victor Ruiz was a bad man. So who did he anger enough to be killed?"

"Torturing him first."

"To make a statement, for information, or to make him feel as much pain as possible?"

"Could be all three. Could be drug related."

"Let's go check the garage. Maybe we'll get lucky."

"I hope so. We could use a break." Liliana halted in front of what was left of the detached garage. "We certainly didn't find much of anything in the house. It was too far gone. Maybe there will be something in here that will help us figure out who Victor Ruiz is."

"Besides being a criminal, according to Luis Morales. I called the Texas Ranger in Brownsville to look into Ruiz. See if he can find out anything about the man. Vague assumptions by the neighbors aren't enough." Cody opened the side door into the partially destroyed building, its roof gone.

"Some of this is still intact." A tan van parked in the garage had pieces of the caved-in roof on its top as did the concrete floor.

Cody's inspection of the back of the vehicle revealed a cleaned area with wooden benches along the panel sides of the van. No windows except two darkened ones in the front seat and the windshield. A black curtain separated the front from the back. "Someone didn't want anyone to see inside here."

"Wonder what he used this for. So far Officer Vega hasn't discovered any place that Ruiz works. So where's his money coming from? What's he living on? He paid cash for his house."

"Does he have a bank account?"

"Not that Vega can find in town."

"Maybe he hasn't transferred it here from Brownsville. We might know more when the ranger in Brownsville calls me back. I'll dust for fingerprints. I couldn't pull any from the house. Maybe in here."

"Ruiz might not be his real name. Fingerprints would be good to have. *Señora* Emilia gave the sketch artist a good description of Ruiz, so we have something to go on."

Cody took out his kit to dust the door handles and the steering wheel first.

Liliana began searching the rubble on the floor, mostly charred pieces of the roof. In the back of the garage was a padlocked lid on a freezer. She had a bolt cutter in her car. After retrieving it, she snapped the lock off and lifted the top to peer inside. Cold air blasted her face. Stacks of frozen food lay before her. But she knew appearances weren't always what they seemed. She started removing the cartons and containers until she reached the bottom level—full of different sized guns and rifles.

"I've got something here. Lots of weapons. I even see a .38. Maybe it's the gun that killed our Jane Doe."

"I've got a couple of fingerprints on the steering wheel and driver's door."

An hour later, after transferring all the additional evidence to Cody's SUV, he slammed down the lid on his lock box, then closed the back of his car. "At least we have some evidence to plow through in the next few days. It's a start."

Liliana started for her Chevy. Her day began early and was ending late. If it hadn't been for *Señora* Emilia's cinnamon rolls, she wouldn't have eaten anything for lunch. Pausing at her car door, she glanced at Cody. He gave her a smile and slid behind his steering wheel. His engine roared to life, then he pulled away from the curb.

Liliana studied the destruction before her. Something nagged her. She couldn't put her finger on it, but it churned her stomach, an uneasiness shivering down her length. She felt watched.

5

Watching from a distance as the new Texas Ranger and Liliana Rodriguez leave the crime scene, I relax the tense set of my shoulders. They don't have a clue who killed Anna. They don't even know who she is. The thrill of pulling the trigger that second, then third time on Anna surges through me. I saw the life go out of her eyes—eyes that mocked me only a moment before. Her lips pursed in surprise—silenced forever.

And now the same with Victor Ruiz. He thought I was a nobody. He took my money and didn't care that Anna wasn't going to stay with me. He knew she was double-crossing me, and he got what he deserved. I can still remember the coyote's screams of pain. Victor might have been a bully, but he couldn't take it for long. He'd given up Anna's lover—or at least a clue to where she was going.

Only a couple of people knew whom she was coming to see. I've taken care of the coyote I paid. Now I need to track down the other one. Then I'll be safe and can go back to being nobody.

But the thought of being a nobody leaves a nasty taste in my mouth. For the first time in my life, I feel like what I do matters. How can I go back to being invisible?

The coyote didn't deserve to live. I made a difference. Too bad no one will know what I did to make Durango a better place to live.

Thirty-six hours later, after a Sunday spent trying to settle into his apartment and run a few clues down, Cody gulped down the last of his coffee then put the mug into the sink. *Thank goodness Sunday was a quiet day. After two murders in two days, we certainly didn't need a third one.* "Ready, Kyle? We need to get to school to enroll you."

When he didn't hear anything from his son, Cody went into the hall to call out again and found Kyle standing by his bedroom door, a scowl on his face, clutching his backpack.

"C'mon. We have an appointment with the school counselor to set up your classes."

"I don't wanna go. I just left my old school. Can't I take a couple of days off before I start a new school? Just because you don't, doesn't mean I can't. We still have some boxes to empty. My room's a mess."

Since when had his son cared about a clean room? "Prolonging this won't make it go away."

Kyle raised his head and stabbed him with a hard glare. "I can homeschool myself. I don't need to go to high school here."

If his son wasn't so dead serious, he would have laughed at the suggestion right on top of wanting to stay and clean his room. "I know how you feel. It's scary going to a strange school, especially in the middle of the year."

Cody hadn't thought it was possible Kyle's scowl could deepen, but it did. "You don't know how I feel. At the very least, you could have let me stay in Houston and finish my sophomore year at my old school. Nate said I could stay with him."

"No." Cody ground his teeth to refrain from saying anything about the man his ex-wife had married. Forcing deep breaths into his lungs, he moved toward Kyle. "You are my son. I can't leave you behind. And I do know how you feel."

Kyle snorted. "Yeah, sure." He plowed past Cody in the narrow hallway and strode toward the front door.

Tell him why you moved him across Texas to live in the middle of nowhere.

Cody quickly followed before his son stopped and came up with another reason he didn't want to go to school. When Cody climbed into his SUV, for a second the lingering scent of lilacs teased his senses. A reminder of Saturday and Sunday with Liliana that had ended with no real clues to the identity of the killer or killers caused him to pause in starting the car. Yesterday afternoon they had gone back to both crime scenes. Nothing new had revealed itself. The debris in Ruiz's house wouldn't be removed until tomorrow under police supervision.

His son shifted in the front seat and said, "Let's get this over with," as though he were a criminal forced to stand in a lineup.

Cody backed out of his parking space in front of the apartment building. "When I was a kid—"

"Hold it, Dad. Not some story about how you walked through two feet of snow to get to school."

Lord, patience. He's hurting and lashing out at me. "I grew up in San Antonio. There's rarely two inches of snow there. So no, you won't get that story. What I wanted to say is that when I was fourteen we moved to Austin and I had to leave behind all my friends. Dad lost his job and—"

"Stop it. Losing a job is different from losing a mother. So you don't know what I'm going through. Yours is still alive."

The muscles in his neck knotted, spreading pain down his back and across his shoulders. "No, but nine months before we moved, I lost my little brother. That's probably why my dad lost his job. He fell apart, started drinking."

"Granddad?"

Maybe if I ease into the subject of Nate, Kyle will listen.

"Yes. The family fell apart. My mom moved us to Austin where her parents lived."

"But they aren't divorced. They live together now."

Cody turned onto the street that led to the high school. "Yeah. It took Mom leaving to finally get through to Dad. He stopped drinking, pulled his life together, and came to Austin. Mom didn't take him back right away. He got a job and had to prove to Mom that he had changed. But I understand what it's like to have your life totally disrupted."

"You had a brother killed? How old was he?"

"Five. He ran out in front of a car."

"Why didn't I know this?"

"Because Mom and Dad never talk about it. That's their way of dealing with the tragedy. It didn't help me, though. I needed to talk about it." Cody pulled into a parking space at the school and angled toward his son. "So if you need to talk about your mom, I'll listen. It's hard losing someone close to you."

"I can't talk to you about Mom. You two divorced. Barely were on speaking terms." Kyle shoved open the passenger door and exited the SUV.

And Kyle blames me for that. This didn't go well at all. So much for trying to explain about Nate. Maybe after we form a stronger bond, Kyle will be ready to listen to the truth about Nate and his suspicious activities. All I know is that Nate won't see Kyle again if I have anything to do about it.

With a sigh, Cody quickened his pace and caught up with his son as he entered the two-story, brick building. The bell for class rang as Kyle went through the metal detector. The security guard took his son's backpack and began searching it.

Cody showed the man his badge and was waved on through. Without looking any further, the guard zipped up Kyle's backpack and handed it to him. Waiting on the other side, Cody checked for the main office where they were to sign in.

"I thought he was gonna pat me down until you showed him your badge." Kyle slung his backpack over one shoulder, trailing after Cody toward the office. "I guess there's one advantage to having a cop for a father."

At the counter, Cody wrote their names on a sheet of paper. "We're here to see Mrs. Lopez."

"I'll let her know you're here," an older woman said, coming from around her desk and walking toward the back of the complex of smaller offices.

A boy thrust open one side of the double doors into the reception area and stomped inside, throwing his body into the nearest chair and slouching in it with his legs sticking out and blocking the pathway. The teen dropped his head and stared at his stomach.

A man stepped out of the assistant principal's office and said to the teenager, "José, I'll see you now."

"I haven't done anything wrong. Why do you always pick on me?" the boy said in Spanish and remained where he was sitting.

The assistant principal cut the distance to him and nudged his feet. "Sit up." Glaring at the teen, he waited until he finally complied with the request then continued in English, "I want to hear your side before a decision is made. Now you have a choice. Either tell me about the incident, or I'll make my decision on the facts that I've been given without your input."

The boy shot to his feet. "So you can appear to be fair. No way." He pushed past the man and rushed out the office, the double set of doors banging closed.

The assistant principal glanced at Cody, noted his silver star on his shirt and said, "I'm sorry you had to witness that." He moved forward. "I'm Mr. Gonzalez. May I help you?"

Cody rose and shook the man's hand. "We're waiting for Mrs. Lopez to enroll my son in school."

"Are you taking over for Al Garcia?"

"Yes. Did he have a lot to do with this school?"

"Not much professionally. We were friends. He'll be missed. I was surprised he retired. He hadn't planned on it at least for five more years, but he wasn't the same after he was shot."

"That can happen." Al had been driving into Durango from his office in the Highway Patrol building when he'd been ambushed and wounded in the leg. Al had been investigating rumors of a smuggling ring in the area.

The secretary returned to the counter. "Mrs. Lopez is available now."

Thirty minutes later, Kyle was enrolled in Durango High School and had his schedule in his hand. Mrs. Lopez walked Cody and Kyle out into the reception area where a student would be waiting to show Kyle to his locker and his next class.

"Manny will come to each of your classes and take you to your next one. If you have any questions, he should be able to help you with what you need. He's one of our aides who does this for any new students. Ah, there he is now."

Cody peered toward the double doors as a teenager with black hair, brown skin, and a tall, thin build came through the entrance. Kyle stiffened next to him. His son's permanent frown cut even deeper into his face.

"I can find my own way around. I went to a high school twice this size. I don't need any help," Kyle whispered to Cody.

Mrs. Lopez stopped a few feet from Manny and swung toward Kyle. "We do this for all our new students. It helps them not feel so overwhelmed with a new place."

"That's okay. I have seven minutes to get to second period. I think I can manage." He stalked away from Cody and Mrs. Lopez and passed Manny without a word.

"I'm sorry for my son's behavior. This move has been difficult for him. Thank you for your help today." Cody tipped his tan hat then hurried to catch up with Kyle. When he did, he clasped his arm, halting his progress. "This isn't the time or the place to have this conversation, but this evening we'll talk about your behavior this morning. You might be upset and angry at me, but you do not take it out on others who have nothing to do with your situation. Son, sometimes in life you have to grin and bear it."

Kyle yanked his arm from Cody's grasp. "I didn't ask for a student to show me around like I don't know how to find room numbers or ask directions if I need to." The bell rang. "Now I need to get to class. I wouldn't want to be late because you delayed me."

Students poured out into the hallway, and his son disappeared into the crowd. When Cody noticed the stares he was receiving, he pivoted and made his way out of the building. At his SUV, his cell sounded. Noting it was the police station, he quickly answered it. "Jackson, here."

"There's been another murder. Chief Winters wanted me to call you."

He'd know Liliana's voice anywhere. There was a huskiness to it as if she'd inhaled too much smoke. "Where?"

"Out south of town, not far—the second dirt road on the highway to Seminole Canyon State Park. It leads to a two-hundred acre ranch."

"I'll be there." Cody pocketed his cell, wondering how long it would have taken her to call if the chief hadn't told her to notify him.

❦

Miguel Salazar covered his mouth with a quaking hand, his face leeched of all color as he stared at his cousin's body. "Who would do this?"

"That's a good question. Any thoughts on it?" As Officer Hudson strung up the yellow tape from the barn to the wooden house thirty feet away, Liliana moved back from the body, indicating to the man who had found the body to follow her.

"I felt for a pulse to see if he was alive. He was warm. He hadn't been . . ."

Liliana paused. "You touched his neck?"

"*Sí*, but that was all."

That could possibly account for the blood on his boots and clothes. "Did you wipe your hand off on your shirt?"

He nodded. "I didn't know what else to do. I need to change. I need to get these clothes off."

His gaze transfixed on his cousin, Miguel stumbled as he backed away. He went down on one knee. The action caused him to fold in on himself, sobs coming from the man. She was acquainted with Miguel but didn't really know him well. She certainly hadn't realized he had a cousin named Carlos who lived out here. She hadn't realized anyone had bought this property recently.

She gave Miguel a few moments to gather his composure. He struggled to his feet and turned away from Carlos lying sprawled on the ground in front of the barn. "How long has Carlos been here?"

"A couple of weeks at the ranch. My wife's uncle bought it but got sick so Carlos worked out an agreement with him. Carlos had been staying with members of the family."

"Does anyone live here with him?"

Miguel peered down at the ground by his feet. "No. He's single."

"How long has he been in Durango?"

"A few months. He used to live in New Mexico." Miguel glanced over his shoulder, mumbled, "I think I'm going to be sick," and slapped his hand over his mouth again. He heaved several times, tears shining in his eyes. "I don't—understand. I . . ." He swallowed hard. "Can I leave? I can't stay here. He's riddled with bullets."

She didn't think she would get much more from Miguel as long as he could see his cousin's body and the funeral home wouldn't be here for a while. "Yes, you can go down to the station. When I'm through here, I'll finish interviewing you."

"Salud!"

"Officer Hudson, can you take Miguel to the police station? Give him something to change into and process his clothes."

"My clothes? Why?"

"You touched your cousin. You are part of the crime scene."

"I can't go home, take a shower, and change into my own clothes?"

"No, but I'll be there as fast as I can."

"You don't think I could do this?" The man waved wildly toward the body.

"Did you?"

His mouth dropped open. "No!"

"Then you'll have no reason not to cooperate with us."

"Come with me, Mr. Salazar," Officer Hudson said, heading toward his patrol car.

"Why can't I follow in my truck?"

"Someone will bring you back out here to pick up your truck."

As Officer Hudson drove off, Cody's blue SUV came around the curve and pulled into the yard. She waited for him before proceeding to the body to examine it up close. "This is probably not how you envisioned being welcomed to Durango."

"Not in my wildest dream—three murders in four days." Cody brought his camera and began shooting some pictures of the body and crime scene.

As two more squad cars rolled into the yard, Liliana squatted near the body and ran her gaze slowly down Carlos, categorizing the injuries she saw. Multiple gunshots to both kneecaps, right shoulder, stomach, and probably the last one was to the heart. From the blood spatter and damage to the body, it appeared Carlos might have been killed from a distance.

In her mind, she visualized how she thought the crime might have gone down. From the trail and pattern of blood, Carlos came out of his house and headed toward the barn or his movements could have been reversed. There was no way to tell for sure. He fell, shot most likely in the shoulder, but got back up and began moving toward the barn. Went down again. Blood pooled in the dirt.

"The shooter toyed with Carlos before killing him."

After walking to the barn and extracting a bullet lodged in the wood, Cody turned toward her. "This is a 7.62 NATO round used in M16 rifles. From the entry and exit wounds and the blood splatter on the barn door, I think the shots came from there." He pointed toward a cropping of rocks perched on top of a small rise about three hundred yards away.

"A sniper?"

"Possibly. We'll need to check that out, then the house. But it's looking like there were no witnesses around."

"He lived alone."

"You know him personally?"

"No, but I'm acquainted with the man who found the body—his cousin, Miguel Salazar. We'll interview him later at the station. Officer Hudson took him there."

"Why was Miguel Salazar out here?"

"He came to visit."

"Nothing else? On a Monday morning? Where does Miguel work?"

"He works in construction. Miguel was upset. He kept staring at his cousin and shaking his head. I thought it best to get him away from the crime scene. Since he touched Carlos to feel for a pulse, I wanted to process his clothes. He had blood on his boots, too."

"Are you thinking Miguel had something to do with this?"

"A large percentage of the murders in this country are committed by people who know the victim."

"I know the statistics, but this doesn't feel like that."

"And it doesn't feel like a random murder either. Why would a killer come all the way out here to kill a random person? Toy with that person?"

Cody swiveled toward Liliana. "I agree. Like the other two, this is personal. The killer knows Carlos and has a reason to kill him."

"I don't think it's Miguel. He seemed genuinely scared."

"Why scared?"

"Good question. One we'll need to ask him."

Liliana inspected the body again as the ME approached with Officer Robertson. In the front jean pocket something blood-soaked stuck out of it. "Look." She pointed at what she'd seen then carefully with her gloved hand pulled out a folded piece of paper.

Cody bent over her and stared at the paper covered in Carlos's blood. Taking the tweezers he handed her, she carefully opened it to reveal a letter.

"The signature looks like the name 'Anna' but no last name." She rose and held it out for him to see better.

"It's all in Spanish."

She read the first line out loud in English, "I will be there soon. I am counting the days until I see you again." The next part of the letter was unreadable from the blood.

"I don't see a date."

"I don't either. So this Anna could have come and gone. Miguel said Carlos was alone. He said nothing about a woman."

"Once we know what the whole letter says we might have more information about when she was coming. Maybe from where." Cody held open the evidence bag while Liliana slipped it inside.

"The letter may mean nothing, but I'm hoping it's a piece of evidence because we sure could use some."

"Let's get this scene processed then check out the place I think the killer was."

⚜

An hour later, after the ME took the body to do an autopsy, the area had been combed for any pieces of evidence. "Not much for us to go on," Liliana said as she and Cody headed toward the cropping of rocks. "I hope we find something here. We could use it."

"What bothers me the most is that you haven't had any murders in Durango for a few months and suddenly in four days you have three." Cody's strides cut the distance at a quick pace. "On the surface they don't appear to be done by the same person. Different weapons used. The MOs are all over the map."

Even though it was the end of March, the sun bore down on Liliana with an intensity that reminded her of early summer. Sweat beaded her brow, and she brushed her hand across it. "I hope this isn't a pattern. It's been quiet for a while, although we have had a rise in robberies."

"What kind?" he asked as he began climbing the hill.

"The majority are homes, a few businesses. I think it's the same people responsible for most of them."

"Didn't Garcia work a series of murders last fall?"

"That was outside of Durango—along Highway 90. They were related to drug running. We're pretty isolated out here. Which can be a bad thing. Certain people like that fact."

"But it can be good. You know who the strangers are in the area."

"If you see them. What about the ones you don't? We're starting to discover Victor Ruiz aka Victor Torres, thanks to the police in Brownsville, wasn't a nice man."

"Yeah, he's suspected of bringing illegals into the U.S. from Mexico. Things were getting too hot in Brownsville. I guess that's why he changed his name and town. So had he opened shop here in Durango smuggling people across the border or was he doing something else? He had a drug charge in his past."

"It would have been nice if the .38 had been used to kill Jane Doe. That would have been one crime solved. Do they have the ballistics on the other guns in the freezer?"

"The full report should come in this afternoon."

Liliana stopped at the base of the rocks overlooking the barn and house and peered down at the indentation in the dirt. "A tripod?"

"Probably, and I bet it wasn't for taking pictures." He gestured toward the ground that had been swept. "Covering his tracks using this." With gloves still on his hands, Cody picked up a branch tossed to the side on the grassy part of the hill. "The crime lab guys are going to give me grief, but I'm bagging and tagging this as evidence in hopes there might be some kind of DNA evidence or fibers on the branch."

"I know what you mean, but we're desperate for evidence we can use. I especially want to know what else was in that letter."

"I'll be driving everything we gathered today to the lab in San Antonio first thing tomorrow morning and put a rush on it. I don't like the fact there have been so many murders close together—seemingly unrelated but violent."

While Cody took photos of the area, Liliana made a slow circle then walked a few paces to the other side of the hill. "He probably parked down there."

Cody stooped to investigate the ground closer, looking beneath some rocks. "No shell casings left here. He took them with him." Standing, he covered the distance between them. "Let's go check it out. It'll be hard to cover up tire tracks."

Carrying the bagged branch, he descended the steeper slope on the backside of the hill. When he offered his hand to assist her over a deep rut, Liliana ignored it and jumped the gully, landing a few feet from him. She wobbled but quickly regained her balance. Being only five feet three inches tall had its disadvantages. People underestimated her strength and capabilities.

At the bottom, tire tracks left an impression in the dirt.

"After we go through Salazar's house, I'll take a casting of these impressions. At the moment, besides the bullet lodged in the barn door and the letter, there's little else to go on."

"You forgot the branch. It could be a valuable piece of evidence." She suppressed the smile for a few seconds but couldn't for long.

"Are you gonna give me grief too?" Wading through tall weeds and cacti, Cody followed the tracks and made his way to the dirt road that led to the small ranch.

"No, never, especially since we both know long shots can come in from time to time."

When they reached the road, the tire tracks became lost among others. "Too bad we can't follow them to the killer's place. Sure would make this job easier." Liliana started back toward the house.

"It doesn't look like the guy went close to Salazar's home. Before our tracks covered up his, it appears the killer turned toward the highway."

"He murdered him from a distance then left. Maybe we'll find something in the house that will point to someone who would like to see Carlos dead." Liliana mounted the steps to the porch of a small, rundown place where their victim lived.

Inside the adobe brick structure, the front door opened into a tiny living area with a kitchenette off to one side, equipped with a small refrigerator, two burner plates, a sink, and two chairs. A chipped plate with bits of dried egg on it sat on a table along with an empty mug—as though Carlos had finished his breakfast and gone right out to the barn without cleaning up.

Looking closer, she noticed drawers weren't completely shut, the counters in the kitchen were cluttered with items from the cabinet. "Either Carlos is a lousy housekeeper or this place has been tossed."

"The killer came down from his perch after he killed Carlos and searched the house? Then walked back to his vehicle behind the hill and left?"

"I guess Miguel could have. Although I don't think so. He was visibly shaken. He didn't take anything with him."

"That you could see."

"We should check his truck parked out there before we leave."

"And take fingerprints. If the killer went through this place, we may find them."

Cody's long strides chewed up the distance between the kitchen and the doorway into the lone bedroom in the house. "I'll take this room. You process the living area."

Because she so recently found Maria in a couch, that was the first place Liliana looked, tossing the cushions to the floor and checking every crevice. Nothing. Next, she went to the TV table and pulled out the drawer. Empty. Had there been something inside that the killer took?

She took out her fingerprinting kit and began dusting for prints. Lots of smudges. Some areas wiped clean. Had that been Carlos or the killer?

She finished her search in the kitchen, opening and investigating each drawer and cabinet. For a lone bachelor, he had a lot of food. Was he expecting a visitor? Miguel? Anna? What were they missing? Again, she processed the kitchen and gathered a few good prints.

Cody came back into the main room. "There wasn't anything in the bedroom or bathroom, except a couple of changes of clothes. He bought a new pair of white pants and a white shirt. The price tags were still on them. But that was all."

"A new outfit. More food than a single man usually has in the house. Most of the men I know who live by themselves have pretty bare shelves. Not Carlos. I wouldn't be surprised that he went shopping yesterday. So what was he planning? Expecting Anna? If so, why didn't Miguel know? He acted like they had been close."

"Maybe that will be the key. Figure out what he was planning, and we'll know what's going on."

"I'm thinking Anna is at the center of this."

"We don't know why she was excited about seeing him, but I bet it is because they were lovers."

The word hung in the air between them for several heartbeats. The intense look Cody gave her rendered her speechless for that brief moment. Swallowing to coat her dry throat, she turned away. "I think we've found just about all there is to find here."

"Yeah, you're right," Cody said after a long pause, his voice deeper than usual.

He moved toward the exit and held the door open for Liliana. She left the house without looking at him. For some reason, she needed a few seconds to gather her composure. The intensity pouring off him stole her breath. She drew in gulps of the warm spring air, filling her lungs to capacity.

"I'll meet you at the station after I make the tire casts." Cody strode past her toward his SUV.

She watched him leave then realized she was all alone in the middle of nowhere, arid land for miles around. What was Carlos growing here? She didn't see any crops—only about thirty scrawny cattle.

Before this investigation was over, she would know everything she could about Carlos Salazar. Who had a grudge against him?

❧

As Liliana pulled into a parking space at the back of the courthouse where the police station was housed, her cell beeped. After switching off her Chevy, she answered it.

"This is your friendly reminder about Joanna's birthday party at five. The first thing she asked me this morning was if you were coming to her party."

"Elena, am I that bad that you have to resort to reminding me?"

"No, not usually but I heard about the third murder and I know how you can get so involved in a case that you forget about your family."

"One time does not make a pattern."

"I can't disappoint my daughter. You're her favorite aunt."

"I'm her only aunt."

"Still makes you her favorite."

Liliana pushed open her driver door and stepped out of the Chevy. "I'll be there. I won't let Joanna down." Besides, she intended to let Samuel know how important her sister's well-being was to her without openly accusing him of what she thought he was doing. "See you this evening."

"Are you bringing Mama?"

"Yes and Rafael. Baseball practice should be over by then."

"See you all later."

Liliana slipped her cell back into her pocket and started for the back door. Juan stepped outside with a large plastic trash bag and swung it one-handed into the dumpster near the exit. Juan had cerebral palsy but worked hard not to let his affliction get in his way. She admired his courage and determination. "How's it going?" She stopped beside the janitor, greeting him with a smile.

But Juan didn't return her grin as he usually did. Instead, deep grooves creased his forehead. "Not so good." His words slurred slightly and a drop of spittle glistened at the corner of his mouth.

"What happened?"

"My nephew got in trouble at school today and left. He's telling my sister he isn't going back."

"He's giving up the baseball team? I thought he loved playing."

"I thought it would be his way to college. He has decided he wants nothing to do with school." Juan moved toward the back door and opened it with his right hand while his lifeless left arm lay folded and plastered against his side then waited for her to enter. "Do you think your brother could talk some sense into José? He might listen to Rafael. He doesn't think I know what I'm talking about."

"I'll say something to Rafael. I'm picking him up this evening. My niece is six years old today, and we're having her birthday party tonight."

Juan's mouth tilted up. "*Gracias.*"

Liliana entered the building. "Anything for you. You ignore my messy work space."

Juan chuckled as he shuffled past her. "You are *mi amiga.*"

Liliana sat for the first time that day at her desk. The long morning and afternoon at the crime scene underscored her exhaustion. *That's what I get for not sleeping last night.* For that matter the night before, too. She'd certainly seen her share of dead bodies and had been elated at the lull in murders over the winter months. But the death of a woman with child bothered her more than usual. She'd been six months pregnant. The baby never had a chance. The way the killer had shot Jane Doe shouted it was very personal. A rejected lover?

Officer Hudson paused next to her. "Miguel Salazar is in the interview room and a reporter called from the *Durango Daily.*"

She was almost afraid to ask, "Anything else?"

"Other than the mayor has been on the phone with Chief Winters for the past fifteen minutes, nope."

"I'm considering going to Colorado, hunting down Brock, and hauling him back here."

"You could always track him using his cell."

"I wouldn't put it past him that he conveniently left it at home."

"Ha! Me neither."

As the back door opened and Cody came into the police station, Liliana flipped through her messages, decided they could all wait, and rose.

Cody set his cowboy hat on an empty chair behind Liliana's desk. "Ready to see what Carlos's cousin has to say?"

"We've given him enough time to stew."

"It was interesting how he complained about missing work once we wanted to take him in for questioning, and yet he had all the time to go out to see his cousin to chat. I'll take the lead on the interview."

"Miguel goes to my mother's church. He's super-protective of his family. From what little I've heard about him, work and family are about all he does."

"Is he married?" Cody's long strides shortened the distance to the interview room quickly.

"Yes, with one boy, eighteen months old."

Cody cocked his head toward Liliana. "How well do you know the Hispanic community in Durango?"

"Very well. I have a big family, and they're quite social."

"But not you?"

"What makes you say that?" Liliana started to reach for the doorknob. Cody clasped it first but didn't turn it.

Instead, he angled his head until their gazes connected across the foot that separated them. "The way you said it. Like it was something they did, but not you."

She toyed with whether to answer him or not. When she decided against it, she nodded toward the door. "I have a party to go to at five, and I can't be late."

He laughed. "I wouldn't want to keep you from your—social life. A party sounds so much more fun than what I'm going to do." He twisted the knob, but the door remained closed.

"Okay, I'll bite. What are you going to do tonight?"

"Try to put together an edible meal for myself."

"What about your son?"

"He texted me that he would be studying at the high school library tonight until it closes at nine. He's grabbing a sandwich and heading to school at five. He already has a big project. I'm sure tonight I'll hear all about that." He pulled the door open.

"Is that normal?"

"Studying or complaining?"

Liliana entered the interview room, glimpsing Miguel with his forearms on the table, twiddling his thumbs. "Studying. I know complaining is normal for a teenage boy. I have a seventeen-year-old brother."

"Yeah, it's normal, just not at the library. But we only live a couple of blocks from the high school. In Houston, it was miles away." Cody switched his attention to Miguel and slipped into the chair next to the man.

Miguel hunched his shoulders and tried physically to get as far away from Cody as possible without moving the chair.

"*Señor* Salazar, I'm Ranger Cody Jackson, and I'll be working on your cousin's case along with Detective Rodriguez here. We just have a few questions for you then you can leave. I understand you have a job to get to. When were you due at work today?"

Miguel blinked then dropped his gaze to his hands folded on the table, his thumbs pointing to the ceiling. "One."

"That's an odd time. What are your hours?"

"Usually seven to four, but today I took the morning off."

"Ah. Do you normally do that?"

"No."

"Then why today?"

"Well," he started twiddling his thumbs again, the seconds evolving into a full minute before he finished, "I wasn't feeling well this morning."

"But well enough to go see your cousin. What would your boss say about that?"

"I was heading to work when Carlos called and wanted to see me."

"Oh, I see. What did he want to see you about?"

"He didn't say, but he was excited."

"And you don't know why?"

Miguel shrugged and looked toward the ceiling. "No telling with *mi primo*."

"Yeah, no telling." Cody glanced at Liliana.

Within his gaze, she saw an invitation to step in. She moved forward and leaned across the table. "Miguel, we need your help. Who would do this to Carlos?"

This time the man swung his attention to Liliana. "I don't know. He doesn't do nothing to others. He works hard, minds his own business."

"What does he do?" Liliana sat in the chair across from Miguel.

"Raise cattle for my wife's uncle."

"All I saw was thirty or so."

Miguel let out a deep breath slowly. "I know it don't look like much. But he is—was doing better than my cousins in Mexico."

"Who isn't?"

"*Sí*, that's why Carlos was so happy to be here. A dream come true working the ranch for my wife's uncle."

"But someone ended his dream." Liliana cocked her head. "How was your wife's uncle going to make any money off of just thirty or thirty-five cattle?"

"Before he got sick, he had started buying some to build the herd up. But he got sick before he really could."

"Who is this uncle?"

"Alfredo Flores."

"Ah, wasn't he Cesar Álvarez's foreman?"

"Yes. *Señor* Álvarez gave *Tío* Alfredo the land when he retired. It isn't good for a whole lot, but it can support about fifty head of cattle. That's all my wife's uncle wanted. *Señor* Álvarez is generous with his retirement benefits to his long-time employees."

"Where is *Señor* Flores now?"

"Staying with my wife's mother."

"Write down the contact information for him." Cody slid a pad and pen toward the man who scribbled it down on the paper.

Liliana removed her card from her pocket. "Please call me if you can think of anyone who would want to hurt Carlos. If he's mixed up in something illegal, we need to know."

"Carlos? His younger brother and uncle died of a drug overdose. He won't—I mean he didn't touch drugs."

"It can be a quick way to make money—and get killed."

"Not Carlos. He wanted to start a family." Miguel slipped her card into his shirt front pocket.

"Did he have a girlfriend?"

His gaze slid down to a spot in the center of the table, Miguel didn't say anything for half a minute. "Not that I know of. He was fixing up the ranch first. I think he hoped *Tío* Alfredo would sell it to him in time."

"Would someone have robbed him?"

Miguel shook his head. "He didn't have much. Was his TV still there?"

"Yes."

"He had a fifteen-year-old black truck that barely ran. I saw that when I came to the ranch. The only other things on the ranch were the cattle and two horses. From what I saw they were still there."

"So robbery wouldn't be the motive."

"No."

"Who is Anna?" Liliana asked, observing closely his body language for any sign of recognition.

Miguel opened his mouth then snapped it closed. "Anna? There is a woman at church named that. What's she got to do with me or Carlos?"

"Are you talking about Anna Delgado?"

"*Sí.*"

Anna Delgado was fifty-five and a friend of her mother's. She wouldn't have written those letters to Carlos. "Does he know anyone else by the name of Anna?"

Miguel lifted his shoulders in an exaggerated shrug. "I don't know. It's a common name. How would I know everyone my cousin knows?"

Liliana rose and stretched out her arm toward Miguel. "I appreciate your help. Sometimes, you'll think of something later. Please call if you do."

Miguel closed his hand around hers and shook it. "*Sí,* if I can think of anything else. Am I free to go?"

"Yes." Cody walked to the door and opened it for the man.

After Miguel left the interview room, Cody turned to Liliana. "He's lying. He knows who Anna is. Possibly even who might have killed Carlos. Why would he keep that a secret unless Miguel or Carlos were into something illegal?"

"I don't think he is. He has lived here for his whole life. We went to school together. He was a few years older than me, but he was a good kid."

"Yeah, and from what you've said he's a good man. I still think he's lying, not telling us something. Good men can fall from grace."

"And bad men can change." Although she said those words, she really didn't believe that. Her father hadn't, and she didn't think Samuel would. Maybe Miguel was protecting his family.

"True. But something is happening in Durango. What has changed?"

"The weather has gotten warmer. Otherwise, I don't know."

"In other towns around here, I would say probably nothing happened, but Durango is one of the safer towns near the border."

"We have our share of trouble."

"But not like other places. That's one of the reasons I picked Durango instead of working nearer Brownsville."

"You had a choice?"

"Yep." He flashed her a smile. "I was planning on kicking back and relaxing for a change. Maybe only work eight-hour days instead of twelve to fifteen. I'm not so sure that's gonna happen. The first full day I'm here there's a murder."

Liliana made her way to the doorway. "I guess you'll have to save up your vacation time if you want to rest and relax."

He fell into step next to her. "What do you do for rest and relaxation here?"

"We have a movie theater, a bowling alley. Soccer is a popular sport, even for the men. There's riding, hiking, and boating around here."

"What do you do for leisure?"

Pausing in the main room, she swung toward him. "Family takes up most of my free time, but when I get a chance, I like to take my camera and go hiking or biking."

"You're a photographer?"

"I wouldn't go so far as to say that. But I like to take pictures."

"Do you like to ride?"

"Yes, when I get a chance. Why?"

"Maybe you could show me some of the countryside when things settle down around here."

"Do you have a horse here?"

He nodded. "Yep. Star of Texas. A quarter horse I'm boarding with Al on his land right outside of town—sixteen hands of muscle and attitude with enough stamina to track all-day and still run down a fugitive like a bloodhound. If I was staying, I'd buy some land so I wouldn't have to board Star."

"You aren't staying?"

"At the most, I'll leave when Kyle graduates in two years."

So he's passing through. She shouldn't be too surprised by that. Durango wasn't a post most Texas Rangers would want. Usually they got new rangers or ones like Garcia who were close to retirement and from this area so they didn't mind being struck out in southwest Texas. "Then why are you here, if it's only for a short time?"

"I needed to get my son away from Houston and certain people who weren't a good influence on him. Also, I am here to solve Al's shooting."

"We haven't been able to do that. Al and I have talked about the case and there aren't many leads."

"Then you won't mind a fresh pair of eyes on it. I owe Al. He helped me a lot when I first started out in the Texas Rangers before he moved back here. I don't like the fact someone tried to kill him and has gotten away with it."

Liliana stabbed him with a sharp look. "I don't like it either."

"But as far as my son's concerned, he thinks I've been banished to the parts unknown."

"This town has a lot to offer. I wouldn't consider it being banished."

"*Banished* is my son's word. He thinks I should have turned down the assignment. He doesn't know I sought it out when Al had to retire rather than come back to work."

"Why haven't you told him?"

"The right moment hasn't come up."

"Right moment? That seems like some kind of excuse not to tell your son why you came to Durango."

One of his eyebrows rose. "You do speak your mind."

"I don't like to play games." For most of her childhood, she'd had to live behind a facade, keeping herself suppressed because her papa expected a daughter to act one way only.

"Until his mother died a few months ago, Kyle lived with her except every other weekend. We spent a lot of our time together reacquainting ourselves. Then there were weekends where I had to work and we had even less time. It has been an adjustment for both of us—living together seven days a week. Kyle has a stepfather he looks up to and wants to be exactly like."

"Does that bother you?"

"Yes, because this man is being investigated for being a part of a white supremacist group. For years, he's been slowly indoctrinating my son with that kind of garbage. I'm losing Kyle—maybe already have—but I'm gonna try my best to make up for the years I wasn't around. This isn't only his stepfather's fault, but mine, too."

"How old is Kyle?" Liliana asked as Juan brought a cup of water and poured it on her plant. She smiled her thanks, glad he remembered to do that or the cactus would die from lack of water. Hard to do but she was capable of doing it—had with two other plants.

"Fifteen. He'll be sixteen in a month then he'll want to drive. Being a highway patrolman before coming to the Texas Rangers, I have seen my share of accidents caused by young teens driving with little experience. It scares me to know he'll be joining those ranks soon."

"That's the way I felt when my brother started driving a year ago. He had three wrecks in the first six months. Mama had me take him out each weekend until I was satisfied he could drive capably. He couldn't get the car until then. He wasn't too happy with me that I wouldn't say okay for three months."

"After dealing with Kyle, I can imagine. One good thing about Durango is that there are a lot fewer people on the roads for Kyle to hit."

She laughed. "The glass is always half full. I like that."

Cody snatched up his cowboy hat and set it on his head. "I'm heading to my office."

"I want to speak to Pedro and Maria again. They should be home from school by now."

"Do you think Mr. Martinez will let you speak to them?"

"That's why I'm going now before he gets home from work. If he's there, he probably will, but that doesn't mean they'll tell me anything."

"I hope he's thought about it and changed his mind. I hope the kids aren't in any danger and the parents take enough precautions to keep them safe."

"At least the chief managed to keep their names out of the paper."

"Yeah, but the neighbors in Rancho Estates know about it." Cody tipped his hat. "I'll be gone most of tomorrow hand delivering the evidence to the state lab in San Antonio and in my usual charming way encouraging them to work on it in a timely fashion."

"Maybe you could hang out with them for a few hours while they run the tests."

He winked. "In our dreams. But I'll stress there have been three murders in four days with a chance it could be the same person."

"Do you believe that?"

"It's a possibility."

"Yeah, but we just need to find the connection."

"You've got my cell number if you need to talk tomorrow."

The Texas Ranger sauntered toward the back door, stopping to speak for a few minutes with Officer Hudson, who was first on the scene that morning at Carlos's ranch. When Liliana glanced down at her watch, she hopped up. After going by the Martinez's house, she had to pick up her brother and mother then get to her niece's birthday party. Elena didn't like it when they were late.

～❧～

"Joanna didn't think you were coming," Elena said as she opened the refrigerator and removed a tray of vegetables. "Make yourself useful and grab the lemonade and tea." Bumping her hip into the door, she closed it and started for the dining room.

Liliana clasped her older sister's arm and stopped her. "Slow down. Joanna is outside playing with her cousins. It's not time to eat yet."

Elena tugged herself free. "I like to get things set up ahead of time, so if there's anything that goes wrong at the last minute, I can take care of it."

"We're family. We don't care."

"I want this to be perfect for Joanna."

Liliana took the vegetable tray from her sister. "Stop. Take a deep breath. What's going on here? Joanna won't care. Does this involve Samuel?"

Stepping closer, Elena leaned toward Liliana, gripping her upper arms with trembling fingers. "My husband has nothing to do with this."

Liliana unclasped her sister's hand and held it up between them. "Then why are you shaking?"

"Too much caffeine. I'm going to have to cut back on the coffee."

"I've got a suggestion. Go be with your daughter. I'll see to the food being put out for the buffet. I'll have it all ready in fifteen minutes."

"No. No. I can't let you do that. This is my job. Not yours."

"A sister can help a sister."

"Stop it," Elena screamed. "This is my house. I have to keep it up." She shook, opening and closing her hands while she looked around as though searching for something that had eluded her.

Liliana grabbed her. "Calm down, Elena," in the most composed voice she could muster while inside she raged. Her heart raced. Her throat went dry.

6

"I'm fine. I'm fine." Tears shone in Elena's eyes and rolled down her face.

Liliana gathered her big sister into her embrace. "Tell me what's going on. Please, Elena."

"It's just that this party has thrown me behind. I have so much to do. I didn't get the laundry done like I should have. The garden needs to be weeded. I still haven't cleaned the bedrooms. Joanna made a mess in here, and it took longer to clean up. I . . ." Her sobs increased as she clutched Liliana.

Anger insinuated itself into her heart. This was Samuel's doing. Her sister was afraid to do anything wrong. She knew the signs. She had lived with them as a child.

When Elena stopped crying, she finally pulled away, wiping her cheeks. "I'm sorry. I got your shirt wet."

Liliana brushed her fingers over the wet spot. "I'm not worried about that. But I am worried about you."

Her sister peered out the large window in the kitchen nook. "I need to finish putting out the food." She scrubbed her hands down her face. Her gaze latched onto something out in the backyard, then she grabbed the vegetable tray and scurried toward the dining room.

Liliana followed the direction Elena was looking and saw Samuel standing with the other men, her two uncles and several cousins, talking and laughing. Rafael, who was eleven years younger than Liliana and never really exposed to their father's abuse, was in the middle of the male group while Mama and the females in the Rodriguez family sat in a circle, no doubt gossiping. The dozen children played on the swing set and trampoline.

While inside, Elena was falling apart.

Elena came back into the kitchen and went to the refrigerator for some more food. Liliana picked up the two pitchers with lemonade and tea and headed into the other room.

Ten minutes later with all the dishes on the table, Liliana stepped back and surveyed the feast. "What army are you feeding?"

"Our family is an army." Elena finished lining up the bowls and plates with the salads first, then the meat and vegetables. The last was the dessert, a large cake with Joanna's name on it. "Do you think *Tío* Ricardo will mind we aren't having any Mexican food? He complained last time." She straightened one platter that was crooked, sighed, and moved toward the back door.

"*Tío* Ricardo always complains. He would if you made Mexican food. He would say he was tired of eating it all the time. His wife has her hands full with that one. Never satisfied."

Her fingers around the doorknob, Elena looked at Liliana. "I haven't been sleeping well lately. I'm overtired. That's all. Nothing else is going on. Understand, Liliana?"

"Perfectly," she replied while her nails dug into her palms.

Elena opened the door and went outside to round up everyone for dinner.

"Why the frown, *niña?*" her mother asked Liliana when she approached her in the kitchen.

"Elena is working too hard. She's exhausted, stressed," Liliana whispered in Spanish.

"Tsk. Tsk. You know Samuel has asked us nicely to speak in English. He's still trying to learn Spanish. We must honor his request when we are at his house."

Exactly, but then Liliana wondered how much Samuel really knew. He had been living here for eight years and "learning" the language. As President of Durango City Bank she would have thought he would be fluent by now. "*Madre, perdóname.* I forgot."

"You don't think I know what you are doing. I'm going into the dining room and celebrating my oldest granddaughter's birthday. I hope you will behave yourself."

"I always do, Mama."

Her mother snorted, adjusting her black shawl about her shoulders. Dressed in black since the day Liliana's father died four years ago, Mama ambled into the other room while the back door opened.

Liliana was left alone in the kitchen with Samuel.

His gaze pierced through her. "Is something wrong? You seem upset."

As if the man cared. "Three murders in the last few days takes its toll on the police."

"Yes, I can imagine. I wanted to speak with you and see what's going on with the investigation."

"I can't talk about it. Besides, the investigation has just begun."

His eyes hardened like the rocky faces of the mountains in the Big Bend National Park. "But I thought you would have it solved by now. I heard Chief Winters talk about how good you are. He told the mayor that you and the new Texas Ranger for this area would have it solved in no time."

"While I'm flattered Chief Winters feels that way, it's not that simple. I'll tell you one thing, though, I'll make sure my family is protected no matter what or should I say who hurts them. *La familia* is important. You do understand *familia* is Spanish for *family*?"

He squinted, his gaze running down the length of her then back up to her face. Cold. Calculating. "I think I got that."

"*Bueno.*" Liliana started to skirt around Samuel in the kitchen.

At the same time she moved, he did, too. Into her path. A large man, over six feet three inches, with muscular arms, Samuel blocked her exit. "I can ban you from this house. I demand respect in my own home."

Demand? She bit the inside of her mouth to stop from retaliating and forged a smile on her face from a deep well of willpower. "I never said anything about not respecting you. You are my sister's husband and her protector. A man who harms his own family is worse than a rabid dog. You know what we do to vicious dogs? I trust you feel the same way I do about family. Is that not so?"

The rigid lines of his jaw spoke of his suppressed anger. "Yes," he muttered between clenched teeth. "One day you'll go too far."

Stepping back, she tilted her head and let her gaze roam down his length. "I was just thinking that. Funny how we know each other so well." She made a wide circle around Samuel and forced herself to walk from the kitchen in a leisurely pace while inside fury shook throughout every part of her.

The next day while Cody was heading for San Antonio, Liliana knocked on *Señor* Flores's sister's door. When *Señora* Gloria appeared, she smiled.

"Child, what are you doing here? I never see you except at church with your mama."

Liliana returned the grin. "My mama knows half the women in Durango."

"That's because she has never met a stranger. So to what do I owe the pleasure of your visit?"

"I need to speak with your brother. Miguel told me he is staying with you since he got out of the hospital last month."

The remnants of her smile disappeared completely. "Ah, Alfredo is not doing too well. His heart attack has left him relying on family, and he isn't happy about that." *Señora* Gloria waved her hand toward the hallway to her left. "May I inquire why you need to speak with him?"

"As I'm sure you've heard, Carlos Salazar was murdered at the ranch your brother owns."

"Yes, but Alfredo wouldn't know anything. He hasn't even been to the property since his stroke two months ago."

"This is really just routine. Since he's the owner of the ranch where there was a murder, I have a few questions and then I'll be on my way."

"He tires easily. If he doesn't hear you, it's because he usually refuses to wear his hearing aid anymore. You may have to shout." The gray-headed woman swung the door to her brother's bedroom open then stepped to the side. "If you need me, I'll be in the kitchen."

"*Gracias.*" Liliana entered the cheerful room with light flooding it from the large window overlooking the backyard.

The man sitting in the chair staring out that window at a birdbath and feeder was a shell of his former self. Once he had been strong and muscular, tanned a golden bronze. Now skin hung off his thin arms and his pasty face was surrounded by half the black hair he had a few months back.

"*Señor* Flores, I need to have a word with you." Liliana's voice rose to a near shout.

"Why are you screaming?"

"*Señora* Gloria told me you aren't wearing your hearing aid."

"She's been harping on me to wear it so I am. I am fifty-five and falling apart. I know you. You're Pablo Rodriguez's daughter."

"*Sí.*"

"I miss him. We used to drink together."

She tensed, trying to keep her expression even, but the mention of her father sparked a fear she'd had as a little girl. She'd worked hard to bury that fear and never to feel that helpless and scared again.

"Sit." After she took the hardback chair across from him, he continued. "Why are you here?"

"Do you know about what happened at your ranch yesterday?"

A scowl aged his face by five years. "*Sí.* What are you doing about it?"

"Investigating it. Do you know anyone who would want to kill Carlos Salazar?"

"I hardly knew the man. Miguel is the one who suggested Carlos work the ranch since I can't anytime soon. I get winded walking out to get the mail."

"Has anything unusual happened at your ranch since you acquired it?"

He scratched his chin. "Come to think about it, right before my heart gave out on me, one evening when the sun was going down behind the mountains, I saw lights in my pasture near the house. Kids like to ride across the fields back there on motorcycles or dune buggies. Went out the next morning and two cows were gone. The fence was down and you know it didn't appear the cattle did it. I saw tire tracks in my field but at the downed fence there were a lot of cattle tracks—more than two would make. I told Miguel to keep the kids off my land."

"That's strange. Did you ever find your cattle?"

"They were about five hundred yards away, eating, just two happy cows, oblivious they weren't where they should be."

"How many cattle do you have?"

"Forty."

"Forty? I didn't see that many at the ranch."

Señor Flores straightened in his chair, one hand gripping its arm. "Two months ago when I had my heart attack I had forty head. I'd planned to buy about ten more. That's about all my land will support. Besides, I didn't want too much work."

"I'll count the next time I go out there, but I don't think there are forty."

"Miguel hasn't told me there's a problem." He put his hand on his chest as it rose and fell. "Talk to Miguel. He was stepping in for me with Carlos. He didn't want to worry me about anything." He took another deep inhalation, his eyes sliding closed.

"Did Carlos ever see the lights?"

"Don't—know. I didn't—ask. He didn't tell me." Resting his head on the back cushion, he gulped in a deep breath. "As much as I like a pretty lady visiting—I'm tired."

"*Gracias.* I won't bother you anymore."

"No bother. I used to do so much more. Forty years working as a ranch hand and foreman, you would think I could talk more than ten minutes."

"Rest. You'll be back working on that ranch in no time."

"Tell that pretty mama hello for me," *Señor* Flores said, without opening his eyes.

Liliana left after telling *Señora* Gloria *adios* and strolled toward her car on the street. She intended to ask Miguel about the cattle. What has happened to ten cows? Why didn't he say anything to *Señor* Flores? Was Miguel protecting him or was something else going on? She couldn't shake the feeling Miguel was keeping something from them.

As she rounded the front of her Chevy, she noticed her back tire was flat. Great! Tossing her purse on the front seat, she started toward the trunk. Until she spied why the tire was flat. It was slashed, along with the other back one.

An alarm clanged against her skull. She pressed herself against her car and scoured the area for a sign of anything unusual. Nothing out of the ordinary. In fact, no one was outside in the yard. Deserted.

Keeping an eye on her surroundings, she called headquarters.

❧

Later that afternoon, after she had her two tires replaced, she went to the construction site to see Miguel. When he wasn't there, because he was picking up supplies for his employer in San Antonio, she headed for the second crime scene. Chief Winters had supervised the removal of the debris yesterday at Victor Ruiz's house since she had been at Carlos's ranch processing that crime scene.

Before the charred ruins of Ruiz's house, Liliana took several steps closer, the burnt smell still clinging to the air. From what little they could tell, the perpetrator jimmied the back door and entered that way. He probably caught Ruiz off guard, maybe sitting in his lounge chair where he was found tied to it with barbwire. The autopsy report confirmed he had been tortured. What information did the killer want? Did it tie to Carlos's murder the next day or the woman's the day before? She could understand Victor Ruiz being murdered. He'd led a violent life, and as the police were discovering, with a long list of people he had crossed. Digging into Carlos's life might produce some answers, or maybe when and if they discovered who Jane Doe was, her identity would point them in the right direction.

Liliana stared toward the field behind Ruiz's home across the rubble that had been a one-story house. Was that the way the perpetrator had approached or had he come from the front and around to the back door where he wouldn't be seen when he broke in? Did he park nearby or walk a distance?

Ducking under the yellow tape, she entered the ruins. Chief Winters said nothing else had been found in the debris carted off yesterday. Ruiz paid cash for this house. Didn't have a job in Durango. What was he living on? His ill-gotten spoils from Brownsville or had he set up here? Doing what? Drugs? Smuggling people into the country? Or something entirely different?

Across the living room she saw the remains of the chimney, one of the few things still standing. How many times would a person use that here in this part of Texas? Not many. She slowly made her way toward it, checking the floor. There had been carpet that had burned in the fire with only a few pieces left. Those were removed yesterday—leaving only the concrete slab the house was built on.

At the fireplace, she bent down to check it out. Somehow, a couple of logs were intact inside. They looked real—not the fake kind. She touched one. Real. She guessed the stones had protected the logs. The irony was the one thing that should have burned in the house didn't while the rest around it did struck her. As she started to pull her hand away, her fingertips brushed the bottom, encountering a ridge.

She wiped the thin layer of ash away, noting the disturbed concrete. Taking the logs from the low grate, she then removed the concrete and realized something was wrong. This wasn't a normal bottom of a fireplace. Sweeping more ashes away, she revealed loose blocks. After she pried the nearest one up, a safe lay beneath the fireplace flooring.

Five minutes later, she placed a call to the station to inform the chief. One of Officer Hudson's skills was his ability to open most anything. She hoped he could do this. Why would Ruiz hide something in his fireplace in a safe?

While she waited, she turned from the fireplace and scanned the street. She kept coming back to the three murders in four days. Instinct told her they were somehow connected. But Jane Doe was up close and personal—somehow directed at the unborn child. The second, Ruiz, was up close and personal, but the torture meant so much more. Did the murderer want information or to make Ruiz pay for something? The third was what seemed out of the ordinary. From hundreds of yards away. If it was the same killer, why that method? Was there a reason he didn't want Carlos to know who was murdering him? It couldn't be fear. Ruiz, a suspected coyote, was a scary man to cross. Carlos was by all appearances an ordinary person, and if she believed his cousin, not into anything illegal like Ruiz.

There were too many questions and not any answers. Her insides twisted into a knot of frustration. Three days ago she'd been standing here, trying to figure out the same things. Who had the nerve to murder a man like Victor Ruiz? From what they were uncovering about Ruiz, few liked the man but even fewer would have tried to kill him because of his reputation for ruthlessness. Was there someone even more dangerous who had moved into the town?

When Officer Hudson arrived, he went to work on the safe. In due time, he succeeded in opening it. He and Liliana stared down at stacks of one hundred dollar bills—lots of stacks. On top of them was a small ledger.

"This answers what Ruiz was living on," she murmured and picked up the pad.

"Does that tell you how he got so much money?" Officer Hudson asked as he withdrew the twelve bundles of money— each stack probably ten thousand dollars.

Liliana whistled. "Whatever he was doing, he was doing well." Flipping the ledger open, she scanned the dates, names, and numbers. One stood out: March 23rd, Crip, $5,000. The day Jane Doe was found.

⸎

After a frustrating day getting nowhere on the cases, Cody relished the feel of his horse beneath him. Although he wanted to check out what happened to Carlos's ten cows—a nagging feeling it was connected somehow to what was going on in Durango—he needed this ride. There was something rejuvenating about being on his gelding in the early morning before the heat built up. He didn't get to do this nearly enough.

Cody examined the ground then looked back at the small herd grazing not far away in the enclosed field. "Where did the cows get out? This looks intact."

"Carlos probably repaired the fence," Liliana said.

"But there are still ten cows gone from the herd. You said Flores had forty cows before his heart attack. Now he has thirty."

"I know. He didn't know about where those cows went. I plan on bringing Miguel in to interview again."

"What if Carlos sold the ten cows for money?"

"Another question is did Carlos see the lights in the field like *Señor* Flores did? He thought it was kids fooling around. What if it wasn't? Something else is going on?"

Cody pulled back on his reins and hopped down from his gelding. "I think I know how they are getting out. This is a gate. Not obvious but all a person has to do is unhook the barbwire and the cows or anything else can go through." Cody pointed to the ground. "See all the tracks here." He opened the "gate" and swept his gaze over the ground on the other side of the fence. "Obviously this is how the cows left. Let's see where the tracks lead to. Maybe we'll find some of the cattle."

"That was months ago."

"Maybe. He said only a few cattle were gone. That's not ten. So something must have happened in between then and now."

"Who opened this gate?

"Maybe the tracks will lead us to the person." Cody mounted his gelding.

"You just want to ride your horse."

He tipped his hat then spurred his mount through the gate. "Yep, ma'am."

"How about closing this—gate?"

"Go ahead." Cody slowed his horse and focused his gaze on the ground before him.

Liliana hooked the barbwire back in place and closed the distance between her and Cody in a gallop. "What did you find?"

"Besides tracks from more than a few cattle—feed. Not much but even a little is strange here."

"Like someone was throwing down a trail for them to follow?"

"Exactly."

By a stream on the other side, Cody found more feed. He frowned.

"What's wrong?" Liliana asked.

"The cattle stopped here and fed, but some of them—three—went off this way." He pointed toward the south. "Let's go that way."

"I talked to the ICE agent this morning before we left. Nothing so far on the ID of our Jane Doe."

"She may not be from Mexico. Just because she wasn't in any of our databases doesn't mean she isn't a U.S. citizen." Cody pulled back on his reins and studied the hard ground.

"True, but even the face recognition program hasn't turned up anything in our system, and there hasn't been a missing person's report filed for a woman who fits Jane Doe's description."

"Sometimes that happens."

"Sad that no one is missing this woman. Who was the father of her baby? Why hasn't he come forward?"

"Do you think there's a connection between Carlos and Jane Doe? Does Victor Ruiz fit in to their murders somehow?" Cody set his gelding in a steady walk as they trailed the hoofprints of some cows from Carlos's property.

"I haven't found an obvious connection between Ruiz and Carlos."

"So let's start looking for a less obvious one."

"Who is Carlos Salazar? What do we know about the man?"

"Only what Miguel has told us. Very little. I'm having Officer Hudson see what he can track down in New Mexico." Liliana guided her mare through the opening in the rocks that led into a narrow canyon adjacent to Carlos's ranch.

Cody followed her through. "Whose land is this? Part of Cesar Álvarez's ranch?"

"Without a map, I'm not sure, but I think so." A film of perspiration coated her forehead. She removed her cowboy hat and ran the back of her hand across her brow.

"Hey, I think I see some cows halfway down this canyon." Cody set his gelding into a gallop.

Liliana scanned the cliffs hemming them in. Goosebumps flashed up her arms and encompassed her whole body even though the sun had baked the landscape in hot temperatures, unusual for the last few days of March.

She increased her mare's gait until she caught up with Cody ten yards from three cows grazing on some lush vegetation ringing a spring. "No wonder they didn't come home. They found food, water, and freedom."

"I'm not sure freedom means that much to them, but food and water are important. And we still don't know how they got out."

"Why didn't Carlos let someone know he was losing cattle?"

"There are some in Durango who would rather not approach the police—they take care of problems themselves."

"Like Mr. Martinez?"

"Yes. The other day when I tried to interview the children again, Mrs. Martinez sat between them with her arms around each one. If they started to say something, she pressed them close to her. Both Maria and Pedro couldn't remember anything."

Cody took his hat off and waved it at the cattle, using his horse to urge them toward the canyon opening. "I've encountered that before. Don't people realize we're here to help them—protect them?"

"That hasn't always been the case in some of these people's lives. They have discovered street justice often works better than the judicial court system." Liliana helped in keeping the cattle moving forward. Goosebumps still covered her. She didn't like this place.

Cody came to a halt at the end of the canyon and twisted around in the saddle to stare back the way they came. "I did discover there is a cartel in Mexico with the evil eye as its symbol. It's meant to strike fear in the people who encounter it. They wear a tattoo on their right forearm. The problem is that that cartel isn't one in northern Mexico. At least not yet."

"Another player in the game? Great." After having two tires slashed a couple of days ago, Liliana couldn't shake the sensation she was being watched. She rubbed her hand up her left arm, forcibly trying to rid herself of the goosebumps. The chill clung to her like the sweat to her forehead earlier.

"It seems we have more questions than answers."

"I'll be interested in seeing what that whole letter from Anna said. What little I could read at the crime scene indicated a love letter, but Miguel didn't say anything to us about a love interest for Carlos. If they were so close, you would think Miguel would know that. In fact, he couldn't tell us anything about an Anna in Carlos's life."

"The more we discover, the more I think Miguel isn't telling us everything."

"Which warrants us bringing him back down to the station." Liliana spurred her mare faster. There was something about the box canyon that had given her the creeps.

Lunch in hand, Kyle spied an empty table in the courtyard at the high school and hurried toward it. After taking a seat, he dug into his pizza, starved because he'd dragged his feet getting dressed, missed breakfast, and literally had to run to catch the school bus. A quick survey of the area reinforced his anger at his dad. Mostly unfamiliar kids were clustered in small groups talking with one another. Seeing a few familiar ones from his classes, all engrossed in their friends, churned his feeling of loneliness.

I hate Durango. I hate this school. I hate my dad.

He fumbled in his backpack and pulled out his notebook. When he opened it, he saw the calendar for March. He put an X through Monday, Tuesday, and Wednesday. Three days down and too many to go. The twenty-ninth on the page mocked him. School didn't end for two months.

"Hi." Manny, the office aide from Monday, sat across from him. "I saw you by yourself over here and thought I'd come invite you to join us."

"Us?" His anger at his situation still coursing through him, Kyle gripped his pencil.

"It's not easy being the new kid." Manny tossed his head toward a group of six students a couple of tables away.

A white teen from his English class waved. The others looked like a gathering of the United Nations. Kyle stuffed his notebook into his backpack and rose. "Sorry. I've still got to go to the library." Taking a huge bite of his pizza, he started for the large trash can and tossed the half-eaten lunch into it.

As he walked away from Manny, he sensed gazes boring into his back. He found a quiet place, leaned against the brick wall, and began texting a friend in Houston. He'd better not be stuck here too long. Somehow, he had to get back to Houston and civilization.

"I saw you blow off Manny back there."

Kyle lifted his head, ready to defend himself if he needed to. His hand clenched around his cell phone as he stared into the face of a guy in his history class. "You're Aaron."

"Yep. I tried to get you after class to see if you wanted to eat with me and the guys, but you were gone."

"Hungry. Didn't want to spend all my time standing in line waiting for something to eat."

"You threw most of your pizza away."

"Guess I lost my appetite."

"Know what you mean. Manny can do that to me. Don't care for him and his buddies. Why don't you join us?"

Kyle looked around and didn't see anyone except a group of girls by the doors going into the building. "Where?"

Aaron walked in the opposite direction from the doors, gesturing back at Kyle who still leaned against the wall. "This way. Our own private place."

Around the corner and behind some tall bushes stood a small gathering of four others besides Aaron—all white. When Kyle saw the teens, he sighed. Maybe it wouldn't be so bad if he found a few friends until he returned to Houston. One way or another he would be going back there before school started next year.

~ ❧ ~

I paced from one end of my living room to the other. I don't like the fact a little girl saw me kill Anna. So that noise I heard wasn't the wind blowing through the open window. It was Maria Martinez.

What to do?

I can't hurt her. She's innocent. So far she doesn't remember anything. She probably didn't see my face. I had my hat on.

But what if she does start remembering something important? What do I do?

I'll decide that if it happens. The police have no idea who killed those people. I want to keep it that way. I have work to do in Durango. I'm still in control.

⟨⟩

Early Friday, Liliana sat across from Miguel, who drummed his fingers on the top of the table in the interview room. Studying some notes to give him some time to stew, she pulled her own thoughts together about how she would handle this questioning. She'd discovered Miguel had volunteered to go to San Antonio for his boss on Tuesday and then Wednesday and Thursday he'd taken off to arrange Carlos's burial in Mexico where the family was from originally. She'd been at his house first thing this morning to make sure he didn't disappear again today.

She'd only had one cup of coffee. Taking a sip of her caffeine-laden drink, she looked up at Miguel. "Why didn't you tell us about the missing cattle at Carlos's?"

"What's there to tell? A few wander off from time to time."

"Did Carlos ever tell you about seeing lights in the field behind his house at night?"

"No," he clipped out, his fingers striking the table moving faster.

The sound distracted her for a moment after spending a restless night trying to sleep. But the three murders kept flying through her mind like a ping-pong ball in a fierce game. "Did he ever have to fix the fence?"

"I don't know. He didn't tell me the day-to-day activities he did at the ranch."

"What did he talk about? You two were friends, cousins."

Miguel ceased his drumming and slid his hand off the table. "Just guy stuff. Nothing important."

"Why didn't you tell *Señor* Flores about the missing cattle?"

"In case you don't know, he isn't doing too well. I didn't want to give him anything to be concerned about. It happened a couple of times. Cows are dumb animals. They don't always want to stay where you want them to. What's missing cattle have to do with Carlos's murder?"

"Maybe someone was shopping for his dinner and taking one from time to time. Maybe Carlos caught him and the man killed him. We can't rule anything unusual out."

Miguel snorted. "It was a few cattle. Certainly nothing to kill him over."

"I've seen people kill for less." Liliana spread the re-created letter from Anna that the state lab had faxed to Cody out on the table before Miguel. "Tell us about Anna."

The third victim's cousin stared at the sheet then raised his head. "Anna? We've been over this the other day. I don't know who you're talking about."

She studied the man for a long moment, almost ready to believe him except that his eye twitched, then his gaze slid away to a spot behind Liliana. "You don't know anything about Carlos having a girlfriend?"

"My cousin dated many women. I guess one could have been called Anna. And that lady could have written him a letter." He centered his full attention on her. "Is this why you had to see me again? A woman? What's she got to do with Carlos's murder?"

"We don't know if she has anything to do with it, but this is a copy of a letter found on Carlos when he was shot. We want to get a good picture of the man who was murdered. It helps us find his killer. You want us to find his killer, don't you?"

"*Sí.*"

"Carlos never mentioned anyone named Anna?"

Miguel shrugged. "Not that I recall."

"When we checked out Carlos's house, it looked like he was expecting to entertain. Who? Anna? You? Someone else?"

Miguel's mouth tightened. "Who's standing behind that mirror?" He pointed to the two-way one behind Liliana.

"Ranger Jackson."

"I feel like I'm the criminal here. Carlos was *familia*. We were like *hermanos*." Miguel rose. "So unless you're going to charge me with something, my lunch hour is over and I need to get back to work."

"So Carlos never mentioned anyone named Anna?"

Her question halted the man reaching for the handle. "I thought I already answered that earlier." Anger reinforced each word with steel.

"Just checking for the record, because if we discover you lied in a murder investigation, charges could be brought against you."

Both of his dark bushy eyebrows shot up. "I haven't done anything wrong. Anna is a common name. I guess Carlos could have mentioned someone by that name. He talked about a lot of women. He's a ladies' man."

"Okay. Then write down the names of the women you remember him talking about." Liliana slid a sheet of paper toward the end of the table near Miguel.

He glared at it then made a production out of checking the clock on the wall. "You going to pay me for lost wages?"

"I'll call your boss and tell him you were at the station and will be a few minutes late. I'm sure he'll understand being questioned by the police in a murder investigation."

Miguel squeezed his hands into fists, glanced back at the door, then stomped the few feet to the table. After he scribbled down a couple of names, he said, "There," and slammed the pen down on the metal top.

Only two names were scribbled on the paper. "For a ladies' man, that's not very many names."

"That's all I can come up with. He wasn't here that long." He fled from the room, leaving the door open.

Cody appeared in the entrance. "I thought family was important to him."

"So long as you don't ask questions. When I caught him at his work site and asked him to follow me to the station, he wasn't too happy with me."

"That's what happens when you purposely try to catch him off guard." Cody dropped a report on the table in front of Liliana. "The tracks at Carlos's ranch matched the tires from a compact car."

"Not a light truck?" she asked, thinking of the black pickup Pedro had seen pulled out of the field onto the road. Brady had confirmed what his friend had said.

"Nope. That would make our job easier."

"I don't know about easier, but at least it would mean two of the murders were connected possibly. I guess a small black pickup narrows things down just a little more than a compact car."

Cody chuckled. "If you say so. Do you know how many pickups are in the town? In the short time I've been here, I've seen a lot."

"Yeah, I know. I have several cousins who own a small black truck."

"That coupled with a tan cowboy hat still makes our haystack pretty tall and that needle small. Hungry?"

"When Miguel was talking about lunch, I was afraid that my stomach was gonna growl and embarrass me."

His laughter eased the stress from the unsuccessful interview. "C'mon. My treat after the unproductive morning we've had."

"Speak for yourself." She made her way down the hallway. "According to Miguel, his cousin is a model citizen."

"According to Miguel, his cousin didn't know anyone named Anna."

Coming into the large room, Officer Vega passed Juan setting a trash can on the floor, saw the white board Liliana had started on the murders, and frowned. "Rodriguez, I wouldn't work too hard on Ruiz's case. We're better off without him around. There's probably a long line of suspects that wanted him dead."

"If you know of any that stand out to you, by all means give me their names."

"Hate for you to waste your time. Just more scumbags. He had his hands in anything that would make him a buck. Legal or illegal."

"Hey, maybe all the scumbags will kill each other off and we can go on vacation," Officer Hudson at the counter said. "Wouldn't ya like that, Juan? No more trash to empty, floors to sweep."

"And no more money."

Officer Vega burst out laughing. "He's got you there, Hudson."

Liliana walked toward the front door. "Have fun, boys. Chief will be back soon from lunch with the mayor and councilmen. You know what that means."

Nancy, the police chief's secretary and dispatcher, entered from the back. "Yeah, and he just pulled up."

Liliana reached for the handle, but Cody stepped forward and opened the door for her. "Good time to leave."

"Why?" Cody asked.

"Chief always comes back from these monthly luncheons ready to bite off the nearest person's head. I try to stay low, especially with all that's going on."

"Yeah, as if we would ever have to worry about not having a job because there's no crime. Sadly that problem isn't gonna happen."

"So people like Victor Ruiz are our job security?"

Cody stopped at the curb and slanted a look toward her. "Yeah, I guess they are. I hate to think we need the bad guys."

"I wouldn't mind moving on to another job if that were ever the case."

"I'm not sure what I would do." He nodded toward the cafe across the street.

"Best food in town." Liliana jogged across to the other side. "I'd be a photographer. What are your interests?"

"Work. And more work. All I've ever known is law enforcement. And don't you dare mention all work and no play . . ."

As she entered the cafe, she threw him a grin. "I don't have to. You already have. Feeling a little guilty?"

"Not me." He scanned the restaurant. "This must be a good place. Only one table is free and the dirty dishes are still on it."

The door opened behind Liliana. "Even though it's technically after the lunch hour, Mom's Cafe is usually busy all the way until mid-afternoon so let's grab it before someone else does."

Liliana sat across from Cody as a young man approached the booth and began gathering up the dirty dishes and utensils. "Hi, Sean. I've missed you the last couple of times you've delivered food to the station. How's school going?"

Sean kept his head down and finished stacking the plates. "Had—had—to drop—o—ut."

"I'm sorry to hear that. I hope you don't give up on college."

After putting the dishes into a big plastic bin, he began wiping down the table. "May—be one—day," Sean stammered then quickly left, favoring his right leg. With his head still ducked down, he ran into a customer getting up from a booth.

"Watch where you're going," the barrel-chested man said to Sean.

He mumbled something and continued his flight toward the kitchen.

"Sean's had a hard life. Lost his father and mother when he turned eighteen. He's been working two jobs to go to school but was laid off from one of them a couple of months ago. He stutters when he's nervous, and I have a feeling he has a hard time in job interviews. He's been limping lately. A bike accident."

"Who do you not know in town?"

"There are a few. I like people."

"Is that why you became a cop?"

"Yes and that I didn't like some of the injustice I saw." A picture of her father materialized in her mind, and she shoved it away. She had dealt with that long ago. Put it behind her, or so she thought. Maybe Elena's situation was dragging it to the foreground again. How long had Elena been covering for Samuel? "How about you? Why are you a cop?"

The waitress came to the booth and set the waters down then placed the dog-eared menus before them. "I'll give you a few minutes."

When she left, Cody picked up the menu. "Any suggestions?"

"Everything. I haven't gotten anything here I haven't liked. This cafe has gotten a fair share of my wages along with most of us from the station."

"What are you getting?" He perused the menu.

"A salad."

"That's all?"

"Yep. You wait until you see the portions. You get your money's worth. This is a family-owned cafe. Our waitress is one of the daughters. You haven't answered my question. Why did you become a cop?"

Cody set the menu on the table and looked directly into her eyes. "Because if it hadn't been for a cop, I'd probably be in prison by now."

Liliana nearly choked on the water she was sipping. She coughed, glad at that moment the waitress returned and took their orders. It gave Liliana time to recover from his revelation. "Why?"

"At fourteen, I had a chip on my shoulder and was angry at the world. My little brother died, my mother left my dad, and I had to leave the town I grew up in. By the time I was fifteen, I rebelled and ran with the wrong crowd. A cop caught me joyriding and instead of taking me to jail, he took me to my home, but he didn't let me off. I ended up doing community service in a program he was involved in. Every time I pass through Austin, I go see him. He still helps confused kids get back on track. I want to make that kind of difference."

"I know we aren't the only police department in the area you work with. How are you going to find the time to do it all?"

One corner of his mouth quirked. "That has always been my problem. This is a demanding job. At least the way I do it."

"You told me that your son isn't happy about this move."

"That's putting it mildly. He doesn't understand what my job is."

"With all that's on TV you would think he would."

"No. He thinks when the hour is up I should be home. I wish it were that easy."

"That's one of the reasons I'm not married. Most people don't understand the amount of time this job can take, not to mention the emotional toll it can have on you."

"I've been there. I know what you're saying." As the waitress put their orders down in front of them, Cody waited then continued after she left. "I've decided to go back out to the area behind Carlos's ranch tomorrow and take a look around. Something is still nagging me. I felt watched."

"I did, too."

"Interesting. Probably nothing, but . . ." He shrugged.

"But you're going to satisfy your curiosity?"

"Yep, want to come again?"

"I'll pass. I'm revisiting each of the crime scenes."

"One thing TV doesn't get across is all the legwork a cop has to do on cases. Often dull and boring."

"But necessary to rule out various leads in a case."

Cody picked up his hot roast beef sandwich. "I'm also working on Al's shooting. He's reviewing his notes on the case. I thought I would pay him a visit this weekend and see if he remembers anything else."

"We ran into a dead end. There's a lot of money involved in smuggling, possibly palms greased. I don't think those people would let a Texas Ranger," she tapped her chest, "or a police officer stand in their way. I figured Al's questions were rattling someone's cage."

"Such a cynic." He took a bite of his sandwich.

"It's hard not to be when you work in law enforcement." Liliana stabbed some lettuce in her taco salad. But she realized that wasn't the only reason she was jaded. Her childhood had forced her to look at life differently. She couldn't help but blame her mother partially for the situation Elena found herself in with Samuel. She'd never stood up to her husband, and now Elena thinks she is at fault for what was happening.

༄

"How was school today?" Serena asked as she wheeled herself into the gym at the apartment complex.

Kyle stopped his crunches and mopped his face and neck. "Okay. I met a couple of guys."

"That's good."

"How come you don't go to Durango High School?"

Serena's smile faded. "Some people can't accept people who are different."

"What do ya mean?"

"I went to a private Christian school until my dad lost his job and had to take one that cut his salary in half. I started high school last year at Durango High and quit at the end of first semester. I—I was having problems."

Kyle scrambled off the floor and grabbed a set of weights. "What kind of problems?"

She gripped the wheels of her chair and pushed herself toward the shelves that housed the different weights. "Bullies. There were some who didn't think a girl with a disability should be at the school."

"You're kidding."

"I wish. Now I'm homeschooled and doing much better. The only thing I miss is not seeing friends as much. It gets kinda lonely at times."

"You said you went to a Christian school. Do you go to church?"

Serena stopped in mid-action reaching for the twenty-pound weights and looked at him. "Yes, I belong to the Church of the Redeemer. It's a few blocks from here. They have a great youth group, and I get to see my friends then. I guess you figured out there aren't many kids here at these apartments."

"I hadn't noticed." He hadn't noticed much about the place except the great gym.

"They're a couple of others here—a guy named Manny. He goes to Durango High and there's a girl who's thirteen. She goes to the middle school. Oh, there is another guy, but I haven't talked to him."

"Manny Chavez?"

"Yes, have you met him?"

"Yeah." He remembered Aaron and his friends discussing Manny and what a big shot he thought he was because he was the star on the baseball team.

"Nice guy. I've heard rumors that if he keeps playing like he does, he'll be recruited by a major league baseball team."

"He's that good?"

"Yes." She clasped her weights and started to do some exercises he'd shown her.

"Hold it. You aren't lifting it the right way."

"I'm not?"

"Here, let me show you." Kyle positioned himself behind her wheelchair, leaning down to grasp her arm. Serena's scent of apples wafted to him, which sparked a memory of his mother baking an apple cobbler the week before she died.

He released Serena's arm and backed away. Her aroma stirred remembrances that brought the past months' pain to the forefront.

Serena dropped the weight, and it bounced on the carpet. She twisted about to search for him.

He kept retreating. "Sorry. I've got to go." He spun around and hurried from the gym.

Another scene flashed into his thoughts. Of the police officer notifying Nate and him that his mother had died in a car wreck while the drunk driver walked away from the crash with just a few bruises. Even knowing the man was going to prison for killing his mother didn't make this hollow feeling go away. It burrowed deep into him, leaving nothing but emptiness in its path.

∼⌒Չ∼

A blaring sound reached into Liliana's mind and yanked her from a deep sleep. She fumbled for the receiver and knocked over her flashlight. The phone rang again. And again.

Finally she snatched it up and said, "Hello?"

Silence.

Elena? "Hello? Anyone there?" She glanced at the red numbers on the clock. 1:15.

A menacing cackle cut through the silence on the other end.

Liliana swung her legs over the side of the bed as she fumbled for her light switch.

Crash. From her living room.

Another hideous laugh then her line went dead.

Tossing down her phone, Liliana grabbed her gun on the nightstand and hurried from her bedroom. She pressed herself against the wall and sidled toward the end of the hallway. She paused at the entrance into the living room, listening for any unusual noise. Nothing, except the hammering beat of her pulse.

She waited another moment then reached around the wall into the room and flipped on the light as she swung into the doorway. Gun up, now both hands cradling the handle, she panned the area. Her gaze fell upon the rock on her tile floor then the busted window five feet away, glass strewn across the floor.

For a few seconds relief wilted her against the wall until the black letters *RIP* on the rock snagged her attention. She could no longer ignore what was happening. The slashing of her two tires yesterday was more than a warning to her to back off. Someone was sending her a threat.

7

Cody stood on the elevated spot in the box canyon where they'd found the cattle on Thursday, his gaze drawn to a high ridge on the west side. Had he seen a glint yesterday from up there? Prickles rose along the back of his neck. Something wasn't right.

Prepared to scale the cliff if he had to, Cody removed the climbing gear looped around his saddle horn. He secured his horse before hiking to the wall of the canyon. After examining the rocks shooting straight up, he mapped the route he would take to the top then proceeded up the stone face.

Fifteen minutes later, he pulled himself over the ledge and clambered to his feet. Wind whipped by him, stirring the dust in the air. The sun rising higher in the eastern sky bore down on him, and he welcomed the breeze.

He squatted, getting down near the ground for a different angle for his search. Again nothing—until he spied something caught in a crevice of a rock. Did he imagine the gleam of the sun striking off something? The glass off a pair of binoculars? It had been such a fleeting feeling. He wasn't sure. Why would someone be up here, watching him and Liliana? He inspected the ground around him. Hard. No footprints.

Then he saw it. A cigarette butt. He pulled out an evidence bag and started to gather the butt when he noticed another one beneath it. The more he dug the more he found. A total of ten butts of the same kind of cigarette. A smoke hole? Strange place for one. Who? Why?

His gut tight, he rose and slowly made a full circle. Now he wished he'd brought binoculars with him. Something didn't feel right. The rough terrain on the other side of the ridge of the box canyon stretched for miles toward the border between the United States and Mexico. Not far from here another sheer rock face jutted upward, creating another higher ridge.

He knelt again at the stash of cigarette butts and collected them, then began his descent to the floor of the canyon. He'd wasted enough time with this hunch. But this whole situation with the missing cattle, the "gate" in Carlos's fence, wouldn't let go of him. He would have to make an appointment to see Cesar Álvarez who was out of town right now, and he intended to talk with Al again about the rumors he'd been investigating when he was shot.

As he headed back to Salazar's ranch, the feeling he was being watched again snaked down his spine. He glanced back several times and the last time he saw a glint in the middle of the higher ridge as though sunlight bounced off something. Spurring his horse faster, he let it run.

⌘

When Liliana pulled onto the dirt road that lead to the abandoned house where Jane Doe was shot three times, she drove slower than usual, trying to figure out why this place. It was isolated but was not far from a large subdivision. She studied the houses in the distance then swung her attention in the opposite direction. The field, dotted with clusters of trees and carpeted with tall weeds and cacti, stretched south toward the border—maybe from this point ten miles away.

The two things all three of the murders had in common were that they occurred in the southern part of Durango and the victims were of Hispanic descent. Did that mean anything?

According to Maria, the man and woman were talking when they came into the house. Only after a few minutes did the rapid-fire Spanish and angry exchange happen. So had the man planned to kill the woman from the beginning? Was that why he'd chosen this place? How did he know about it? Did he live around here? In the Rancho subdivision?

A lot of people carried guns in the area. Had the man come prepared to shoot Jane Doe or was he used to carrying a weapon and pulled it because the woman made him mad? That murder seemed filled with a passion—of hatred.

A dull throbbing pounded behind Liliana eyes. Too many questions she couldn't answer. The more she thought about it, the more she couldn't get a handle on what was going on. She needed to talk to Maria again. Somehow. Walk the child through the exchange the two had before the man killed the woman.

She parked in front of the house. The yellow crime scene tape had been broken into two pieces, each dancing on the wind like a conductor leading an orchestra. Turning toward the housing subdivision a hundred yards away, she decided to get a list of people who lived in Rancho Estates. Check each one's background. She didn't think this murder had been planned, which meant it could have happened near where the killer lived.

Did Maria know more than she realized, especially if it was one of her neighbors?

Her eyes swept back toward the abandoned two-story house. Something flickered in the corner of her eye. She zeroed in on the living room window. Open. Nothing was there.

Creeping forward, she withdrew her gun. Maybe it wasn't anything but the wind moving the branches of the bush in front of the house. Or maybe . . .

She eased up the porch steps and noticed the door ajar. Thinking back to what Pedro and Brady had described the day they'd found the body, Liliana composed herself with a calming breath. Every sense became alert. She heard the flap of the yellow tape behind her. The sound of a lawnmower in the distance. Cars passing on the road not far away. A door closing.

The back one.

She gave up being quiet. She jumped from the porch and raced around the side of the house as two boys ran into the high weeds between the subdivision and the abandoned house.

"Brady. Stop," she shouted.

One boy, the one she recognized, slowed while the other disappeared into the brush.

Brady looked back at her then in the direction his buddy had gone. His body readied itself to spring into action.

"I know where you live. Don't make me chase you down." She fell into a jog and holstered her gun.

The boy stared at his feet, scuffing one into the dirt, stirring the dust. "I didn't do anything wrong."

"Why were you in the house? It's a crime scene."

He kept his head down. "I don't know."

"Who was that with you? It's not Pedro."

"We haven't played together since Saturday."

"I thought you two were best friends."

"Not anymore. His mom won't let him leave the house. He hasn't even gone to school this week."

"He hasn't? Is he sick?"

Brady lifted his shoulders in an exaggerated shrug. "His kid sister hasn't either."

"Why were you in the house? 'I don't know' isn't an answer."

"Promise you won't take me in."

"I can't promise you that. But if I don't get a straight answer, I'm going to have to escort you home and have a word with your parents. Why aren't you in school?"

"Parent-teacher conference day."

She'd forgotten. Rafael had mentioned something about that. "So you just decided to revisit the crime scene. I would have thought after what you saw here that you wouldn't come near this place."

Brady raised his head. "That's why I did. Robbie called me a scaredy-cat. I had to prove I wasn't."

"Who's Robbie?"

"My older brother. He's watching me while Mom and Dad are at work."

"Then he needs to do a better job of it. This house isn't safe structurally. I want you to promise me you'll stay away from here."

"But I'm not an ole scaredy-cat."

"I know. That day you were brave, and I'll walk you home and tell your big brother just that."

"He'll still call me a baby."

"If he does, let me know. I'll set him straight."

"You will?"

"Yeah. Let's go this way." Liliana skirted the tall weeds. "Do you ever see anyone hanging around here? Maybe someone from the neighborhood?"

"Besides Pedro and me?"

"Yes."

"Just kids. Sometimes a parent looking for one of us." Brady stopped at the stream. "But really we don't come here often."

"Why not?"

"Because of the stories about this house."

"Really. What?"

"There was a murder here years ago. I think that's why the people abandoned it last year. Ghosts. I've seen lights on at night. I can see this place from my bedroom window."

❧

Cody shook Al Garcia's hand. "It's good to see you."

The former Texas Ranger limped toward his recliner and eased down. A grimace passed across his face. "Still stiff but the docs say that should get better. I think they're humoring me."

"Your shooting is one of the reasons I'm here in Durango. I wanted to get your take on it. I'm determined to find out who shot you. When someone attacks a Texas Ranger, they attack us all."

One of Al's eyebrows rose. "With all that's happening right now, three murders in four days? My incident is old news compared to the recent crime spree."

"Yeah, Durango has given me a right proper welcome."

Al laughed. "One I'd want to forego."

"Me, too. But someone didn't give me that chance."

"You think it's one person who did all three murders?"

"Maybe, or three different people. We haven't found anything definite to tie them together yet. But . . ." Something was just out of his reach. A thought that flittered in then out so quick Cody couldn't grasp it.

"We've had our share of murders. Who hasn't, if they live on the border these days? But three murders in four days in

Durango is still unusual. This town has been lucky to avoid some of the violence. Others in the area haven't."

"Why?"

"I'd like to say because of my presence and a good police force, but you and I both know that doesn't always make a difference. We've got good men stationed all up and down the border, and we are still having problems."

"Something else going on here?"

Al shrugged. "People come and go. Durango has its share of transients, but overall the population is pretty stable. Now that you've been working with the Durango Police Department a week, how's it going?"

"Fine. They have some capable officers."

"Yeah, I hear you've partnered with Detective Rodriguez."

"Well, not exactly, but her partner is on vacation and we're working the murders together."

"What do you think of Liliana?"

How should he answer that question? His first thought was she was distracting. But that wasn't her problem but his. He found her attractive. But also so much more. "She is inquisitive, dedicated, and good at her job."

"You've discovered all of that in a week?" Al laughed again. "I'd add demanding of others but even more of herself and easy on these old eyes. But to save you a whole lot of heartache, she's a tough one who doesn't let people into her personal life. I've seen a lot of men try and get nowhere."

Cody shifted on the chair across from Al, the ex-ranger's sharp gaze following his reactions with interest. "Tell me about what happened to you that day you were shot."

"I'd left my office to go to the Durango Police Station to talk with the chief about some rumors that had surfaced."

"What rumors?"

"New person working this area." Al leaned forward, his elbows on his knees, his hands clasped together.

"Could that have been Victor Ruiz, our second murder victim? We found information that confirms he was smuggling people over the border here. His last one was for Crip for $5,000."

"It's a possibility. But I thought this ring was involved in smuggling guns, ammunition."

"Tell me what happened when you got shot. I've read the report several times, but I'd still like to hear it in your own words."

Al straightened, raking his hand through his full head of black hair with touches of silver at the temple. "I didn't have a blowout, but about halfway to town my tire was completely flat. I got out to fix it. It happened as I finished changing my tire. A blue Dodge passed me on the road, the window went down, and a gun that I later found out was a .44 Magnum was aimed out of it. The next thing I know I'm shot and down. I think they would have come back except a couple of cars were coming. That's what saved me. In one, the man's wife was a nurse."

"I read the Dodge was found abandoned a few miles down the road."

"It had been stolen from El Paso. It had been wiped down. No fingerprints. Even the owner's. Later I found out the tire I changed had a slow leak caused by a nail I could have picked up anywhere."

"But you don't think you did?"

Al shook his head, staring at a spot beyond Cody. "I think it was planned. Not a random shooting."

"Why?"

"Because I had seen that blue Dodge earlier that day."

"That wasn't in your report."

"I know. I've had the time to go over the events that led up to the shooting, and only recently have I remembered a couple of things that I didn't right after I got shot."

"Besides thinking the Dodge had been tracking you that day, what else?"

"Right before I headed to the station in Durango, I stopped to get some gas and went to get my usual morning coffee. When I came out and headed to my truck, a guy dressed in a black hoodie was running away from the pump area. I didn't think too much about it because my car was in a row closer to the front and nothing seemed out of the ordinary."

"Now you're not so sure?"

"Now I'm wondering if that was when I got the nail in my front right tire. I even called the gas station to see if they had a surveillance tape from two months ago. They didn't."

"Anything else? Anything about the guy running away?"

"You'll be the first to know if there is."

Cody rose and extended his hand. "It was nice talking to you. Your case is important to me and the department. I won't forget all you did for me my first year in Dallas."

"You didn't have to come all the way to Durango to thank me. A phone call would have been enough. I was surprised to hear you were taking this assignment."

"Remember that manhunt we were involved in that first year? If it hadn't been for you, I might not be here today. That fugitive had his gun aimed at my chest when you came along."

"That was nothing. You'd have done that for me if our roles were reversed."

"Yeah, but that doesn't change the fact that I owe you my life." His friend planted his cane in front of him and struggled to stand, but Cody waved him down. "I can let myself out."

Al sank back. "I'm still getting use to this weak leg." He patted his right one. "My knee was shattered. I had it replaced but recovering has been slower than I wished. Take care of yourself. I thought these past few months of peace and quiet might stick around, but that doesn't look like the case with these recent murders."

As Cody left the small house on the outskirts of town, only fifteen minutes from the highway patrol station, he turned toward Carlos's ranch. Lights in the field, strange things happening, and rumors of smuggling made him wonder if they were all connected. That end of town wasn't far from the border.

⋘

"You and I kept missing each other yesterday. I heard you got the ballistics report back on the guns found in Ruiz's freezer." Parked next to Cody's SUV on Sunday afternoon, Liliana came around her Chevy to mount the four planks of wood that comprised the step to Carlos's porch.

"Yeah. Nothing that will help us. I wanted one of those .44 Magnums to be the gun that wounded Al."

"How did your meeting with Al go?"

"Al thinks there may be a gun smuggling ring in this area."

"Yeah, he's talked to the chief about it. But there hasn't been anything concrete for us to go on yet."

Cody reached for the door to unlock it, but it opened beneath his touch. "This doesn't bode well."

Liliana withdrew her gun and entered behind Cody. A few steps into the small house, he halted. She scanned the disarray before her. Every drawers' contents littered the floor. Cushions were cut and the stuffing pulled out.

In the distance the revving of engines sounding like motor-cycles blasted through the air. A window stood wide open, the curtains flapping in the breeze.

Cody picked his way through the chaos and looked out of the window. A trail of dust indicated where the intruders were going. "I think we interrupted someone."

Liliana came to his side and peered out in the direction he pointed. "Let's go after them. I know they have a good head start, but we might be able to figure out where they're going. This is still a crime scene so why were they here?" She surveyed the large room. "From the looks of things, if they were looking for something, they probably found it. Carlos didn't have anything to steal."

"That we know of. Let's go. I'll drive." Cody strode toward the door. "I know we won't have much time. It's getting dark, but maybe we can catch a break."

In Cody's SUV, Liliana put a call into the station to have a couple of officers come out and process the cabin again. "I'm hoping whoever trashed Carlos's house wasn't wearing gloves."

"We can only wish. I'm thankful some criminals aren't too smart."

"Yeah, but those that are make our lives interesting."

Departing the relatively smooth and flat yard, Cody slid a look at Liliana. "Hang on. There's gonna be bumpy ground up ahead."

Liliana gripped the strap on the passenger door. "This is the second time a crime scene has been disturbed today. Don't people honor the yellow tape that says do not cross?"

"Since Ruiz's house is lying in ruins, I'm guessing you're talking about the abandoned one at Rancho Estates. What happened?"

"Brady's older brother dared him to go back to the house. They both did. I read Brady's brother the riot act when I brought Brady home. He ran off and left his little brother after all that happened at the house."

"I'm hoping when this is over with, that the house is leveled."

"Chief is working with the city to get in touch with the owners who live in San Antonio. I think something will be done. It's a danger to any kid who thinks it is a place to play or to dare one another to visit. Brady is sure there are ghosts there. He's seen lights at night."

Cody passed through the makeshift barbwire gate that blended well with the rest of the fence. "Bums? People passing through?"

"Probably. Or kids like *Señor* Flores thought were in his field. I've told patrol about it. They're going to keep an eye on the place until something can be done."

Cody's car bounced over a series of deep ruts. "They came this way, but I don't see any dust now." He slowed his vehicle and finally came to a stop. "I'm getting out to check the tracks."

Liliana joined him in front of the SUV.

Cody squatted and examined the tire tracks. "Motorcycles. Two."

Liliana walked forward and squinted into the setting sun. "I think they're headed toward the series of canyons where we found the cattle. See?" She gestured toward some dust faintly coloring the western horizon.

"We need to check that area out more thoroughly. Something's going on out there."

"It won't be tonight. It'll be dark in half an hour."

"Tomorrow?"

"Yes. There's nothing more we can do now. We should be able to follow the tracks tomorrow."

Back in his SUV, Cody turned around and drove back toward Carlos's house. Halfway there his cell phone rang. He answered.

Liliana stared out the side window, but she didn't have to see his face to know it was tensed in a frown as he conversed with his son.

"Tonight? I don't know with all that's happened lately. You have a test tomorrow, and you're just starting to study?"

The silence in the SUV that followed that statement hung in the air like thick, storm clouds.

"I expect you home by nine." When he disconnected, he snapped his phone closed and stuffed it in his pocket.

"Your son?"

"At least he called to tell me he was going to study with some friends he's met at school. A history test tomorrow."

"That's nice he's getting to know some others."

"He mentioned an Aaron Taylor. Do you know him?"

"I know Aaron's oldest sister. She was a year behind me in school."

"Does she live here?"

"No, she moved away a couple of years ago after she got married. The last time I saw her was at her wedding. Sad affair. Her family didn't come."

"Why not?" Cody parked his SUV next to Liliana's car.

"Because she married a man with a Hispanic background and the Taylor family felt she married beneath her."

Frowning, he angled toward her. "Does Aaron believe that?"

"I don't know for sure, but his father is very vocal and controlling."

"So Aaron is bad news?"

"I can't answer that either. He's never been in trouble with the law. Other than that, I don't know."

The earlier tension returned. "I'd hoped this wouldn't happen when we moved here."

"What?"

"Kyle seeking out people who are prejudiced. Kyle looking at what is on the outside of people, ignoring the inside. As I told you, his stepfather has no tolerance for people who are different from him. Over the years, Kyle has become more and more like him no matter what I do. I've talked with him, but he doesn't listen to me. I thought when he came to live with me that going to church would help. It hasn't."

"I'm sorry. Fighting prejudices isn't easy, especially if Kyle grew up seeing that example every day."

"I never realized how bad it was until a few years back when Kyle became more vocal around me about his feelings. I had a conversation then with my ex-wife, but that only made matters worse. It put more stress on a strained relationship."

Headlights came into sight as a car drove into the yard. "Let's get this house processed then get something to eat. Okay?" Liliana kept her hands clenched to stop the urge to reach out to Cody. The pain in his eyes touched her. She wanted to remove that look. It was hard enough raising a teen. Beating yourself up over past mistakes did little to improve the situation. She knew that firsthand from dealing with her family.

Cody opened the car door. "Sure. Working right now is probably the best thing for me. Going to this Aaron's house and forcing Kyle to come home won't solve the problem."

"No. More likely it would drive him closer to this Aaron kid."

Exiting the SUV, Cody captured her gaze over the top of his Ford. "That much I remember from being a teenager."

~

"When we talked of grabbing something after processing the house, I didn't think you meant cooking something." Cody held the screen open as Liliana unlocked the back door to her house.

"When I get stressed, I cook. I've been cooking a lot into the late hours of the night. I freeze most of it, but I have a casserole made and ready to go that won't take long to heat up. If you want, we can go out to a restaurant."

"No way. I never pictured you loving to cook."

"I'm almost afraid to ask how you pictured me in my off hours." Liliana entered her kitchen, tossing her purse on the desk then removing her holster.

"Taking photos and being with your family."

"I like doing those, too. But the cooking is usually late at night when I can't sleep." She withdrew the casserole dish from the refrigerator then put it in the microwave. "Not long now. I don't know about you, but after making our way through Carlos's house, I've worked up an appetite."

"I'll have the lab process the evidence, but I don't think we have anything new."

"Trailing the motorcycles tomorrow will probably be a better lead. With two of them that poses the question about how many people are involved." Liliana fixed a pot of coffee to go with the enchilada dish.

"Yes, to add to all the other questions we have."

"Miguel said Carlos lived in New Mexico before this and moved around a lot. So far we haven't found out much before he came here. He couldn't remember the last place he lived. If we figure out where he lived, maybe something there will give us a clue as to why Carlos was targeted."

"There's always the possibility the two incidents aren't connected."

"I don't see that. I know that homes of people who have died have been broken into before, but Carlos didn't have anything of value except the TV, which was still there at the house. We went through it on Monday."

"But not like the intruders did."

"They were looking for something hidden."

"Which usually means valuable or illegal."

"Or both." Liliana set the table in the kitchen alcove. This was a first. Entertaining a law enforcement officer and discussing business. Brock's wife insisted no work talk during off hours so when they got together socially she and her partner never did.

"If it's valuable, why would Carlos be living like he was?"

"So you think illegal?"

"Makes more sense."

The microwave beeped. Liliana grabbed her hot pads, removed the glass dish, then put it on the table. "My partner's wife gave me this recipe. This is the first time I've made it. Just saying that in case it isn't good."

"Whenever I cook, I always say a disclaimer even if I've cooked the dish before." After filling his plate, he bowed his head for a moment.

Liliana waited until he finished before taking her first bite. "Even as a child I rarely said prayers at a meal unless we were over at my grandmother's. Papa never did."

"How about your mother?"

"She did whatever my father wanted."

"I find it's a way I can make myself pause throughout the day and spend a moment with God. Sometimes with our job I can get so wrapped up in what's going on that pausing helps me keep my focus where it should be."

"And that makes everything fine?"

"No, but it helps me deal with all the problems. How I approach things makes a world of difference."

"The problems with your son?"

"It's not easy to admit to myself I've failed my son." He gripped his fork like the hilt of a sword.

"Have you? What I've seen is a father trying his best. Have you made mistakes? Probably. What parent hasn't? Kyle is a teenager. I know what my younger brother can be like right now. Moody. Wanting to do the opposite of what Mama asks of him. A handful, to say the least."

One corner of his mouth quirked up. "Being a part-time dad has been difficult, especially when my ex-wife and I didn't agree on how to raise our son."

"Just keep being there for him. He'll figure it out hopefully." If only she'd had a father who had cared like Cody did. She toyed with the food on her plate, the memory of her father clenching her stomach into a hard lump.

"I need to tell Kyle I asked for the transfer. He thinks we'll go back to Houston as soon as I figure out who shot Al. I have to confess when he jumped to that conclusion I didn't tell him otherwise. I thought when I got him here he'd make friends and forget about going back to Houston." He took a large gulp of his iced tea. "I have to set the record straight with him, but I've been dreading it."

"I know what you're going through." The lump in her belly swelled into her throat. Visualizing the fear on her sister's face, fleeting, but there, produced the same feeling of dread. She had to do something about Elena, a woman who didn't want her help. "I'm worried about my sister and the way her husband treats her. I think she's being abused, but she insists that isn't the case." She finally took a bite of her lukewarm dish. Its spicy flavor sparked her taste buds but not enough to spur her appetite. Elena thought she'd covered her reaction to Liliana's probing about her relationship with her husband, but she hadn't. Liliana couldn't forget the glimmer of fear she saw.

"What are you going to do?"

"Make her see what's happening. It's our dad all over again." She'd never shared that with someone outside her immediate family. The fact she had with Cody stole her breath. She slid her glance down to her plate. *Why now? Why Cody?*

Silence ruled. When she lifted her gaze, it met Cody's softened one. He covered her hand with his. "That has to be hard to deal with. For yourself. For your sister."

"For the longest time I denied what our father did to us. He took his fits of rage out on us. I tried to justify those actions. Elena and Mama are still trying to. I've seen domestic abuse in my job. I know that's what's happening to Elena. And I can't do anything about it. She won't let me."

"I know what it's like to want to help and the person won't let you. Kyle needs to talk about his mother, but he won't to me. I hope your sister will to you. That'll be a start."

"Acknowledging there's a problem. I agree. She isn't there yet. She thinks she's the problem, not Samuel. I've even said something to her husband—not overtly, but I think he got the point the other day. In a perfect world he'd heed the warning and behave."

"But this isn't a perfect world."

"No." Liliana took a bite of her casserole, forcing herself to eat since she had skipped lunch. "Are you going to tell Kyle about asking for a transfer?"

"Yes. I didn't mean for it to be a secret, but I've never found the right time." Cody finished the last bit of his dinner and washed it down with a swallow of tea.

"Maybe Aaron will be the right friend for Kyle."

He rose and carried his dishes to the sink. "I don't have a good feeling about this teen, but I hope I'm wrong. My son tends to be a follower, not a leader."

After bringing her plate to the sink, Liliana faced Cody, her back against the counter. "I've got a feeling I'll be up late again tonight."

"Why?" He moved a little closer.

"Too many questions about these cases." *Too many about the man before her.*

"So more cooking then?"

"I'm afraid so."

The twinkle in his eyes captured her attention. "Anytime you need someone to take some of those dishes from your late-night cooking frenzy, I'd be glad to."

"Have you been peeping into my house? Frenzy is a good description." She laughed, but it died on her lips as he came nearer. Inches from her.

"You really intrigue me."

His aftershave lotion—a faint whiff of lime—teased her with thoughts of making a key lime pie. But that lasted only a few seconds because her heartbeat kicked up a notch as he leaned toward her, grasping the edge of the counter on one side as though to give her a way to escape if she chose.

She didn't. She inched forward until their tea-flavored breaths mingled. She licked her lips together, wanting so much more than this. Then his other hand clasped the counter, effectively trapping her. A thrill shot through her. When his mouth whispered against hers, she nearly melted into him. From a well of willpower, she kept herself upright, anticipating the complete mating of their lips.

Instead, her cell rang, jolting her back to the real world where she didn't have time for a relationship, where she remembered what her mother and sister had gone through with their husbands. As she fumbled to withdraw her phone from her front pocket, Cody stepped away, putting several feet between them.

Noting it was her sister calling, Liliana answered, part of her still dazed by the effects of just a brush of his mouth across hers. She gripped her phone tight to disguise the trembling his near kiss had caused. "Hello," was all she could think to say to Elena.

"Liliana, is that you?"

Strange question. Did she sound that different? "Yes." Before she could say anything else, her sister began crying into the phone. "What's wrong, Elena?"

A few more sobs before her sister managed to say, "You told me to call if I needed you."

"I'll be right there. You're at home?"

"No, I have Joanna and Sammy with me at the Quick and Go around the corner from our house. Come get me before Samuel gets back."

"Stay inside the store. Don't leave until I get there."

"I'm outside at the phone booth. I can't go in. Hurry." Elena clicked off.

The urgency in her sister's voice scared her more than chasing down a criminal. For Elena to call her meant it was bad. She hurried toward her desk for her purse and gun.

"What's wrong?"

Cody's question reminded her she wasn't alone. How could she forget he was in the kitchen too? When she looked at him, she wanted to tell him everything, but the words stuck in her throat, making it impossible to say anything.

She put her holster and gun on and scrambled to find her keys in the bottom of her purse. "My sister needs me," she said finally in a voice that came out on a raspy thread.

"I'll follow you in case you need me to help."

She'd taken two steps toward the back door when he'd spoken. She halted and spun toward him. "No!"

Deep frown lines grooved his face. "If she's in trouble, I might be able to help."

"It's a family concern I can take care of myself." She continued toward the back door. "But thanks for offering."

For part of the trip to the Quick and Go, Liliana thought maybe Cody was ignoring what she said and tagging along. But when his SUV turned off at Canyon Road, she blew out a deep breath. She really liked him. Probably too much. If he had followed her to the place, it would have put a damper on their working relationship. She'd revealed a little of her childhood to him, and now she wished she hadn't exposed herself so much to him. It left her vulnerable, especially in light of what Elena was going through.

Liliana turned into the parking lot in front of the Quick and Go. She saw Elena with Joanna and Sammy on the side of the building just out of reach of the glow of security lights at the front of the store. As soon as she glimpsed Elena, her sister moved back into the shadows even further. Liliana panned the area to make sure she didn't see Samuel, then she hurried toward her sister. She heard Joanna crying as she neared the trio. Elena held Sammy, her three-year-old, while Joanna clung to her mother.

"C'mon. I'm taking you all to my house." Liliana grasped Joanna's hand and the child transferred from clinging to Elena to her. Her niece buried her face against Liliana's side.

She started toward her car, throwing a glance over her shoulder at Elena as she stepped into the light. The sight of her sister's face sent fury through Liliana.

8

Cody had wanted to follow Liliana to where her sister was but knew that would have been a mistake. She was a private person who didn't share a lot. But this evening he'd gotten a glimpse into the real woman behind the badge.

He would have kissed her if the phone hadn't rung. It was probably a good thing it had. He didn't need to get involved with anyone in Durango. He didn't intend to stay long. Only a temporary stop—at the most until Kyle graduates in two years. Besides, he and Liliana worked together. Not a good idea.

But she was intriguing, and he loved a good mystery. What made Liliana so fiercely independent? As she had talked with her sister, he'd seen a wall fall into place, and she distanced herself from him. And there was a lot more about her relationship between her and her father. He'd heard the pain behind her words, and all he'd wanted to do was protect her. But Liliana was a private person and made it clear she didn't need his help. He would respect that, but it didn't stop him wondering what had upset her so much.

He parked near his upstairs apartment and noticed the lights were still off in his place. Glancing at his car clock, he noted his son was fifteen minutes late. He immediately called him on his cell, and Kyle answered on the second ring.

Laughter followed by male voices sounded in the background as Kyle said, "I'm coming home now. We lost track of the time. Sorry. Aaron's giving me a ride."

"Fine. Are you ready for the test?" Cody exited his SUV and headed for his apartment.

A short pause then his son said, "Yeah, as much as I'm gonna be."

Cody mounted the stairs to the second floor. Kyle's hesitant tone of voice nagged at him. His son hadn't mastered the art of lying. Had he even been studying? Did he have a test tomorrow?

After disconnecting with Kyle, Cody let himself into his apartment, flipping the hall light on. He removed his holster and started for his bedroom to put his weapon away in his lock box. After securing it, he thought of taking a quick shower. It might refresh him enough for the confrontation he'd probably have with Kyle.

No, Kyle would be home any minute, and he just wanted to get it over with. He walked back toward the living room.

A noise like something being scuffed against the tile floor alerted him right before someone barreled into him, slamming him against the wall. The air swooshed from his lungs, momentarily stunning him. Quickly regaining his senses, he shoved at the very tall man who was trapping him. With all the strength he could muster after a long, tiring day, he drove the assailant into the living room—into the back of the recliner.

His attacker swung at him, his fist connecting with Cody's jaw at the same time Cody threw a punch to the man's stomach. The assailant grunted while the room spun before Cody's eyes. Trying to regain his faculties, he stepped back, ending up against the drawn curtains of the window overlooking the pool and office of the apartment complex. While the man dragged in gulps of air, Cody assessed him—noting the six feet ten inches of him, the dark olive skin, the black hair cropped close to his head, the piercing brown eyes, and the deep cleft in his square jaw. He had a tense, lethal look Cody had seen a few times. The giant had come to kill him.

The ringing in Cody's ears subsided. His blurred vision cleared. Cody flicked a look toward the sliding glass door out to the balcony. It was slightly open. Ten feet away.

His assailant started toward him, still breathing heavily.

The front door opened. Cody glanced across the room. Kyle stood in the entrance, the light from the second floor landing silhouetting him.

"Kyle, get out of here. Call 9-1-1."

His assailant pulled a switchblade and snapped it open all the while increasing his speed toward Cody.

"Dad?"

"Go." Cody flung himself to the side and swept around as the man changed direction and came at him again. The giant swiped the knife through the air, backing Cody into the wall, six feet from the sliding glass door and possible escape.

Cody took a precious second to check to make sure Kyle had followed his directions. The entrance was empty. When he swung his attention back to the intruder, all Cody saw was the knife plunging toward him. With desperation and quick reflexes, he caught the man's wrist, stopping the blade a few inches from his chest. A battle began for control of the switchblade. The attacker's superior strength overrode Cody's attempts to turn the knife toward the intruder. All he could manage was to keep it from coming any closer.

His gaze snagged the dark one glaring at him from a smooth shaven face, etched with harsh lines of determination.

The blare of sirens penetrated Cody's focused attention on his assailant. Help.

The sound must have registered finally on the man's brain. He jerked up, throwing a quick look at the wide-open front door. Then he renewed his effort, pouring into it all the extra seventy pounds he had on Cody.

The blade inched even nearer. Cody's fingers locked tighter about the wrist, but his hand quivered under the strain.

The sirens came closer, entering the apartment complex.

"Dad!"

His gaze flickered toward Kyle standing in the doorway again, his hands clenched at his sides.

"Don't," Cody shouted, tearing his concentration off the assailant for a few seconds.

Suddenly the knife slipped lower and pierced his flesh at his neck. Cody went down on one knee. Kyle ran at the assailant, pummeling his fists into his back. The man roared, wrenched his knife up and out of Cody's grasp.

The giant rotated toward Kyle. Blood flowing from the cut on his neck, Cody ignored the pain and scrambled to his feet. Kyle backed toward the kitchen. A dead end.

The sound of the sirens and the flashing red lights illuminating the outside doorway lured the assailant's attention toward the entrance. His gaze flitted between Kyle and Cody.

"Stay, son," Cody muttered as he assessed how to overpower the man who still held the long switchblade.

Again, the man's look skipped between Cody and his son. Then, with reflexes that were fast for such a large man, he whirled and raced toward the balcony door. Cody flew after his assailant.

"Dad, don't," Kyle screamed, pure panic in his voice.

Cody slowed as the assailant jumped over the railing.

"You're bleeding." Kyle covered the distance between them, his eyes huge, his hands trembling.

Cody looked down. Red bled through his white shirt, fanning outward. "It's nothing," he quickly said to calm the fear on his son's face, pale as though he didn't spend any time outside. "Really." He opened his shirt to reveal the three-inch slice from his neck toward his heart. With adrenaline pumping through him, he hadn't realized the extent of the wound. He shed his shirt and held it up to stem the flow of blood. "Son, I'll—"

The rush of men into the apartment cut off his words. Two officers and the police chief came to a stop, taking in the scene.

Chief Winters closed the space between him and Cody. "What happened?"

After giving a brief description of the giant, and Officers Hudson and Vega going after the assailant, Cody went through what had occurred since he arrived home with Chief Winters. When he finished, he looked at Kyle. "Please get me another shirt and a washcloth."

"But, Dad . . ." Kyle scanned the chief's face then pivoted toward the hall to the bedrooms.

When he was gone, Cody said in a lowered voice as he paced, "I don't think this was a robbery."

"Why?"

"I think he was waiting in here and once I put up my gun, he came after me. Surprised me when I came back into the living room."

"You haven't been here long. Who?"

"Could be tied to the murder cases . . . or I began asking questions today about the attempted murder of Al Garcia." That nagging sensation he got when something didn't fit exactly right prompted him to add, "Or it could be because I went back out to where we found Salazar's cattle and took a look around."

Kyle reentered the living room, clutching a gray T-shirt and a cloth.

"We'll talk later," Cody whispered then continued louder, "Now that I've had time to think more, I have a better description of the assailant than I told Hudson and Vega. About six feet ten inches, 280 pounds but not flab, muscles. Almost black eyes and hair. A big nose, broken at least a couple of times. Square jaw with a cleft in his chin."

"I can draw him. I got a good look at him, too."

Cody shifted toward Kyle. "You can?"

"Yeah. I love to draw and have been taking a lot of art courses."

He'd known Kyle was taking an advanced art class at Durango High, but he didn't know that his son loved to draw. That bit of news only made him realize how much he didn't know about Kyle. "Chief, after I get patched up, my son and I will get a sketch worked up for you." *And me.*

"Good. We'll take a look around, see if we can get any fingerprints to go with that sketch while you go to the hospital. You've got to have that cut looked at."

The adrenaline rush receded, bringing forth the throbbing pain. Weary and weak, Cody nodded. "I need a ride to the hospital."

Hudson reentered the apartment. "He got away. Sped away on a motorcycle, no license plate."

"Hudson, take Ranger Jackson and his son to the hospital, then come back." Chief Winters strode toward the balcony to examine the door.

Cody allowed Kyle to help him. As they left, Cody shuddered with the thought that Kyle could have been home before him and encountered the assailant first. The realization this day could have ended far worse scared him more than when he'd been fighting the man for the knife.

⌘

Sitting on the couch in the emergency room waiting area, Liliana held Joanna and Sammy against her. Her nephew finally curled up next to her, laid his head in her lap, and went to sleep. Joanna was sucking her thumb, something she did when she was upset.

Liliana wanted to be inside the ER room with Elena as the doctor tended her wounds—some on her face but a lot on her arms and torso. Samuel had used her as a punching bag. But she needed to wait until her mother came to watch the children. They needed her more than her sister at this moment.

Joanna lifted her face toward Liliana and pulled her thumb from her mouth with a smack. "What's taking so long? Mama said she had an accident. Where's Daddy?"

"I couldn't get hold of him. Don't worry. I'm here for you and your mama. Grandmama will be here soon."

"She hurt herself bad. I came home from school and found Mama crying. Sammy was still taking a nap. I didn't know what to do. I tried calling Daddy, but Mama didn't want to bother him." Tears shone in Joanna's brown eyes.

"Next time you can call me. Anytime. I'll be there for you, Princess."

"Oh, *mis bebes*." Liliana's mother hurried into the waiting room and sank down next to Joanna on the other side of the long couch. When she took the little girl into her arms, Joanna burst out crying. "It'll be all right." She patted the child's back.

Sammy stirred in Liliana's lap, rubbed his eyes then looked up at his grandmother. He scrambled to his feet and threw himself into her embrace, too.

Liliana spied the ER doctor who tended Elena in the entrance to the waiting room. They had worked on cases before when a victim of a crime had been brought to the hospital. She rose and went to him. "How is she?"

"Who did this? She keeps telling me she took a tumble down the stairs. This is the second time in the last year."

"I know and I'll deal with it. Are you keeping her here?"

"She insists on leaving, which is okay if someone will keep an eye on her. She has suffered a concussion and a bad beating, but nothing is broken. This time. She also has a cracked rib, which is going to hurt for a while. I've given her something for the pain. She isn't going home, is she?"

"No. She's coming to my house. I'm taking care of her."

"Good. If she takes a turn for the worse, bring her back immediately. I won't worry about convincing her to stay, then." He looked right at her, his jawline rigid. "The person responsible should be locked up. It wasn't a tumble down the stairs."

"I'll do the best I can. Can I see her?"

"Yes. I've asked her to stay for a while to make sure the medicine is okay for her. She did agree with that. She's in room three."

"Thanks, Doc. If her husband calls, don't say anything to him. Don't even let him know she's here."

"I wasn't going to."

"I knew there was a reason I liked you." Liliana turned back to her mother and leaned down to whisper, "Stay with them. I'm going to see Elena."

She nodded, and Liliana left her to continue calming both children. Her mother was good at that. Much better than she was.

Her face turned away, Elena lay in the ER room numbered three. As Liliana neared the bed, she noticed her sister's eyes closed—one because it was swollen shut. She almost backed out, hating to disturb her, but she halted when Elena shifted, crying out at the movement. Liliana hurried to her.

"You've got a cracked rib. Take it easy. Doc just gave you something for the pain. It might be a while before it takes effect."

Elena tried to smile, but it died immediately. "I can tell you it hasn't yet."

"When you leave here, I'm taking you home with me."

"I can't. He'll get angry."

"Why didn't you tell the doctor what really happened? Let them take pictures of your injuries?"

Elena lowered her head and stared at the white sheet covering her. "It's no one's business but my own."

"Do you want your children to grow up like we did? Always afraid? Joanna and Sammy deserve better than that. We deserved better than that."

Elena flinched. "You know how to hurt me worse than him."

"If it'll get you to leave him, then I'll continue to speak the truth."

"How can you say that? Marriage is for life."

"Not if he's beating you up. One day he'll go too far and kill you. I repeat, do you want your children left with a man like that?"

"He's their father."

"You need to press charges against him tonight or tomorrow. You need to get a restraining order against him."

"No! I can't. I don't want people knowing what happened."

"Remember what we went through growing up. Do you want that for your children? When we got older, Papa started taking his frustration out on us, too."

"But I messed up." Elena's one good eye filled with tears.

"Yeah, marrying Samuel." She was fighting for more than her sister now, and she couldn't be less than brutal. "Get out. I'll protect you. You and the kids can live with me. He'll quickly figure out he can't mess with me." Liliana put her hand on the handle of her gun nestled in its holster.

Elena wailed. "Don't do anything you'll regret. I can't worry about you, too."

"You worry about me? I may want to show Samuel he can't mess with the Rodriguez women, but I wouldn't do anything illegal." Liliana stepped closer and took her sister's hand. "You and the kids are coming home with me tonight. No argument. I know a lady you need to talk with. She'll help you with what you're going through. Promise me you'll do this."

"I don't—"

"If you don't, I'll make your husband's life difficult in Durango. I'm not without resources. Everyone will know what's going on."

"No! I know I have to come home with you. I just don't want Samuel to retaliate." Tears running down her face, Elena tugged her hand free from Liliana's and swiped it across her cheek. She winced when her fingertips touched the bruised skin.

"If he steps foot on my property, I'll press charges against him," Liliana said in such a convincingly tough voice she hoped Elena believed every word.

Her sister sank back against the pillow, closing her eyes. "I want to leave here. Please see if the doctor will let me go now. I've caused enough of a scene for today. I can only imagine what the people here are thinking."

"You've caused nothing. Don't worry about them. You have enough on your plate without doing that. I'll track down the doctor and see what I can do."

"Who are the kids with?"

"Mama."

"Does Mama know that . . ." Her sister looked at her feet, twisting the sheet in her hands.

"Say it, Elena. You have nothing to be ashamed about. You didn't do anything wrong."

"That Samuel—hit—me."

That was a start, but the hesitant way Elena had spoken sent up a warning. Liliana's battle to get Elena to leave Samuel wasn't over. "I haven't told her, but Mama knows. She went through the same thing." And stayed in the situation. Anger knotted Liliana's stomach. "I'll be back."

She left before she said something she would regret. She'd thought she'd forgiven her mother for staying with her husband when he had first physically abused her and then turned it on Elena and Liliana.

But I haven't.

Out in the hall, she stopped, curling her trembling hands at her sides. Leaning against the wall, she drew in gulps of the antiseptic-laced air until she felt composed enough to talk with the doctor and face her mother. When she pushed upright, the doors to the emergency room burst open and Officer Hudson with Cody and a young man came into the ER. Clad in a gray T-shirt, Cody held a white cloth, stained with blood, against his upper chest.

She hadn't thought the day could get any worse. It just did.

જ્જ

Now that Elena and the kids were sleeping in the spare bedroom, Liliana needed to leave and check on Cody. Trying to forget her earlier thoughts concerning her mother, Liliana pasted what she hoped was a smile on her face and said, "Mama, I appreciate you staying here until I get back, but you must promise me you'll not answer the door or phone if it's Samuel."

Her mother bit her bottom lip. "He's such a nice young man to me. How could he do that to Elena? Maybe she did—"

"Don't, Mama. Elena didn't do anything. Just like you never did when Papa hit you. No man has the right to beat his wife. I don't care if he's upset with her. There's no reason for it that is acceptable."

Her mother lifted a quivering hand to pat her neat bun as though there was a stray hair out of place. "When they work hard and things aren't like they want, when they come home after a long day, don't you think—"

"I'm going to the hospital. I shouldn't be gone long, but I need to find out how Ranger Jackson is. With Brock gone, he's been my partner on these murder cases."

She sighed. "I hope he's all right. Too much violence around here."

The irony of what her mother said nearly caused a laugh to escape. Mama had lived in the middle of violence a lot of her adult life. "He's tough. I'm sure he'll be okay." *I hope.*

But the sight of the ashen cast to Cody's tan features wouldn't leave her mind as she drove toward the hospital. At a stoplight, she called the ER to see if Cody was still there. He would probably be worse than Elena about staying overnight. Sure enough, the nurse on duty told her he had left twenty minutes ago.

Liliana made a U-turn on Alamo Boulevard and headed toward Cody's apartment complex. When she pulled up, she saw Officer Hudson sitting in a patrol car outside Cody's apartment building.

She tapped on the window, and Hudson rolled it down. "What's going on?"

"We're keeping an eye on the place. Chief Winters doesn't want another Texas Ranger hurt in his town."

"Did the chief find any evidence in the apartment?"

"One smeared print on the railing on the balcony and a shoe print on the ground below where they had recently watered."

"No other prints from the perpetrator?"

"No."

"He didn't wear gloves. Strange? This has a feel of a pro."

"Maybe he doesn't care. He didn't disguise himself."

"Because he intended to kill Ranger Jackson."

"Yeah, that's what the chief thinks."

Liliana mounted the stairs to the second floor and rang the bell. When the door opened, Cody stood in the entrance, still pale. She could see part of the bandage he had over his wound sticking out of the neckline of his fresh black T-shirt. "I didn't get to say much before they whisked you into the ER room. How are you doing?"

He stepped to the side. "Come in. I didn't get a chance to ask why you were at the hospital. Your sister?"

She nodded. "She's at my house now." Her gaze swept the living room, any evidence of a fight cleaned up except some drops of blood on the carpet and tile.

"Chief Winters just left. I haven't had time to take care of everything."

"In the hospital it didn't look like your son was hurt. He's okay, then?"

"Physically, yes. I'm not so sure otherwise. When the doorbell rang, he escaped to hide in his room. I think he's on overload. He's trying to sketch the assailant and his perfectionism is getting in the way." The tired lines around Cody's eyes and mouth spoke of the effect the assault had on him. He moved slowly into his living room and sank onto the couch. "It's been a long day, but I'm not sure I'll be able to sleep tonight."

"So a long night for you, too." She could understand that. She didn't think she'd be able to sleep either—not after Elena's and now Cody's injuries. After sitting across from him in a chair, she nearly collapsed back, the feel of the softness beneath her welcoming her to relax for the first time in hours.

"Kinda hard to sleep too soundly when you know there's someone out there who wants you dead. And believe me, that man did. I could see it in his eyes."

"Why?"

"Good question. I intend to ask him when I find him."

"Do you think this has to do with the murders we've been investigating?"

"I don't know. It's interesting that I'm attacked the day after I was out at the box canyon looking around and then checking into Garcia's case."

"Maybe those guys didn't like us following them from Carlos's house."

"If that's the case, watch your back. The flat tires and rock thrown into your house may be connected to what happened to me."

"Your assault was with lethal intent. Those incidents that happened to me were more like harassment." Was it Samuel? That wouldn't surprise her if she found out it was.

"Or a warning—we didn't heed."

"Believe me, I'll be careful, but I'm more concerned about my sister."

"What happened to her?"

The concern in Cody's eyes underscored how different he was from a man like Samuel, luring her to trust Cody with the truth. "As I suspected in the past, her husband has beaten her up. She finally admitted it to me. He isn't gonna take it lightly that she's left him."

"Are you going to arrest him?"

"Her admitting it to me tonight is a step in the right direction, but with Elena I think I have a long way to go to get her to admit she needs help. Or press charges against him."

"Why do you say that?"

"Because we went through it as children. Elena has bought into the scenario that she's the one who causes Samuel to go off. She's the one in the wrong. Not him."

He sat forward, anger slashing across his face. "I'll help you bring him in—with pleasure."

"I'm going to try to convince her tomorrow, but I won't be surprised if she doesn't agree." She hated saying it out loud, could even partially understand where her sister was coming from. She could still remember the remnants of thinking she'd done something wrong like Elena. "I left home at eighteen and got help. Elena stayed until she married Samuel. For years she's lived with that mind-set."

"I'm sorry to hear that. As a cop I've had to deal with domestic situations involving abuse. Many didn't turn out well."

"Knowing Samuel, he won't let her go graciously. I have someone she can talk to here in town, but I can't be with her 24/7."

"Do you know a place she can stay in Austin or San Antonio?"

"Maybe but I don't think Elena will leave Durango."

"Dad, I think I've got a good sketch of the man." A tall, lanky teen came into the room from the hallway. He slowed his pace when he saw Liliana, and his eyes darkened, narrowed slightly. "I thought the police were here again. There's a patrol car out in the parking lot."

"I didn't come with the patrol car, but I am a police detective here in Durango."

"Kyle, this is Detective Rodriguez. We've been working on the murders together."

Kyle stared at her for a few extra seconds then turned his attention to his dad and handed him a sketchpad. "What do you think?"

"You've got him. This is good. Thanks, son. We can use it to put out a search for him."

"Really?"

"You bet."

"What if he comes back?"

"There's no element of surprise now. He won't."

"He might."

"You're safe." Cody laid his hand on his gun at his side. "I think he was trying to scare me. That's all."

The furrow of Kyle's brow announced he wasn't buying his father's explanation.

"It's getting late. Don't you have a test tomorrow?"

"I can't go to school after this." The creases deepened as Kyle clamped his jaws together so tight a tic twitched right below his cheek.

"That's the best place for you."

"And what are you gonna do?"

"I have a job to do. I'll be doing it."

"You can't. You . . ." The teen's fear vibrated off of him. He whirled around and rushed from the room.

"If you need to talk to him, go. In fact," Liliana started to rise, "I can—"

His wave dismissed her words. "If I have learned one thing in these past few months, it's to give Kyle time to cool off. Tonight he got scared. He lost his mother three months ago, and he saw how close he came to losing me. At least that's what he thought. I wasn't going to go down without a fight."

"You honestly don't think the man will come back?"

"If he's smart, and we both know sometimes they aren't, he'll be long gone by now. No, I don't know one way or another because I don't know why he came after me. Kyle doesn't need to worry about it, though."

"Are you doing enough for both of you?"

"Yep. I can't have a patrol car sitting outside my apartment. I need someone I can leave Kyle with while I'm working and he's not in school. At school he should be fine."

"Is there anyone you can send him to?"

"No, and I refuse to send him back to Houston. I want him near in case I need to protect him. If something big is going down here, we both know it can have far-reaching arms. Besides the fact that Nate, Kyle's stepfather, isn't the type of person I want my son around, he wouldn't know how to protect him. He'll do more harm than good."

"Let me see the sketch." She half rose and leaned toward him. When she had the pad, she studied it. "He looks huge."

"He is. To the point he would stand out. Six feet ten. Two hundred eighty pounds. Not flabby. Ever seen him around?"

"No, but he's distinctive."

"Yeah, not someone who would blend into a crowd."

"Are we still going back out to Carlos's ranch and follow those tire tracks tomorrow morning?"

He gestured toward his bandage. "This isn't gonna stop me."

She pushed to her feet. "Then I'd better head home and let you get your beauty sleep."

"Yeah, me and this Wilson Combat are gonna cozy up." He touched the handle of his gun.

"I'll meet you at the police station at ten. I want to make sure Joanna gets to school and make a few calls on Elena's behalf. Maybe have a word with Samuel even if she doesn't press charges tomorrow."

"Is that gonna work?"

"I'm hoping she got scared today. Her bruises and injuries can't be explained away. It was a beating, and it looks like one."

"Ten works for me, too. After I take Kyle to school, I'm going to see Al again."

"You think the assault tonight is connected to him?"

"It's a possibility, but I called him when I first got home to warn him about what happened. He offered for me to stay at his place. I think I'm gonna take him up on it. That way I won't worry about Kyle when I'm trying to find my assailant." Cody flicked his wrist toward the sketch now lying on the coffee table in front of him.

"How's your son going to feel about that?"

"I don't think he'll be throwing any parties anytime soon." Cody followed her to the door. "And I still have to tell him. Not something I'm looking forward to. I know the first thing he's gonna say. He'll want to return to Houston and Nate."

"It's frustrating when you want to do something to help someone, and they don't want you to."

"I'm finding out that's often the role of a parent." He opened the door for Liliana. "I feel like today has been forty-eight hours."

She laughed. "I know what you mean. See you tomorrow." It seemed a lifetime ago that they'd been standing in her kitchen and his mouth had brushed across hers.

She waved to Hudson then slid behind her steering wheel and started her car. Fifteen minutes later, numb, ready to fall into bed, Liliana drove down her quiet street to find her brother-in-law's Lexus parked in her driveway.

9

Cody knocked on his son's door. "Kyle, I need to talk to you."

When the door swung open, his son immediately walked away from it and sat on his bed with his cell in his hand. "You're working with a Sp—"

"Don't, son. We've had this conversation. I'm working with Detective Rodriguez as well as the whole Durango Police force. A lot has happened in the past week. She's very good at her job and an asset to the department."

"You looked at her . . ." He snapped his mouth closed and leaned back against his headboard, texting.

"Put the cell down while we talk. We can't ignore what happened tonight."

Kyle flung his phone onto the navy blue bedcover. "Yeah, if I hadn't come home when I did, you would have been killed," he muttered, keeping his gaze averted.

"Next time I tell you to leave, do it. I can't be worried about you when trying to fight someone."

"Oh, so it's my fault."

"I didn't say that. Just follow my directions. I know what I'm doing." *At least as a cop. Not so much as a parent.*

"Fine." Kyle reached for his cell.

"Tomorrow I'm taking you to school and picking you up."

"I can ride the bus."

"I know, but I'll feel better if I do. Humor your dad. After school, we'll come back here and pack some clothing. We're not staying here for a while."

Kyle sat up straight. "We're going home to Houston."

"No, we're gonna stay with Al, the ex-ranger who owns the small place where I'm keeping my horse while we're here."

"Al Garcia?" his son said so slowly he drew out each syllable. "I don't know this Al Garcia. Someone else besides you can solve his case. If not, then why can't I go back to Houston and stay with Nate? I'd be safe there."

He'd been expecting Kyle to ask, but he still didn't have an easy way to explain his reservations about the man who had been part of his son's life for years. "No, I couldn't work effectively to solve the murders and find the man who attacked me tonight if I had to worry about you in Houston."

"Worry about me? I'm fine with Nate. He has a lot more guns than you do."

"Protecting someone isn't always with guns."

"Betcha wouldn't have minded one earlier."

"I've only shot one person in my whole career. It isn't something I take lightly, and I only use it when it's the last resort. Until things settle down, your activities will be curtailed. No studying at the library or a friend's at night. I'm sure if you want to study for a test Al won't mind having your friends over."

"I'm not the one the man was trying to kill. Besides, he could have been a plain old burglar looking for money for drugs."

"That's a possibility, but I'd rather err on the side of caution than have something happen to you."

Kyle began texting. "So you dragged me to this—place—and when I start to make friends, you basically ground me. Perfect." The derision in his voice matched the sneer on his face.

"Have you ever thought if I hadn't come home first what could have happened to you?"

Kyle jerked his head up and glared at him. "You brought this into the house. Not me."

Cody was too weary to argue with Kyle or try to make him see he could be in danger. "We'll talk more tomorrow about it." He strode toward the hall.

"Yeah, sure," Kyle mumbled, the rest of his sentence too garbled to hear.

Probably for the best. He couldn't send Kyle back to Houston and Nate. Besides, there was no guarantee if someone was after him that they wouldn't go after his son. Houston wasn't that far away. When he called Al before talking with Kyle, he knew his old mentor would watch out for his son while he was working. Al might have had to retire, but he was still capable of looking out for Kyle.

❧

The loud pounding on Liliana's front door followed by a stream of curse words from her brother-in-law quickened her pace to a jog before Samuel woke up the whole neighborhood. Mounting her steps to the porch, she drew her gun. The glare of the light emphasized the savage look on his face, fury sculpting his features with harsh lines.

"Move away from the door, Samuel," Liliana said in the toughest voice she could muster. After the long day she'd had, this was not what she'd wanted to be doing, but she'd known he would try to see Elena. She'd just hoped it wouldn't be tonight.

He ignored her and continued hammering at the wood as though determined to force his way into the house.

She closed in on him and raised the gun to his head, pressing the barrel against his right temple. "I said back away. You are not going to see Elena. Have I made myself clear?" *Why didn't Mama call me and tell me that he was here?*

"What do you take me for? I know you won't shoot me."

"Don't be so sure about that. I've had to stand by and watch you hurt my sister. Not anymore. She's finally admitted you like beating her up. I've told you how much family means to me. I guess you forgot that. Now, slowly step away from the door."

He did as she instructed, but red mottled his face, his arms stiff at his sides. "You'll regret this. I didn't do anything wrong and you have no right keeping me from Elena and my kids. I can cause you problems. I have connections and money."

"And by the time I get through with you in the rumor mill, your reputation will be destroyed. I'll do anything to protect my family. This time, don't forget it. I feel in a charitable mood, and I'm gonna let you walk away unharmed. But not next time."

His upper lip curled. "You think you're tough with that gun in your hand. You won't always have that." His dagger-pointed gaze slashed through her. "I will get my family back. They are important to me."

As he stormed away, muttering words that burned her ears, she kept her weapon trained on him, chills rushing up her arm and over her whole body. She waited until he pulled away from the house before holstering her gun and unlocking her front door.

Inside, she faced her sister and mother, standing together with arms around each other, their faces a reflection of the terror she'd seen in other battered women.

"I'm so sorry. I'd better go home. He's very angry."

Elena's voice quavered so much Liliana had a hard time understanding her at first. Then when her sister's words sunk in, Liliana had to squash her own anger quickly. Elena didn't need that on top of everything else. Why didn't her sister understand she wasn't at fault for Samuel's behavior? But frustration tangled with her ire, making it impossible to say anything to Elena.

Liliana checked the locks on the door, allowing time to compose herself. "Because he's mad is the reason you can't go home."

"He called me on my cell, but I didn't answer it." She stuck her hand in the pocket of her slacks and pulled out her phone. "Listen. He didn't mean it."

When Samuel's deep baritone voice filled her hallway with words of apology, Liliana's frustration won out over anger. She grasped her sister's cell and turned it off. "I don't want to hear his lies. Don't you understand, Elena, he is not going to change? Being sorry tonight doesn't really mean anything tomorrow."

"When he gets this mad, there's no telling what he'll do. If I go back now, he'll calm down, and it'll be okay."

"Promise me you won't do anything right now. I have some-one I want you to talk to. I'll take you to see her first thing tomorrow after we take Joanna to school. Mama, can you stay tonight and watch Sammy in the morning?"

As though she was shell-shocked, her mother didn't say anything for a long moment, then finally murmured, "Yes."

"He won't come back here. If he does, next time call me or the station. A patrol car can be here in minutes. I'll let the chief know what's going on." She clasped both her sister's and mother's hands. "We have to stick together. Together we are strong, a force to be reckoned with."

"If you say so." Elena hung her head, her shoulders drooping.

"I say so. It's my turn to protect you."

⟦⟧

"Who is this woman?" Elena asked the next morning when Liliana parked in the driveway of a home on the other side of town.

"Jackie Simpson lives here. She's opened her home up to women who've been living in abusive situations and need a place to go when they finally leave their husbands. She's a counselor who years ago went through a verbally abusive marriage that turned into a physically abusive one."

Elena stopped on the walkway to the front porch. "I can't talk to a stranger about my personal problems. I'm regretting even saying anything to you. You must think I'm crazy for even considering going back to Samuel. But he is a good father. He provides well for us. I don't want for a thing. The kids don't."

"Except your well-being, their well-being. Humor me and talk with her. I have to go to work. Spend the day with Jackie and the women who are staying here."

"Are you kicking me out?"

"No. But I want you to see why you shouldn't go back to Samuel. Nothing I can say will make a difference to you. Maybe Jackie will change your mind because I know I can't make you do what I think is best for you. You have to want to do it."

"Fine. I'll stay today, but that's all. Just to please you."

Liliana rang the bell and a minute later the click of the lock being turned sounded. The door opened and an older woman in her early fifties leaning on two forearm crutches moved back to allow them into the house.

"Glad to see you, Liliana. You're right on time. We finished breakfast and we're going to have our group session before some of the ladies leave for work." Jackie smiled at Elena. "You must be Elena. Welcome to Grace House."

"Grace House?" Elena asked.

"That's what I've called my home ever since I started taking in women who needed my help. The Lord showed me grace, and I've extended it to others. Ten years ago someone found me half-dead after my husband ran me down with his car and because of that Good Samaritan's quick thinking I'm alive today. Come on in and meet the others."

Jackie trudged toward a short hallway that led to a den where a group of six women ranging from twenty-something to Jackie's age were seated. One young lady held a baby to her chest.

Every time she visited, Liliana's heart cracked a little more seeing these women and learning what they had gone through. But because of Jackie, there was a place for some of them to go. Before, they'd felt they had no other options but staying in an abusive situation.

Inside the doorway, Liliana shifted toward Elena. "You have my cell number. Call if you need me. For part of the time, I may be out of cell range. If you try and I don't answer, call the station if you need help. Promise me you'll stay until I come get you later this afternoon. We'll go pick up Joanna together."

"Yes." Elena bent close to Liliana's ear. "But it doesn't mean I like this."

"Duly noted." Liliana left Grace House, confident in Jackie. If anyone could change Elena's outlook toward Samuel it would be her.

Twenty minutes after parking her car near the courthouse, Liliana rushed toward the police station, late to meet Cody. She collided with Sean as he was leaving the building.

"So sor—ree. Didn't—s—see—you."

"I should have been watching where I was going." Liliana held the door for the young man from the cafe. "I was hoping I didn't miss your morning food run."

"I—I—can bring—you back—some—thing."

She gave him a big smile. "That's so sweet. I wish I didn't have to leave right away. I'll have to satisfy myself with a cup of coffee from the pot Robertson probably made. I know you're responsible for fixing all the coffee at the cafe. It's great. Maybe you could give Robertson some lessons."

Sean's thin, flushed face split into a huge grin. "Any—any—time." Then he hurried across the street, his gait better, but he was still favoring his good leg. Time was healing his bike injury from a couple of weeks ago, but not the way the guy looked at himself. She tried to make him feel special—to stick up for him when people made fun of his stuttering.

"I think he's got a crush on you," Officer Robertson said from behind the counter. "By the way I didn't make the coffee this morning. Chief Winters did. So beware of what you say about it."

"Thanks for warning me. His may be a step above yours." Liliana breezed past the police officer, listening to his laughter as she headed for her desk and a waiting Cody.

"Looks like you revived your plant." Cody closed a folder he'd been perusing. "What made you get a second plant?"

"I didn't. Juan gave it to me the other day. Of course, this one needs more water than the cactus and I haven't done very well there. Not sure why Juan bothered. It was looking wilted when I left yesterday. I was going to water it today. Someone else did." She glimpsed Juan coming out of the kitchen area. "And I think I know who. He's got a green thumb. I don't."

Cody looked toward Juan. "Why do you have a plant if you forget to even water it?"

"Good question and I don't have an answer. I guess I keep thinking I'll get better. Plants look nice."

"When they're living."

She chuckled. "Yeah, living is good."

"Ready to go? We're using horses again. They're quieter and can go a lot of places an SUV might not be able to."

"Sounds good to me. Am I using Al's again?"

"Yes, the horses are in my trailer. We'll start from Salazar's ranch. Follow the trail from there."

"You think there's something out there besides desert and rocks?"

"Don't you? What were those two motorcyclists doing at Salazar's ranch? Who ransacked his house? Think of what has been happening across the border. The drug war, the trafficking in humans and guns."

"I was hoping what's happening in other parts of the state somehow had bypassed us. I know. A fool's dream."

"What if someone has the illegal activities in this area locked down? You yourself said people have gone missing."

"That's always been the case. This can be a transit area."

"Maybe." Cody rose and swept his arm toward the back door. "We might get some answers today."

"Or more questions."

≈≈≈

"Did ya hear Manny's car got keyed last night?" Aaron sat behind Kyle in history class. "Rafael Rodriguez's, too." He tossed his head toward the student he mentioned. "Couldn't happen to more deserving guys."

"Someone was talking about it in first hour." Kyle angled around toward Aaron. "Did ya do it after you dropped me off?"

Aaron held up his hands, palms out. "I ain't saying I did. But I ain't saying I didn't. Thanks for helping me study last night. I might be able to pass the test this time. I ain't taking this class a third time. I'll drop out before that. Boring subject. Why take history? I don't care what a bunch of dead people have done."

"Beats me. I don't know how you can sit through this a second time."

"By zoning out. But I've got you helping me now." Aaron settled back in the chair as the teacher began class.

Kyle tapped his pencil against his desk. Was Rafael related to the detective who had come to the house last night? Same coloring. But then, they all had dark hair and eyes. A vision of Serena flashed into his thoughts—beautiful brown eyes that gleamed when she looked at him. Made him feel important to her.

When the teacher started passing out the tests, Aaron leaned forward and whispered, "Put your paper toward the right edge just in case I've forgotten something from our cramming last night."

"The test has started. No talking." The teacher pointedly looked at Aaron before he turned to Kyle. "Face forward."

Kyle did, but when he got his test paper, he slid it to the right.

❧

Walking toward the cliffs, his horse trailing him, Cody searched the ground. "Nothing. The tracks have disappeared."

"They come to within about three feet and then are gone." Liliana pointed to the area. "It looks like something swept this place. If so, where did the two motorcycles go?"

"This is the back side of the box canyon where the cattle were." He made a full circle then peered up the tall, jagged cliff. "Unless they disappeared into thin air, about the only place is up." He pointed in the direction. "That appears to be an opening."

"Yeah. About fifty feet off the ground in the middle of the cliff. Not what I would call accessible unless the motorcycles grew wings."

"Have you ever gone rock climbing?"

"A couple of times in my youth."

"Lady, you're in your youth."

"You only have ten years on me. You aren't an old man—yet."

"This body felt like it this morning when I dragged myself sore and bruised out of bed."

"You need to quit picking fights."

"I'll remember that the next time an assailant comes at me with a knife." He walked to his horse and tethered it then took his climbing gear from the saddlebags. Liliana did likewise with her mare.

While Cody was getting his equipment ready, Liliana inspected the stone face. Why would someone hoist two motorcycles up to the opening fifty feet above? There was a separation in the rocks, but no matter how much she pushed or pulled, she couldn't budge anything.

She thought of the tale about *Ali Baba and the Forty Thieves* and murmured, "Open sesame."

"What did you say?" Cody appeared at her side.

"Thinking about a story from my childhood. There's a gap in the rock here. I can fit my fingers into it." She stepped back and threw her head back to study the hole in the cliff. "That isn't very big."

"It could open up."

"Or not." She wasn't big on closed-in spaces.

Cody examined the wall before him, following the gap until he couldn't then picking it up about ten feet to the north. "If this is a door, and I say that loosely, then I don't know how to open it. It could be water has leaked into a crack and over time has eroded it this way. But to be on the safe side, let's hide our horses behind that outcropping of rocks over there."

She laughed. "So you're buying into the Ali Baba story?"

"Nope, but I don't see why we should leave our horses out in the open for someone to come along and see, especially since the motorcycles disappeared around here."

After they secured the animals, Cody handed Liliana a harness. He went first, finding places to put wedges into the rock facade for protection. As Liliana followed behind him, she removed the devices. Halfway up, she raked her arm against the stone facing, pain shooting up it. Thankful the cave was only fifty feet off the ground, Liliana heaved herself up onto the shelf in front of the hole in the cliff. Panting, she rubbed her hand over the throbbing scrape on her arm. She'd live, but she remembered why she hadn't done rock climbing in a while. She didn't like not feeling more in control of the situation. She didn't like dangling from the side of a cliff with only a rope supporting her. As she'd grown up, so much of her life had been out of her control.

On the narrow ledge of the cave, Liliana peered into the darkness. "I can't see lifting motorcycles up here and dragging them into this. The ground isn't disturbed either."

Cody shone his flashlight into the small opening. "Agreed. It was hard to tell from the ground. Since we're up here, let's do some exploring."

She wanted to refuse, seeing the narrow entrance more clearly with the flashlight, but she bit back a no. "You first." If he could make it through, then she could. He didn't seem to be concerned by the walls tapering to a much slimmer width.

The first few yards Cody stooped over to make his way into the cave, but soon he got down on all fours and crawled forward. Heart thudding, Liliana followed suit. The roughness of the stone floor pierced her even with the jeans she wore. As the passage narrowed, sweat trickled down her face and body.

"This better be worth it," she muttered, loud enough that Cody heard and glanced back.

"Okay?"

"I don't like cramped spaces." And it had nothing to do with controlling a situation.

"Now you tell me. You can go back and wait at the mouth of the cave."

"And let you have all the fun? No. I'm in. It's about time I got over this fear. It's irrational." And yet as she said that, she pictured herself hunkered down in her closet as a child, hiding because her papa was on one of his rampages. The sound of the slaps still shivered down her although she was perspiring buckets.

Cody stopped a couple of feet in front of her. "The space between the ceiling and floor shrinks here." He lay flat on the stones and shined his flashlight down the tunnel. "It looks like it opens back up maybe ten yards up ahead."

Oh, good, only thirty feet of terror. But as she shimmied through the passage, she kept her gaze centered on Cody. She was all right when she did that. Her heartbeat sped up, thundering in her ears but she was moving forward. She wouldn't think about the return trip.

When it opened back up to a bearable space, Liliana breathed deeply in the hot air, a musky smell to it. The tunnel continued to become wider and taller until Cody scrambled to his feet and low walked.

In the distance she heard—voices.

Cody paused then twisted back toward her, retracing his steps and whispering, "Turn off your light. Stay right behind me. I'm cupping my hand over my flashlight to dim it just enough to feel my way."

Another fifteen yards Cody clicked off his flashlight, but there was a faint glow up ahead that gave off enough illumination so Liliana could pick her way carefully along the passage. She only scraped herself once against the rocky surface that jutted out. She clasped her upper arm and felt the tear in her shirt. Before this was over with it, was going to look like she'd had a wrestling match with the cliff and lost.

When Cody came to a halt a few minutes later, he leaned back toward her and put his mouth next to her ear to whisper, "I'm edging closer to the ledge. It sounds like some men are below us. Stay back."

She kept track of his shadow in the dimness. He went flat on the stone floor and wiggled closer to the ledge, barely visible to her from her vantage point. Her heart still beat a rhythm faster than normal, and she worked to even its pulsating to a calmer rate. She glanced behind her and shouldn't have. Although the men down below them had lighting, it didn't penetrate the black recesses of the cave, especially back the way she had come. She quickly swiveled forward and spied Cody closing the short distance between them. Her heartbeat continued its rapid pace.

"They're moving crates of guns. I think from what I could hear they're shutting down the operation for a while." His chuckle barely filled the quiet. "Something about a nosy Texas Ranger."

"How many men?"

"I count six—one being the man who attacked me."

"The giant."

"Yeah, all six feet, ten inches. I'm staying to monitor their activity. You need to get help ASAP. Leave and go as far as necessary to get cell reception."

"So how are the men getting into here? It's not the way we came."

"Don't know for sure, but two motorcycles are down there. Hurry, but be careful. Don't know how many are involved. While you're gone, I'm going to do some looking around up here. There may be a way down without rappelling over the ledge."

Eager to get out into wide open spaces, she turned around and headed back the way she'd come, not using her flashlight until she'd gone fifteen yards and gone around a bend in the tunnel.

Although she had more light, the sense of being totally alone inundated her as if the rocks had come crashing down on her. The dizzying speed of her pulse made her lightheaded. She stopped, closed her eyes, and tried to imagine herself in a crowd of people, bodies pressed against her. That she could handle.

It's not that far. I've been this way before. I know what's there.

Then she hit the low part of the tunnel and had to belly crawl as sharp pieces stabbed her palms and down her body as she dragged over it.

Lord, I'm asking for Your help. Cody's depending on me. Again she shut her eyes and thought about riding with Cody across the pasture—fresh air all around, the sun warming her. She inched forward. Slowly.

Just when she thought she couldn't pull herself another foot, the passageway began to widen. Not far ahead, the bright sunlight slanted into the mouth of the cave, beckoning her. She hurried her pace until she was able to stoop, then almost straighten to her full height.

Close to the ledge where Cody had his rope on the floor of the cavern, she reached for it and froze.

⊶❧

Kyle came out of Durango High School at the end of the day with Aaron and a couple of other guys and scanned the cars, hoping to see his dad's SUV. He didn't. Instead, his gaze fell on Al Garcia's red truck—big and obvious. When his dad let him out this morning, he mentioned Mr. Garcia might pick him up if he couldn't get away from work. The fact his dad wasn't here didn't surprise him one bit. Typical.

"My ride's here. See you guys tomorrow." Kyle descended the stairs, glimpsing his father's friend climbing from the pickup and waving with his cowboy hat.

Aaron dogged his steps. "Who is that? Your dad?"

"No way. Someone my dad knows. Dad must have gotten caught up in something."

"Maybe he's found the murderer." Aaron and his friends kept pace with Kyle. "Why they bother, I don't understand. They're probably not even Americans. I heard one was a coyote, responsible for bringing more of *them* into our country."

"It's his job no matter who has been murdered." Kyle bit the inside of his cheek right after he said that.

"Well, he doesn't have to do a good job. At least not in this case. If more of them killed each other, it's one less problem we'll have." Aaron glanced at his companions. "Right?"

The two other teenage boys nodded.

When Aaron slowed then came to a halt on the sidewalk a few yards from the red truck, Kyle looked over his shoulder at him. All three guys pivoted and presented their backs to Kyle as they formed a huddle and conversed.

While Kyle climbed into the front passenger seat, the trio walked away with Aaron peering over his shoulder for a long moment. The reptilian-eyed look he gave Kyle made him shiver.

"Friends?" Al Garcia started his truck.

"I've just met them," came out, then caused Kyle to wonder why he didn't say yes they were.

"They didn't look too happy."

Kyle shrugged. "It's been a long day. Why isn't Dad here?"

"I didn't hear from him. He told me if I didn't to come pick you up."

"What do you mean? He didn't call you? Why not?"

"Probably in an area where there isn't cell reception. No big deal."

Yes, it was. After what happened last night, he didn't like the idea that his father was out of cell range. Someone tried to kill him. What if the attacker found him? What if his dad was lying dead somewhere? Kyle gripped the door handle.

The retired ranger glanced at him. "He knows how to take care of himself."

"Yeah, sure." But the picture of a knife at his dad's neck, slicing into him, wouldn't quit his mind. It haunted him the whole way to Garcia's house. He even pulled out his cell and called his dad. After the fourth ring, it went to voice mail, and he disconnected. His fingers clutching the handle tightened even more.

❧

At the sound of men talking below the cave opening, Liliana crawled forward, straining to hear what they said. Had they found the horses? Were they waiting for her and Cody to come back out? She peeked over the edge, saw a black pickup, and counted three men slipping through a small opening by the gap in the rocks—a gap that had widened enough for men with crates to go inside.

She retrieved her cell to see if she could get reception. No bars. Would the men come back out? Could she make it down and to her horse to ride for help? Ten minutes later, grabbing a fistful of rope anchored around a boulder inside the cave opening, she began lowering it over the side, but laughter and talking paralyzed her. Then suddenly she yanked up what rope she had over the ledge and ducked back.

"That's the last of the guns. Let's go get a beer," one of the men said in Spanish as the grating noise of the stone door reverberated through the stillness.

The one getting into the driver's seat replied, "*Tengo que llamar al jefe.*"

Call the chief? Chief Winters? No, it's got to be the boss.

Liliana waited five minutes after the truck disappeared from her view before tossing the rope over the side of the cliff and hooking herself up to rappel down to the ground. No doubt Cody saw the men come into the cavern below him and probably figured out that she would have to stay put until they left. She looked toward the west and the sun starting to make its descent toward the horizon.

She lowered herself over the edge and two minutes later she was standing below the cave. Leaving the rope dangling down the cliff, she hurried to find her horse she'd hidden behind the boulders. She hoped she wasn't gone so long that another truckload of guns arrived, but she'd gotten the feeling from what the men had said that was the last shipment they'd delivered. In the saddle, she spurred her horse into a run, hugging the area near the rocks until she had no choice but to cross the flat, arid land toward Carlos's ranch. There she knew she had cell reception.

Thoughts of the location of Carlos's ranch sparked an idea. Was his place a front for the shipments of guns? It was the most direct route to the cliffs and the caves and easily accessed from the highway. Had Carlos been involved? Carlos never said anything to Miguel or *Señor* Flores about seeing lights or trucks crossing the ranch. Could he have been paid to turn a blind eye to the comings and goings of trucks at odd hours of the day? Or had he been more involved? She couldn't see him not knowing they had used his place as a way to cut across the rough terrain to the canyons.

About a third of the way to the ranch, Liliana tried her cell. No bars still. She rode as fast as she could but kept checking the phone for any reception. Halfway across the wide-open expanse one bar appeared. Slowing her horse, she punched in Chief Winters's number. He wouldn't be involved. She'd known the man half her life and his integrity had been proven countless times. Bottom line, she had no choice but to trust him.

It rang two times, then nothing. She looked at her cell. She'd lost the one bar. Spurring her mare, she rode hard for a minute then slowed and tried to call again.

Chief Winters picked up on the first ring. "What's happening?"

"We found a ring of gun smugglers using the canyons behind Carlos Salazar's ranch. They're in the process of making a last shipment before shutting down the operation. I think they're using a cavern system that goes under the Rio Grande. They just delivered ten crates of guns to a cave on the west side of the box canyon where we found some of Carlos's lost cattle."

"We're coming. Meet me at the ranch to show us the way."

She knew the wisdom in those words, but she hated leaving Cody by himself in the cavern. Not that he couldn't take care of himself, but he was outnumbered and outgunned.

As the women left Jackie's den at Grace House, Elena remained seated. "I'm not like these others. My husband loves me."

Jackie closed the Bible she'd read during the afternoon session and put it on the table next to her. "Why do you think your husband loves you?"

"Well, that's obvious. He married me."

"There are a lot of reasons to marry and love is certainly one of them, but it isn't always why two people marry."

"That might have been true hundreds of years ago or even today in other countries, but not here in America."

Jackie pinned her with an assessing look. "Why else do you think your husband loves you?"

Although she was only thirty-two, a hot flash suffused her body. Elena held up her left wrist, the diamonds in the bracelet glittering in the light pouring into the room through the window behind her. "He's always giving me gifts. He gave this to me last week for no reason."

"Nothing happened to cause him to do that?"

Remembering what had occurred before Samuel left for work that morning, Elena shifted, the action sending pain from her cracked rib knifing through her. She held her breath, trying not to cause her chest to rise and fall. It didn't work. She fumbled next to her for her purse and grabbed the pain pills the doctor prescribed for her. After taking one, she met Jackie's gaze.

"What do you mean?" Elena raised her chin, fighting the memories of the humiliating words that had spewed from her husband's mouth with the children in the next room.

"Did he hit you?"

"No."

"Did he belittle you, put you down in anyway?"

"He was trying to help me be a better wife. He works hard to give us a beautiful home. We don't want for anything." She ran her finger along the string of diamonds on the bracelet, recalling the feeling she'd initially had when he'd given it to her. Elation that he wasn't angry with her anymore.

"So because he does that, you feel you shouldn't have a say in your marriage?"

"He brings in the money."

"Did you want to work?"

"I don't need to."

"That wasn't my question. Did you want to work?"

Elena lowered her gaze. "A while ago I asked him if I could get a part-time job now that Sammy is almost four. Next fall he'll be in an all-day program for his age group at school."

"And he said no."

It wasn't a question, but Elena said, "Yes. But he's right. He doesn't want his wife working. I shouldn't have told him I needed something more. I made it sound like I was ungrateful to him."

Jackie scooted to the edge of her chair, strain from the movement etching pain into her features. "It's been ten years, but I'm still constantly reminded of not pleasing my husband no matter what I did—to the point he ran me down with his car and sped away, leaving me to die. You know how it all started that day? I wanted to go to lunch with an old friend from high school. He didn't want me to. In fact, he didn't want me to be involved with others. I hardly saw my family and all my friends had fallen to the wayside because I kept saying no to their invitations to do something. I was so lonely and unhappy." She patted both legs. "These may not work as well as they used to and still hurt me even ten years later, but I'm happy and I'm not alone anymore."

After picking up her forearm crutches, she planted them in front of her and struggled to her feet. "Please think about what these women said today and come back. You're welcome here anytime. Please mingle and talk to the others. I have a few calls I need to make before thinking of what to prepare for dinner. It's my night to cook."

Elbows on the arms of the chair, Elena buried her face in her hands. That discussion about her getting a part-time job led to the latest trip to the hospital. He'd made it clear that under no circumstances could she work outside of their home. She'd dared to question his decision. She shouldn't—

Her cell buzzed in her pocket. Without looking to see who was calling, she answered it. When she heard her husband's deep baritone voice tell her he missed her, she sank back against the cushion.

"Elena, love. Are you there? Don't hang up, please."

The word *please*, so rarely used by Samuel, melted her anger. She cradled the phone to her ear and took in shallow breaths to keep the pain to a dull ache. Why did she even want to work, when he gave her everything she could need? "I'm here."

"It's so good to hear your voice. I miss you. Please come home, baby."

"I can't."

"Why not?"

The lack of irritation in his voice gave her a seed of hope. "You hurt me bad."

"I didn't mean it. I'd had a frustrating day at work. A big loan was defaulted. I lost control. I won't do that again."

"How do I know you mean what you say?"

"Trust me, baby. You know I love you. Go outside and take a look."

"I'm not at Liliana's."

"I know you aren't and I'm not there. I'm at home. Waiting and hoping you'll return to me." How did he know where she was? Then she remembered the people he knew being the president of the largest bank in the area. He had extensive connections and resources.

"I don't know. It hurts to breathe deeply."

"Go outside. I'll do anything to make it up to you. I'll even let you volunteer outside the home. That'll give you something to do. I'm at home waiting, love." Samuel disconnected.

Elena kept her cell at her ear for a long moment, not knowing what to do. Then her curiosity wormed its way into her thoughts. It wouldn't hurt for her to go out on the front porch and take a look. She'd leave the door open. She'd be safe.

❧

The tunnel angled downward. Crouching, Cody made his way deeper into the system of caverns beneath the rocky cliffs overlooking the box canyon. The smugglers' voices still drifted to him. They seemed to be waiting for someone or something. More guns?

He came to a fork in the passageway and chose the one on his left. Still using as little light as he could to see the area in front of him, he continued on the path that slanted down at a ten- to twenty-degree angle.

Once, he clicked off his flashlight and glanced around. Pitch black. Not a ray of light coming from any direction. If it weren't for the voices he could still hear, raised in an argument, the sensation of being totally cut off from humans could easily swamp him. Liliana had indicated she didn't like small spaces. He didn't like the dark.

Turning the light back on, he proceeded cautiously. The distance between the ceiling and floor began to shrink again.

Moving far enough away from the ledge he'd perched on to view the men below, he decided to shine the flashlight in full brilliance to check out the tunnel before he went any further.

Its glow illuminated hundreds of bats hanging everywhere. First one, then another, and another squeaked and flew past him. In seconds, the whole ceiling moved and bats filled the air as they zoomed toward the tunnel entrance, their wings flapping, their sounds giving his presence away.

❧

As Liliana neared Carlos's barn and house, smoke mushroomed up into the sky as though a nuclear bomb had gone off. She increased her speed and minutes later charged around the barn into the yard. The crackling of the fire vied with the pounding of her horse's hooves on the hard ground. The scent of smoke saturated the air with a suffocating smell.

She dismounted and called 9-1-1. Her mare pulled on the reins she held, her eyes wide as it stared at the fire across the yard. After reporting the fire, she put her horse in the trailer in the barn. The wind blew the smoke and flames away from the barn so her mare was all right.

But until others came, she turned on the hose and doused the barn and the area surrounding it. The house was gone. All the fire department would be able to do was contain the flames from spreading and becoming a wildfire.

Within minutes, two patrol cars and Chief Winters's four-wheel drive Ford 150 sped down the road from the highway. In the distance, Liliana heard the sirens of the fire trucks not far behind the police.

Chief Winters strode to her. "Do you know how this happened?"

"No, but I suspect it was the truckload of men who delivered the guns. They left here not too long ago."

"Why burn the house?"

"They couldn't find what they were looking for yesterday?"

"The murder cases just get more difficult each day. This is the second fire in a week. Is Victor Ruiz's death connected to Carlos Salazar's?"

"We don't know. All three murders could be, somehow."

"We'll leave as soon as the fire department arrives. I've called the Texas Rangers in San Antonio. They're sending a chopper."

"We can't wait too long. They were moving the guns. May have already." Liliana relived the darkness of the cave, its isolation, the fact it was filled with men who smuggled guns across the border. And Cody was there alone, waiting for their return. What if the smugglers discovered him?

❧

Kyle came into Al Garcia's living room and planted himself in front of the lounge chair where the man sat. "Where's Dad? I called the police station and tried his cell again. No one is telling me anything."

Garcia glanced up and put his book down in his lap. "When I worked this area, I often went out of cell reception. It happens. I'm sure he's working the murder cases with Detective Rodriguez and will call when he can. It's only four."

"You're hiding something from me."

"Why would I do that?"

"I don't know. I seem to be an afterthought to my dad. Someone tried to kill him last night and now I can't get hold of him."

"I know you're concerned about him, but he can take care of himself."

"He isn't invincible, and you don't know how I feel." Kyle spun on his heel and stormed from the room.

This man was a stranger to him. He couldn't stay here. He wasn't the one in danger anyway. He went to the bedroom "assigned" to him, grabbed his backpack, and stuffed it with some of his belongings and all the money he'd been saving for a car. Dad didn't know about that and probably wouldn't approve. But when he got his license, he wanted his own car. He wished he had it now. He could get into it and drive to Houston. Instead, he was stuck in Durango. But that didn't mean he had to be stuck here with Al.

He crossed to the window, opened it and jumped to the ground. He didn't need a babysitter. He wasn't staying.

∾♥∾

"What was that noise?"

The excited question sliced through the darkness, freezing Cody as the last bats flew by him. The slight breeze created by their wings brushed past his face. The rancid ammonia smell of their guano nauseated him.

"Bats . . . getting towards evening . . ."

Cody couldn't hear what else was said as the men in the cavern below lowered their voices. Now that the bats were gone, he crept forward, still hoping that the tunnel that slanted downward would bring him to the lower chamber.

Halfway through a narrow passage he became stuck, not an inch of room on all four sides. A jagged rock hooked his shirt, gouging his flesh. The stone pressed against him like a tight-fitting coffin. His heartbeat sped up, his breathing ragged. He tried to wiggle forward. He couldn't. Sweat drenched him.

With his arms pinned against him, he pushed backwards. And went nowhere. Trapped.

❧

Elena stepped out onto the porch, her gaze latched on to the gleaming metallic blue Lexus that matched the silver one Samuel had. A large red bow sat on top of the car. A box on the porch with the same kind of bow perched a few feet from her. Her name in bold letters on the present drew her forward.

This was the car she'd wanted for the past year, but Samuel didn't think she needed a new one. Although her Chevy was five years old, it only had forty thousand miles on it. She picked up the present and opened it. Inside was a set of keys and a note from Samuel.

Her hand shook as she read his message. "I love you. Will you forgive me? Whether you do or not, this Lexus is yours."

Tears smarted Elena's eyes, the words I love you burning into her mind. He really was sorry this time. Elena descended the stairs to the sidewalk.

"Don't, Elena."

Gasping, she whirled around, her hand going to her chest. "You scared me."

"Sorry. I thought that when I walk I make enough noise to alert anyone. Is that a gift from your husband?"

"Yes. See, I told you he loved me. Do you know how much one of these cars cost?"

"I'm sure a lot. But money doesn't equate with love."

Elena pulled the set of keys from the box and started toward the Lexus. "Tell my sister I have come to my senses."

As Elena drove away from Grace House, she saw Jackie making a call on her cell phone. She'd already tried getting hold of Liliana. She wasn't available, which would give Elena time to work everything out with Samuel. She could be home tonight sleeping in her own bed with a husband who realized he'd gone too far this time and was sorry for doing it.

Cody pushed all the air out of his lungs that he could and shoved himself forward. His shirt ripped, the rock scraping a deep groove into his back. But he kept moving inch by inch. His chest burned. The lack of air made him lightheaded.

Finally, freed from the stone prison, he inhaled deep gulps, filling his lungs with precious oxygen. The stench of the bats still lingering, he shone his flashlight down the tunnel and noted the continued narrowness. He had no choice. He had to go forward and prayed he would make it.

Close to five o'clock, Liliana led Chief Winters and two police officers through the passageway above the hidden entrance into the cavern while Officer Robertson stayed back to alert the Texas Rangers when they arrived. The state police were coordinating with the Mexican authorities to be ready to grab anyone on the other side of the border once they found the location where the tunnel that ran under the Rio Grande came out, if that were the case.

The third time through the narrow passage didn't bother Liliana as much, but then her thoughts were with Cody. What if he had gotten caught? When she reached the section that afforded her a view of the large chamber below, she peered over the ledge, concerned that she didn't hear any people talking. What if they were too late?

A few faint lights lit the cavernous room, but the crates were gone and nobody even stood guard down below. The smugglers were gone and there was no indication where Cody was. Beads of sweat broke out on her forehead and upper lip. Had he been captured by them, and had they hightailed it out of here with Cody in tow?

"Where are they?" Chief Winters whispered next to Liliana.

She shook her head.

"Where's Ranger Jackson? I thought he would be waiting for us."

"If they left, he would follow them."

"Or they caught him."

"When I left he was checking to see where this tunnel led to. He hoped he could find a way down to the chamber where the guns were since we didn't know how to open the cave entrance from below."

"Then let's follow the tunnel and see where it takes us." Chief Winters went first with Liliana following him and the two officers coming up behind her.

When the chief reached a narrow part of the passageway, he stopped and checked it out. "I can't get through there. We need to go back. I don't see how Ranger Jackson came this way."

Liliana examined the tunnel. Although her boss wasn't as tall as Cody, he was overweight. Maybe Cody squeezed himself through the passage. But what if he had found one more narrow than this one? The thought heightened her concern for him. The horror of being trapped consumed her like a fever, perspiration pouring off her face.

She backed out of the passageway until she could stand again, then headed toward the ledge overlooking the chamber. Officer Hudson retrieved the rope at the entrance and tied it around a cropping of rock before rappelling down the cavern wall to the lower part of the cave.

Liliana went next, and the second she landed on the rocky floor she began inspecting the area, trying to figure out where the tunnel might have come out—if it emptied into the chamber. Thinking of Cody being lost in the cave system sent a spurt of adrenaline surging through her.

Finally, behind a group of stalagmites she found a tunnel that came out into the large cavern. She stepped back around the rock formation and called out to the chief. "I think this is where the passage comes out."

He turned toward Officer Hudson, a medium height, thin man. "Check it out from this end. We'll wait. Hopefully our backup will be here by then." Chief Winters clicked on his walkie-talkie and let Robertson know what they were doing so he could tell the Texas Rangers when they arrived.

"Chief, they are ten minutes out," she heard Robertson say.

Ten minutes could be an eternity if Cody was in trouble. *Protect him, Lord.*

First, she examined the stone wall where the men would have come into the cavern. It looked like it was on some kind of roller system, but she couldn't figure out how to open the "door." Officer Vega came over to help look for a lever to open the door.

As the minutes ticked down, she turned her attention to where the men went with the crates and possibly to where Cody was. With flashlight in one hand and her gun in the other, Liliana walked across the chamber to the only other opening into the room—a wide, tall tunnel that could easily be used to move men and guns through.

"Rodriguez, we're waiting for the Texas Rangers. I don't want to rush this operation and lose the smugglers."

Liliana turned toward her boss to protest waiting when gunfire sounded from the tunnel behind her.

❧

Cody ducked behind a large stalagmite, a bullet flying past his ear and lodging in the rocky face behind him. He'd made good time when he'd finally come out of the narrow passageway. For the last fifteen minutes, he didn't even need to use his flashlight. Theirs had lit the way for him.

But one of their men had hung back and seen him come around a curve into a medium-size chamber. The rest of the five smugglers were heading toward the opening on the far side when the sixth one shot at Cody.

They all stopped, dropping the reins of the mules they were leading and dove for cover. Pinned, no way to escape, Cody took stock of his bullets—one eight-round magazine in his Wilson Combat as well as another backup clip. Sixteen bullets. He hoped help would arrive soon. He didn't know how long he could hold them off.

❧

Liliana swung around toward the passage, the thought of Cody lying on the cave floor, bleeding out propelling her forward.

"Wait!" Chief Winters said and lifted his walkie-talkie.

Liliana stopped, but it took all her willpower to follow her police chief's order. Especially when she imagined Cody alone against the at least six smugglers they'd seen in the cavern.

"Robertson, there's been gunfire down here. We're going forward. Get the rangers down here ASAP."

"Will do."

"Let's go." Chief Winters hurried to the small tunnel and called out to Officer Hudson to come back.

Liliana along with Officer Vega plunged into the large passageway with the other two quickly following. More gunshots reverberated through the cave. She increased her pace even though it was hard to tell how far away the gunfire was. Cody needed their help.

Please let us be in time, Lord.

⁂

A volley of bullets riddled the stone face around Cody. Chips of rock flew off and one sliced across his cheek. He resisted returning fire in hopes of luring some of the men out to see if he was still alive. Another round of gunshots blasted the air.

Cody groaned as though hit.

Then waited.

Minutes passed with no sound. He peeked around the bottom of the stalagmite. The mules were gone, no doubt the firepower scaring them away. Nothing stirred in the chamber as more seconds ticked away. Did any of the smugglers escape too?

Suddenly a flash of white to the side of him caught his attention. A small man with red hair charged his hiding place.

Holding his breath, he aimed his Wilson at the smuggler. And waited. A few more steps.

Cody squeezed off a shot. The man went down, his weapon skittering toward Cody and coming to a stop a couple of feet away. One down, five to go.

As he ducked back, a hail of bullets bombarded his hiding place.

He poked his head around the other side of his stone protection in time to see three men making a break toward the tunnel behind them. He popped up and shot the third one before he disappeared into the darkness. The smuggler stumbled and fell to the stone floor. Two down.

"Help is on the way. You can't escape. Give up before I take any more of you down."

His invitation was met with more gunshots.

To his left from the passageway that led back to the entrance someone returned fire. From the shadows, he glimpsed Liliana and Officer Vega.

"Cover me," Cody yelled to them as the chief and Hudson joined the pair.

He ran toward another stalagmite nearer the smugglers' escape route. The two remaining men didn't try to stop him. They were barraged with bullets from Liliana and the others. They weren't total fools.

From his new place, closer to the smugglers, Cody called out, "Give it up. As you know my backup is here. The authorities are closing in from the Mexican side as well."

Someone behind a boulder tossed out his automatic weapon.

"Come out with your hands up," Chief Winters shouted from the tunnel.

A dark-skinned man about six feet tall stood up with his arms in the air and stepped out from his hiding place. "I surrender," he said in Spanish.

His attacker from the night before was still unaccounted for. "How about your friend?"

At that moment, one of the mules carrying the gun crates burst out of the passageway where the other men had bolted. Braying and charging in fright across the chamber toward the other tunnel, the mule didn't stop.

During the commotion, the assailant took the opportunity to make his escape. While Liliana rushed out to apprehend the one who surrendered, Cody aimed for his attacker's leg and released a shot. He staggered a couple of feet but kept going. Cody chased after him and tackled him a few yards inside the tunnel, near where the other smuggler went down. They hit the hard surface of the cave. The impact knocked the breath from Cody's lungs. Last night's intruder grunted but dragged Cody as he tried to break free.

Clamping one arm around the barrel chest of the assailant, Cody managed to level his Wilson at the man's head. "Give it up. You aren't going anywhere alive. Drop the gun."

Seconds passed.

Liliana and Winters rushed into the tunnel.

The attacker let go of his weapon and sank to the stone floor.

∽✑

Two hours later back at Salazar's ranch, the burnt rubble of the house lay in a mound. Cody blew out a rush of air and kneaded the tight cords of his neck. "I don't want to repeat these last two days. Ever."

"I'm with you on that. All I want to do is go home and fall into bed." Liliana climbed up into his SUV, both horses in the trailer ready to leave.

"Not a bad day, though. We caught a gang of smugglers, shut down a tunnel below the Rio Grande."

"I wonder if guns were the only thing smuggled through those tunnels."

"ICE, the border patrol, and ATF will hash that out."

Exhausted, her adrenaline rush gone, Liliana rested her head on the back of the passenger seat. "We may never know all of this. The gunrunners didn't seem very talkative except one who I don't think knew too much." One dead, two injured, and three captured unharmed. It would be days before they waded through all the information gathered. The one who had surrendered had started talking right away but was Mexican and didn't know who was behind the ring on the American side. Cody's attacker had remained silent.

"So who's running the smuggling ring? It wasn't one of the men we caught. From what I overheard they were following orders." Cody rolled his shoulders before starting the SUV.

"Part of that canyon system is on Cesar Álvarez's ranch. We should talk to him."

"Do you think he's the one behind it? Why risk it on his own property? He has over twenty thousand acres. He may not know what's going on in every part of his ranch."

"I agree, especially since this wasn't fenced."

Cody drove past the area where the house had been hours before. One fire truck was still in the yard, monitoring the situation to make sure the fire was completely out and wasn't responsible for igniting a wildfire. "Why burn down Salazar's house? And risk drawing attention to this place? Is the person behind the murders the head of the gunrunning ring? There's a lot of money at stake. This has to be the ring Al started investigating. They're probably responsible for shooting him. We collected a lot of guns today. Maybe one will match the one used on Al."

"I hope so. Lots of questions still unanswered. Like, was Carlos involved with the ring or did he discover what was going on and was killed by them?"

"I think we need to go on the assumption he knew what was happening since we think they cut across his ranch to get to the canyon. We need to have another conversation with his cousin, who I think knows more than he's saying."

"Also Alfredo Flores. He owns the ranch. We can bring both of them in first thing tomorrow." Liliana pulled out her cell and noticed several calls—one from her mama, Jackie, and Elena. A chill encased her all of a sudden. Something was wrong. "I need to call my sister."

She punched in Elena's cell number and waited for her to pick up. It went to voice mail. "Elena, this is Liliana. I'll be over to pick you up at Jackie's soon. I'm sorry I'm late. A lot has gone down today."

"She wasn't there?"

"No, but then she has a habit of leaving her phone in her purse and not hearing it ring. I'm calling Jackie to let her know I'll be over there within twenty minutes. I'll take her to my house then return to the station. I want to sit in on the interviews with the three uninjured men we caught."

Jackie picked up on the second ring. "I'm so glad you called. Your sister has gone back to her husband."

Liliana shot up straight in the seat. "When?"

"About three hours ago. I tried to keep her here, but he gave her a new Lexus and apologized. She is convinced her husband means it and won't hurt her again. We both know that is a lie. The first time he gets angry at her, he'll explode."

Which could have already happened. "I know you did what you could. I'll go over there and try to talk some sense into her."

When she disconnected, she called her mother. "Did you know Elena went back home?"

"Yes. She phoned a while ago to tell me to watch her children tonight. She and Samuel were going to celebrate getting back together. He's having dinner catered in by Durango Steakhouse."

"So Sammy and Joanna are with you at my house?"

"No. Elena said Samuel didn't want them over at your house. He's afraid you'll say something to the kids about their father."

Anger swept through her like a brushfire gone wild. "You're on his side now. Did you forget what Elena looked like last night?"

"She loves him. Let her try to preserve her marriage. The children need a father."

"Is that why you stayed with Papa?"

Liliana heard a breath sucked in then a click as her mother hung up. Gripping her cell, she scanned the area to see where they were. A few blocks from the station. Dread began to replace the anger. She again called Elena's cell then the house. No answer. Her apprehension multiplied.

"Do you want me to go with you?"

"No. She's probably ignoring my calls or more likely Samuel has demanded she ignore them."

Lord, let that be the reason Elena isn't answering. You didn't ignore me earlier. Please don't now. I need Your help on this one. "You need to stay here and see if you can get anything from the gunrunners and make sure someone tends to your wounds." The second Cody stopped, Liliana jumped from his SUV and ran toward her car, fear dogging her every step.

10

*W*atching Salazar's ranch through night vision binoculars, I see the last fire truck pull away and head back to town. I have accomplished taking care of another loose end. If Miguel hadn't come along when he had, I would have taken care of it on Monday after killing Salazar. I don't know for sure what the police discovered in the house, if anything. But they didn't release the crime scene, as if they expected to find something else. Other letters Anna wrote to Salazar? The one didn't reveal anything, but others could have. Now there's nothing to be found.

One more problem to take care of and I'll be safe. Miguel has been down at the station twice. I never thought the two cousins were close, but what if I'm wrong? The thought of taking care of Miguel, a man who has made fun of me, whets my urge to kill again. I like it. I like the control it gives me.

And even more the acclaim I've received for getting rid of a thug like Ruiz. I revel in the news that has come out about Ruiz. The whole town knows he was a coyote—preying on people in need. I made this town a better place. Me. Not even the police could do what I did.

When Cody entered the police station, he checked the messages on his phone. A couple from Kyle and one from Al. Probably both of them wanted to know when he would be at Al's house.

While Chief Winters and Officer Robertson processed the three men they managed to capture unharmed and several others in custody with the Mexican authorities, Cody sat in Liliana's desk chair and called Kyle. No answer—not even an angry one about where in the world was he. Next, he tried Al, who answered immediately.

"How's things going?" Cody asked, watching a gunrunner having his fingerprints taken.

"Okay."

"Is Kyle around?"

"Yes, he's right here with me." Cody heard his friend say, "It's your dad."

His son mumbled something he couldn't understand, then came on the line. "When are you gonna be home—I mean at Mr. Garcia's?"

"I've got some suspects to interview, then I'll be there."

"I'll probably be in bed by that time."

Al came back on the phone. "See you when you can get away. We're fine. You can tell me about what went down today."

"How did you know anything went down?" Cody said with a chuckle.

"I have my connections at the station. You know Chief Winters's secretary is a wealth of information. See you later."

Cody pocketed his cell and stood. The chief had finished processing two of the suspects. Time to get some answers. But the one he was really looking forward to questioning was his assailant from the night before. After he was patched up at the hospital, he would be brought here.

⌒

"Why didn't you tell Dad I left your place and came back here?" Kyle faced Al Garcia in the middle of the living room in his apartment, turning so he didn't have to see the place where his father had wrestled with that man last night.

"Your dad is dealing with enough right now."

"He is? How about me?" Kyle stabbed his finger against his chest. "I have no home. First, I was taken away from the only home I knew to live with my dad. Then he makes me move here, but this place isn't my home." Flailing his arms, he finally focused on the spot that still had drops of blood on the carpet, his voice rising with each word. "I have no place to call home."

"Then why did you come back here when you left my house?"

The question, spoken in such a calm voice, only heightened the anxiety swirling in Kyle's stomach, as though any moment he would throw up. "It's all I have, and now I don't even have this." The words came out of his mouth in such a rush Kyle couldn't stop them. He didn't owe this—stranger an explanation and yet . . .

Kyle spun toward the couch and plopped onto the cushion so hard he bounced once. He stared at the man who, in spite of his attitude, had been kind to him. The sympathy in his dark eyes completely undid Kyle. His feelings of no control, of being lost, overwhelmed him.

"Why did my mother have to die?" The question he'd held inside for the past three months spewed from his mouth, and he didn't care if he was asking the wrong person.

Al Garcia took a chair across from Kyle, his brow lined in thought. "When I was twelve I asked myself that question every day for a year. I never really came up with a good answer. Sometimes there isn't a good answer to a question like that."

"You lost your mother when you were twelve?"

"And father. They got caught in the middle of two warring gangs in New York City. Two senseless deaths. They were in the wrong place at the wrong time."

"That's how I feel. Like I've lost both parents. I can't see Nate. He was my stepfather for the past ten years and was always good to me. Mostly, he was around when I had a problem."

"But your dad wasn't?"

"No," Kyle said immediately, then began thinking about the times his father came to his baseball games or to the art show where he won first place or . . . "well, some of the time. What happened to you after your parents died?"

"I was shipped off to Texas to live with my aunt and her husband. I had never met them and was scared. I didn't want to leave New York. It was my home. I even thought about living on the streets."

"You did?" Kyle had thought about running away lately, but never to live on the streets. He'd even gotten a map and plotted hitchhiking back to Houston and Nate, but then he'd remember stories about the dangers of hitchhiking.

"Yes, but that's a kid thinking nothing can touch him. I ended up in Texas—Del Rio. At first I was so angry at everyone, especially my aunt. I blamed her for everything that went wrong. That changed when my uncle was killed in the line of duty. He was a highway patrolman. He was helping a motorist who was stranded. A car swerved into him and killed him. My aunt and I became close after that. She needed me and I needed her."

"He was a highway patrolman? My dad was, too."

"I grew up and became one not long after I graduated from high school. I learned when I was a kid that change was going to happen no matter what I wanted. I couldn't control that, but I could control what I did about it. My attitude. I couldn't control my parents or my uncle dying, but I could control if it was going to take me down. That's when I turned to the Lord to help me with my attitude. It sure needed work. You see my aunt insisted I go to church when I didn't want to listen to anyone talk about God."

"My dad makes me go with him. I hate sitting there. The preacher going on and on about how God is love. It isn't love that He took my mother."

"I guess all those Sundays sitting in the pew listening to the priest must have affected me more than I thought. When I started thinking about all the things that had happened to me, I realized something. If I had stayed in New York, I would have ended up in a gang, probably wielding a gun like the gang members who murdered my parents. That was the direction I was going. I wouldn't have been there to help my aunt through the death of her husband. I can't begin to understand all God's plans, but I've learned He does love me and has my best interest in mind."

Kyle bolted to his feet. "Sorry, I don't buy that."

"I didn't either for years. But looking back I've seen God's hand in my life and destiny. Knowing He's there for me is about the only way I've gotten through those changes we can't avoid in our life. He's the one solid constant."

"Are you going to tell Dad about this?"

Al pushed to his feet, steadying himself when he wobbled. "Nope. That'll be your call. If you want your dad to know, you'll have to tell him. Let's go." When he shut the door and turned the knob to make sure it was locked, he continued. "I do know one thing. Your dad loves you. He isn't a man who likes a lot of change. This has been hard on him."

"Why couldn't we stay in Houston?"

"He has his reasons. Ask him."

I just might. When Kyle grasped the passenger door handle, someone called out to him in the quiet.

⤥⤦

Liliana marched up to her sister's house and raised her fist to pound on the door, rather than ring the bell. She stopped before making contact with the wood. Dropping her arm back to her side, she inhaled to fill her oxygen-deprived lungs—again and again. Slowly her anger abated to a level where she thought she could manage a conversation with her sister and husband without punching him in the face.

When the door swung open, Samuel blocked her path inside. "You are not welcomed in this house anymore."

"I want to see my sister."

"No."

"I'm not leaving until I do."

"Fine. I'll call the police. You're trespassing on my property." He stepped down from the stoop, puffing himself up like a male peacock showing off his prowess.

She remained where she stood. "Go ahead, and I'll tell everyone who will listen what you did to Elena. I want to see my sister."

He glared at her with such savagery that she was glad she wore her gun. In his eyes, she glimpsed all the things he wanted to do to her. Shivers rose on her scalp and ran down her body.

Suddenly he turned and yelled, "Elena, come to the top of the stairs."

"I want to talk to her."

He ignored Liliana, gripping the edge of the door while he waited for his wife.

Elena appeared in her nightgown. She stared at Samuel for a long moment, then said to Liliana, "I don't want to see you ever again. You've tried to break up my husband and me. Please leave."

"She won't unless you talk to her."

"I don't have anything to say to her. Please come up to bed, Samuel."

"Yes, dear, just as soon as your sister leaves."

Liliana stomach clenched with nausea. Bile swelled into her throat.

"Get out, and if you say anything about my husband, I'll deny every word and before I'm through, the town council will wonder why you're a police officer."

With her gaze glued to her older sister who looked away, Liliana wanted to deny the words she'd heard. How could Elena be saying this? She called her last night. Liliana had held her while her sister had sobbed. "Elena?"

Her sister stared hard at her. "Leave, Liliana. Now."

"I'm going. But, Samuel, if anything happens to Elena, I'll come after you and I'll forget I'm a police officer." Not daring to turn her back on him, she faced him and moved away.

The smile that slithered across his face taunted Liliana. He slammed the door, the sound resonating through the quiet on the street and trembling down her length.

When she made it to her car, she sat parked outside her sister's house on the street. *How can Elena have grown up in the same household and not see the danger she's in with Samuel? Why, God? He's going to kill her one of these days. Do something!*

❧

"Kyle. I've been worried about you." Serena wheeled herself across the parking lot with a small, thin man trailing after her. She stopped near Kyle, the security light illuminating her features that reflected concern. "I heard what happened in your apartment last night. Are you all right? I was hoping to see you in the gym this afternoon after school."

"I'm fine." Dressed in her workout clothes, she must have been at the gym working late. He'd forgotten to call her and tell her he couldn't help her today. Her face was flushed and a fine sheen of sweat covered it. His hand itched to wipe the towel she'd slung around her neck over her face to make up for not calling her. Instead, he clasped the handle and opened the truck's door. The light from its interior shone in her dark brown eyes, their appeal touching him as no girl's had.

The man paused behind Serena's wheelchair. "I'm Serena's dad. You and your father have been the talk of the apartment complex."

"Yeah, I was out on the patio and think I saw the man running away from your place," with that, Serena pulled his attention back to her.

"Ever seen him around here?" Kyle asked, then nearly laughed. He was starting to sound like his dad.

"I didn't see his face, but I saw someone earlier about his size when I left the gym and went to our apartment." She tossed her head back. "That's why my dad's escorting me tonight."

Kyle glanced at Serena's father. "Hopefully my dad will find the man soon."

"With all that's been going on lately, I don't want Serena even leaving the apartment alone."

"Dad, I have to work out."

"Maybe we can do it together," Kyle said before he censored the words coming from his mouth. Why did he say that? Yes, he'd helped her a couple of times, but he didn't need to do it on a regular basis. She'd managed by herself tonight.

"Partner up? I sure could use your help. I need someone to force me to keep going. Dad's worthless. He kept looking at the clock and asking me if I was finished."

"Yeah. That would be nice. Right now, we're staying with Ranger Garcia, but when I come back, I'll help you. We can make some kind of schedule."

She backed herself away. "Looking forward to it. Take care of yourself." Then she maneuvered her chair around and headed for the incline to the sidewalk.

Kyle climbed into the truck. "Don't say anything, especially to my dad."

Al chuckled. "No way. None of my business, but she's pretty."

"She's only a friend," Kyle mumbled, looking in the side door mirror at Serena and her dad going into her apartment.

When his cell rang, Kyle jerked back, not expecting the sudden intrusion. "Dad, where are you?"

"Still at the station. I'm going to be later than I thought. The good news is one of the people we caught is the guy who attacked me."

"Does that mean we can go back to the apartment tonight?"

"Not yet. I still don't know what's going on and the man isn't talking. I should be at Al's in the next hour or so."

"I'll let him know."

⟡

After hanging up from talking to his son, Cody caught Chief Winters signaling him. The last suspect, his assailant, was ready to be interrogated and this was one interview Cody wanted to conduct. As he walked toward the room, his gaze strayed to the clock on the wall. He hadn't heard from Liliana in over an hour. Did something happen at her sister's house? Was everything okay? He'd dealt with spousal abuse before, and it rarely ended well. The fact her sister went back to her husband didn't bode well for the situation.

When Cody entered the interview room, he forced himself to shut down thoughts of Liliana or he wouldn't be effective. He took a seat at the end of the table while Chief Winters sat across from the Jolly Green Giant, the name Cody had dubbed him when they rounded up the perpetrators in the cavern because the huge man wore a green T-shirt. Certainly not for a jolly demeanor. His scowl could wither the blue bonnets blooming right now.

Chief Winters gestured toward Cody. "I think you've had the pleasure of meeting Ranger Jackson last night."

The man grunted.

The police chief opened a folder. "It didn't take us long to identify you. You've got quite a rap sheet here. Why did you move recently from Phoenix to Durango, Dave? A job opportunity?"

Jolly Green Giant shrugged his left shoulder and looked down at his fingernails on his right hand as though assessing if he needed a manicure or not.

Cody fixed his gaze on Dave Bond, an enforcer for the highest payer. Was he responsible for the other three murders? "Phoenix wants you back for skipping bail. But we aren't giving you back. And since you skipped bail in Arizona, you won't be getting a chance to do it here. Who do you work for?"

"Would you believe the Tooth Fairy?" Dave's look pierced right through Cody. "I want my lawyer."

Chief Winters scraped his chair back and rose. "Suit yourself. The first person who talks gets a deal. The ones who don't will be prosecuted to the full extent of the law. We caught you red-handed smuggling guns and with Ranger Jackson's testimony, you'll go down for attempted murder of a police officer. You'll be in prison a long time."

"Wait," Dave said as Cody and Chief Winters reached the door.

11

Liliana came into the police station from the back at the same time Officer Robertson was leaving. "Is all the fun over with?" She tried to inject some humor into her voice, but that was the last thing she felt after her confrontation with her brother-in-law.

"Chief and Jackson are interviewing the last guy we caught today. The one who attacked Jackson last night, a Dave Bond with a rap sheet a mile long."

"I thought he would still be at the hospital."

"It was only a flesh wound, easily taken care of." Officer Robertson grinned. "Although painful. I'm heading home before my wife doesn't recognize her own husband."

"Tell her hi for me. I'll going to listen in on the interview."

Liliana turned down the hall that led to the two interview rooms with the small observation area between them. At the end of the corridor, Juan exited the back part of the station where the jail was. He was rarely here this late since he worked at the police station/courthouse during the daytime. His head down, he dragged his foot more than usual. Which meant he was tired or something was wrong. Or both.

Worried, she covered the distance to him. "It's late, Juan. Why are you here tonight?"

"My nephew."

His words garbled together more than usual, only reinforcing her earlier impression. "Is he okay?"

"José is in trouble again and got hauled in for drinking and driving."

"I'm sorry to hear that. My brother said he hasn't come back to school."

"He wouldn't listen to me then, but now he wants me to pull some strings and get him out of the DUI. Like I could or would. I don't know what that boy is thinking anymore. What's happening around here?"

"I wish I knew. We had a big bust tonight. Caught some people smuggling guns across the border not far from the ranch Carlos Salazar lived at."

"So that's why there's so much going on around here."

"Yeah, it's been a *long* day."

"Don't forget in the middle of all of this to take care of yourself."

"You, too. I'm discovering that some people you have to let go to make their own mistakes and hope they learn before something bad happens."

"You're not having problems with Rafael? I keep wishing José would be more like your brother."

"No, not Rafael," she said with a deep sigh.

"Your sister? I heard she went to the ER last night."

"Juan, is there anything you don't know?"

"I have a big family. My niece works at the hospital. She told me. Is she okay?"

"No, but she's refusing my help."

"Like José. Until he needs me. What would we do without family?"

"Have peace."

"Right." Juan patted her arm. "I'd better leave. Tomorrow will be here soon enough, *mi amiga*."

For a few minutes, she'd forgotten about the murders and smuggling ring as she and Juan had commiserated about their family problems, but she needed to turn her attention to her cases. Then maybe she wouldn't go crazy over something she wasn't going to be able to fix. Her sister had made that clear tonight.

Slipping into the observation room, Liliana watched Cody and Chief Winters hovering near the door as the man who had attacked Cody said, "Wait."

Anticipation flashed into Cody's eyes, but he quickly masked it. Liliana moved closer to the two-way mirror, wanting to catch every nuance on the suspect's face. Sometimes it wasn't what a person said, but how they said it that was telling.

"I was hired through a middleman. I don't know who's paying me to be the muscle. I was told to be cautious about the people I'm dealing with in Mexico. I'm given instructions over the phone. All I know is the other men call him *El Jefe*."

Cody closed the distance between them. "Is *El Jefe* the one who ordered you to pay me a visit last night?"

"No. I did that on my own. I'm the protection for the operation and you were getting too close to it. That was why the shipment today was going to be the last one. I want a deal."

Chief Winters folded his arms across his chest. "You haven't really told us anything so there's no deal."

"I overheard you all talking about *El Jefe*. How creative. You called the man who hired you 'the boss.'" Derision in Cody's voice mirrored his expression.

"I do have a piece of evidence that might help you, but until I'm given a deal and the paperwork is signed on it, I'm not giving it to you. I want immunity from prosecution."

Cody chuckled and slid a glance toward Chief Winters. "That's all he wants."

"That isn't going to happen unless the evidence you have leads to an arrest."

The man lounged back in the chair and smiled. "I can give you the name of the middleman and a recording of *El Jefe's* voice—not well disguised, by the way. I know with modern technology that can be stripped away and matched."

Cody nodded to Chief Winters who said, "You've got yourself a deal. Who's the middleman?"

"I know police lie all the time. There's no way I'll trust you. You get nothing until I have a signed agreement."

"Fine," Cody clipped out, a muscle in his jaw twitching.

Liliana sagged against the two-way mirror. Even if Dave Bond got immunity from prosecution on this case, he wouldn't for the charges in Arizona. He would still go to jail. Maybe tomorrow they would have a lead they could work on. At least they might be able to close the smuggling ring case. That left three murders. She massaged her fingertips into her temples. She should go home and try to sleep, but she didn't think she could.

Taking a deep breath, she turned toward the door and stopped. Cody stood in the entrance. Seeing him, looking tired but hopeful, nearly unleashed the dam that held back her emotions. *He would understand.*

"You heard?" Cody asked, coming into the room and shutting the door.

She nodded, her throat tight from the intensity of his look.

"If we find *El Jefe,* maybe we'll find the person who ordered the murders—at least Salazar. Don't know about Ruiz or Jane Doe."

"What if all three murders are connected?"

"So identifying this *El Jefe* might solve all three murders?"

"It's something to consider."

"I've ordered a DNA profile on Jane Doe's unborn child. It'll take a while even with a rush on it. If we have a suspect, the baby's DNA might be the proof we need to tie the person to the murdered woman."

"You think it's the baby's father?"

"Maybe."

She'd come down to work until she was so tired she would fall into bed, numb, not able to think of the disaster with her sister. But as she and Cody discussed the murders, her mind couldn't grasp anything. It was tired. If only her body would cooperate with her mind. A chair nearby beckoned. Her head throbbing, she sank onto it and rubbed her forehead.

Cody took a seat next to her. "What happened with your sister? Is she okay?"

"No. She just doesn't know it yet." She shook her head. "Or maybe she does and doesn't care."

"Or he has a hold on her."

She tilted her head toward him. "A hold over her? I suppose it could be the money. We didn't have much growing up. He bought her a car today. That was what enticed her to go home to him."

"Money is a powerful motivator."

"But he could kill her one day or leave her like my friend, Jackie. She has to use two forearm crutches to get around. Has for the last ten years because her husband ran her down with his car."

"I don't know what to tell you. You've tried to help your sister, and she doesn't want that help."

"I was told tonight I'm not welcomed at their house." She laced her fingers together. "Ever."

"Are you surprised by that?"

"No, not really but I'm hurt. My sister called me last night. Now I feel like the villain for trying to help her."

Cody grasped her hands, massaging them until she eased the grip her fingers had, their tips red. "Are you going to stop trying to help your sister?"

"No way. He may think he's won tonight, but he hasn't. He can't bully me with threats."

Cody stiffened. "He threatened you?"

"Not physically but he insinuated I would regret saying anything about him to others. He thinks if Elena comes back to him and appears to support him, people will forget that he beat the living daylights out of her. This is a small enough town that I won't have to say anything. It will quickly get around. Juan already asked me about Elena tonight. He has a niece who works at the hospital. Others will say something."

"So you might not have to do anything."

"No, but Samuel will accuse me of spreading 'false' accusations about him and take it out on Elena. I don't think he would be stupid enough to come after me. I'll fight back. Elena doesn't." Although now that she thought about it, had Samuel been responsible for her slashed tires and threatening message tied on a rock? She could see him doing those things.

"Invite me next time you see him. I would love to have a man-to-man chat with him."

She stared at his large hands covering hers and cherished his words. She didn't feel quite so alone all of a sudden. Swallowing the lump of emotions jamming her throat, she looked at him and smiled. "You know I like you, Cody Jackson."

His gaze snared hers and kept it tethered to his. "I like you, Liliana Rodriguez. You're beautiful, passionate about life, and a good cop. Appealing traits in a woman."

She laughed. "Being a good cop is a trait you like in a woman? I haven't heard that one before."

"We understand each other. The kind of hours and life we lead. The main reason my wife and I got a divorce was she didn't understand anything about what my work meant to me. She knew what I was like before we married, but she thought she could change me. Being a cop is who I am. She could never understand that."

"We aren't always easy to live with. Half the time, our thoughts are somewhere else."

"Just half the time?"

"Well, it depends on what type of case I'm working on."

"Me, too."

The warmth of his touch robbed her of a coherent come-back. A bond she'd felt since the beginning of the conversation strengthened and morphed into something much deeper than a casual connection. She was attracted to Cody, and if the intent look he gave her was any indication, he was attracted to her.

"Thank you, Cody, for listening to me. I used to think I had my life figured out. I had it together. I'm finding out that isn't so. Ten days ago my life was plodding along just fine. Now it's been ripped apart."

"Murder will do that."

"Family will."

"True. That's been the case for me. I have so much unfinished business with Kyle. I was his age once and should have a better handle on this."

She shifted so she faced him. "Did you lose your mother? Besides being a typical teenager, he might be dealing with his mother's death. You may have been in his life, but for years she was his foundation. That's been yanked out from under him."

"I've tried talking with him about her, but he shuts me down every time."

"Don't give up. Keep trying. There will come a time when he might be ready."

He settled his hands on her shoulders and massaged them. "I won't. I've discovered in the middle of all of this how important family is. Until he lived with me all the time, I'd forgotten what it really meant to have a family."

The massage melted her insides, beckoning the tension to leave her body. She closed her eyes and murmured, "You're hired. Anytime you want to do this I'm game."

He rose and skirted around her to stand behind her. "Your neck and shoulders are knotted."

"After today I'm not surprised the knots aren't as big as boulders."

She imagined herself on a beach, waves lapping against the shore, the sun's rays driving all cold from her bones, the salty tang in the air refreshing. As his fingers worked the knots loose, the pain ebbed to a dull ache. She sighed at the promise of even more relief.

The door opening in the interview room next to them and Officer Hudson speaking to Dave Bond brought the job back full force to Liliana. She glanced toward Hudson who released first one cuff then the other from the bar bolted into the table. For a moment, she'd forgotten where she was. Suddenly back in the present at the police station, she scrambled to her feet, rotating around to face him.

"Thanks, but I think it's time I head home. I suspect tomorrow will be as long and hard as today was."

Cody cocked one corner of his mouth. "Maybe the bad guys will take this weekend off."

"Ha! I wish. That didn't happen last weekend."

"It's been over a week, and we're no closer to solving the murders than when we started."

"Look on the bright side. We caught a smuggling ring in the process. Maybe the one who was responsible for shooting Al."

"Dave Bond?"

"Yes, he did come after you."

"You're one of those people who looks at the glass as half full?"

"Usually, although it has been hard lately."

"C'mon. I'll walk you to your car." He held the door open for her.

"You don't have to. I can manage on my own if you need to stay."

"No, I'm going to Al's. Tomorrow is starting early. I'm having Miguel brought in by eight."

Liliana stopped by her desk and grabbed her purse. "He isn't going to be too happy." She caught sight of a new fax on the top of the papers littering her work surface.

"I don't imagine he will be. But something doesn't add up with him and his cousin. Just don't know what it is yet."

She glanced around at the large room, then picked up the fax. "You can tell something is going down. We rarely have this much activity at this time of night." After reading the paper, she looked up at Cody. "This report says that Carlos Salazar had a border pass and a couple of months ago didn't return to Mexico. He was an illegal alien."

"So Miguel was lying to us about him coming from New Mexico."

"I suppose it's possible he didn't know his cousin was illegally in this country, but I'm betting he did. What else was Miguel lying about?"

"We'll ask him first thing tomorrow morning. We can't blame Miguel for lying about his cousin. He was protecting himself."

Liliana started for the back exit. "Yeah, I know, but we could have looked into Carlos's background in Mexico before now. It could have made our job easier if he had been upfront with us."

"And I'm gonna tell him that tomorrow." His hand at the small of her back, Cody reached around and pulled the door open. "We've rattled a few cages today. Be careful driving home."

At her car, she turned toward him. "You, too."

He panned the parking lot then returned his attention to her. Cupping her face, he dropped his head toward hers. His lips took possession of hers, and she welcomed it, winding her arms around his neck and bringing him even closer. Like the brief massage, his kiss wiped away the rest of the world for a blissful moment. Soothing peace replaced the earlier stress. She didn't want to leave his embrace, but the sound of a car pulling into the back lot broke the bond.

He moved away. "Take care."

She wasn't even sure how she ended up sitting behind her steering wheel, the engine purring to life. Backing out of the parking space, Liliana headed home, the sight of Cody watching her drive away staying in her thoughts.

⁂

"Did everything go okay today?" Cody walked to the coffeepot sitting on the counter in Al's kitchen and poured some into a Texas Ranger mug.

"Everything is fine. Your son and me spent some time getting to know each other." Al slid his cup toward Cody. "Here, refill mine."

"You mean Kyle didn't spend his time holed up in his room?"

"Nope. I don't think he was too happy I picked him up at school, but he got over it."

"Really? Are we talking about the same teenager?"

Al leaned against the counter, allowing it to support part of his weight. "Yep. About five feet ten inches, dark hair, and blue eyes. Got a cocky smile."

"You saw that. He smiled. When I dropped him off this morning, I would say he was in more than a bad mood, if that's possible."

"It's my charm. Never met a teen I couldn't get on my side." Al's chuckle sliced the air. "Well, maybe that's a slight exaggeration."

"Do you give lessons?"

"Just a couple of tips—care and listen."

"I'm afraid to ask what you two talked about."

"This and that." Al limped toward the table and sat. "Tell me what happened today. I've gotten a few reports, but I'd rather hear it from you. Firsthand accounts are always much better than gossip."

"You listen to gossip?" Cody took the seat across from Al and sipped his coffee.

"Remember the rumors about the smuggling ring. And you busted one tonight. You'd be surprised what you hear through the gossip mill. Like your Jane Doe was from the Chihuahua area in Mexico."

"What!" Cody sat up straight.

"I got through talking to one of my contacts in the Mexican government. He'd passed the info on to ICE. I imagine you'll hear tomorrow."

"What's her name?"

"Anna Medina. There isn't much to tell about her. She lived alone and was a waitress at a popular cantina. Did you realize that the Salazar family has relatives in the same area?"

"A connection between Carlos and our Jane Doe?"

"That's certainly possible."

"We discovered that Carlos was in this country illegally. He had a border pass under the name Carlos Ortega. That's why it took a while. Salazar is his mother's maiden name. One day he didn't return to Mexico, and ICE didn't find him at the place where he worked. He hadn't shown up that day for his job. How did you find out about some of the Salazar family living where Anna Medina did?"

"I've lived in this area a good part of my life. I have my own connections."

"Are you surprised about the cavern under the Rio Grande?"

With a frown, Al set his cup on the table. "Not much surprises me anymore. Over the years, I've heard rumblings but nothing concrete. But then I've heard talk about a lost gold mine in the Big Bend National Park, too."

"It wouldn't be the West without rumors about lost gold mines."

"This area has been relatively lucky to avoid some of the problems in towns along the border."

"Why is that the case?"

"I think the police department is good and more importantly Cesar Álvarez lives here. He owns a lot of the land around here, and he has a lot of money to keep it safe. He has his own private army."

"Is he crooked?"

"Honest?" Al averted his gaze for a moment then looked back at Cody. "He could be. I could never find anything. But then other than the occasional coyote bringing illegal aliens through here, there hasn't been a lot of crime," a long pause, "that we know about."

"He's been out of town until recently so I haven't had the pleasure of meeting him yet. But the caverns are partially on his land so I will."

"Tread lightly. Now tell me what happened."

After taking another swallow of his coffee, Cody related the events that occurred starting yesterday concerning Salazar's ranch.

"It doesn't sound like you had a dull day." Al stood and moved to the sink to pitch the last of his coffee. "Your story has worn me out. I'm heading to bed. I imagine you'll be busy tomorrow. Kyle said something about going riding after school. I thought I would go with him. I have a couple of places I wanted to show him not far from here."

"That's fine. I'll see what happens tomorrow, but I think it'll be okay for us to return to the apartment in the evening."

"At least you caught the guy who went after you, and he admitted it was his idea."

"That's what he says. But a big question still remains. Who hired him?"

"I can't see him going after you. He's probably too busy trying to find another way to get his guns across the border."

"Do you think this smuggling ring had something to do with your shooting?"

"More than likely but we may never know who pulled the trigger."

After Al left, Cody finished his coffee, almost calling Liliana to tell her about Anna Medina. But she'd been so tired tonight. He hoped she went home and fell asleep right away.

Cody walked into the hallway and stopped at the door to the guest bedroom where his son was staying. He knocked.

Wearing his earplugs and listening to his iPod, Kyle opened the door and stepped to the side. "Al said you and the detective caught a gunrunning ring."

"Yep. The best part of it is that the cavern system was extensive, and there are probably several areas to access it. The Feds will be busy tracking down all the tunnels. It's a big score."

His son took the earplugs out. "And you're the one who found it."

"Just following a hunch."

"I'm going riding with Al in the afternoon. When you get off work, can we go back to the apartment? I'm helping someone train for a race in a week."

"Where are you going to run?"

"Not running. Serena is in a wheelchair. I'm working with her to build up her arm muscles in the workout room in the apartment complex."

"Sure. I think everything will be okay tomorrow. I got the guy who was in our place."

"Yeah, Al told me."

Cody studied his son, not sure what had changed but something had. "This morning when I let you out at school you got mad at me because Al might pick you up after class. I got the impression you didn't like him. What's changed?"

"I got to know him. He's done a lot of cool things. He used to ride in the rodeo. Bulls. You have to be tough to do that."

"Or crazy. That can be the longest eight seconds of your life."

"You sound like you've done it."

"I did in my youth."

"Why didn't you ever tell me that?"

"I guess because the subject never came up. There are a lot of things we don't talk about each other. I hope we change that, son. I know I can work crazy hours, but I want us to become a family. It won't be that long before you'll graduate from high school and strike out on your own."

"Don't pack my bags just yet." Kyle stuck his earplugs back in. "I might be one of these kids that never leaves home."

Cody laughed. "That's a fair warning."

He left Kyle for the first time in a long while feeling hope they might actually have a father/son relationship. Al's advice came back to him. He had the caring part down, but he needed to work on the listening. And when their relationship was on firmer ground, he wanted to tell Kyle about the authorities' suspicions concerning Nate.

∽≈∾

"Anna Medina. Finally, we have a name to give our Jane Doe. I've always hated referring to a victim as John or Jane Doe." Liliana stuck the fax they had received from ICE into a folder. It concerned the woman who had been the first murder in the death spree of the past week.

"Our contact in Chihuahua is interviewing people she worked with and her neighbors to see if they can discover anything that will help our case." Cody turned down Miguel Salazar's street.

"She was pregnant. Who is the father? Someone in Mexico? Why was she coming to the U.S. if that were the case?"

"Maybe they'll find out some of those answers."

"Anna Medina has to be the woman who wrote Carlos. We need to see if Carlos went to Chihuahua to see his relatives recently. When the DNA comes in on the baby, we should compare it with Carlos's."

"That will all take time. Time we may not have." Cody parked in the driveway behind Miguel's pickup, the man's small adobe house neat and well maintained.

"I know. I wish testing wasn't so backlogged. For some reason I feel she's the key to all of this. Everything happened right after she was killed."

"Now that we have a possible connection between Carlos and Anna, I agree. Did Ruiz bring Anna into this country? If so, then that's the connection between all three."

Liliana exited Cody's SUV at the same time as he did and rounded the front. "Miguel probably knew about Anna and didn't say anything to us about her or the fact Miguel was in this country illegally."

"That's why I decided to come and personally escort him to the station. Make him feel like he's done something wrong."

"If he withheld information, he has. What else is he holding back from us?"

Cody knocked. A good minute passed before Miguel opened the door, his hair wet, wearing only a white T-shirt and old jeans with scuffed brown boots.

Miguel's quizzical look shifted to worry, his hooded expression tightening about his mouth. "Something wrong?"

"We would like you to come with us to the police station," Cody said in a businesslike tone.

Miguel stepped back, his shoulders tensing. "Why? I've done nothing wrong."

"Then you have nothing to be worried about." Liliana poised herself on the balls of her feet. In the man's eyes she saw a war raging: fight or flight. "We know about Anna Medina and about Carlos being here illegally. If you tell us everything you know about her and Carlos, we might overlook the fact you withheld evidence in a murder case."

"I don't know what—"

"Don't bother denying you didn't know." Cody's voice toughened to a steel thread. "You were going out to your cousin's for a reason. How much time did you spend out at the ranch?"

"He called me that morning to come see him. He's my cousin so I went. That's all. I didn't realize he'd come into the United States illegally until—"

One corner of Cody's mouth lifted in a smile that didn't reach his eyes. "Until what?"

"Nothing." Miguel clamped his lips together, crossing his arms over his chest.

"We'll continue this down at the station." Cody gestured for Miguel to proceed first.

Again that look of indecision appeared in Miguel's eyes. Liliana moved a few feet toward the edge of the stoop, ready to leap if he made a run for it.

Miguel's chest rose then fell in a deep breath. He came outside, pulling the door closed and locking it. "I have to be at work in an hour."

"That'll depend on how well you cooperate." Cody followed behind Miguel.

"Should I call a lawyer?"

"Should you? Are you guilty of doing something wrong?" Cody tossed down the challenge as though he already knew the answer.

"You two have no idea what's going—"

The crack of a gunshot split the air at almost the same time Miguel stopped, remained standing for a second or two then crumpled to the ground. Instinct kicking in, Liliana drew her weapon and dove toward the other side of the SUV, putting the vehicle between her and the direction the bullet came. Cody ducked behind his car at the same time.

"I think it came from the park across the street." Liliana pulled her cell out and called the station, her adrenaline pumping through her body. "This is Detective Rodriguez. We're at Miguel Salazar's house on Pecos Boulevard. He was shot as we were leaving." She peeked around the SUV at the man lying on the ground, face down. "He's not moving. May be dead. I think the shot came from the park across the street. Ranger Jackson and I are behind his car."

"Sending everyone we have and an ambulance," the dispatcher said. "Hang in there, Liliana. Help is on the way."

When she hung up, she looked at Cody. "The shooter had a chance to shoot at least one of us before we got to cover. Why didn't he?"

"We weren't the target. Why Miguel?"

"To stop him from talking to us?"

"We may never know, but after the area is secured, we're going to tear his house apart and see if we can find anything to tell us why him."

❧

The exhilaration of seeing Miguel Salazar collapse, a red stain spreading out from the shot to the chest floods me with power. The police can't stop me. I'll do their job for them—rid the town of its trash. No longer am I nobody. Before long criminals will fear me. Someone needs to do something about this town. And I'm that someone. When this is over with, they will look at me differently.

I'll be somebody. Important.

Time to leave. The police will thank me one day for what I'm doing. After collecting the shell casing, I climb down to the ground and back away from the children's fort on the playground in the park, then make my way toward the grove of trees. Each step I take feels light.

The power grows within me. Demanding justice. Demanding respect.

❧

Cody positioned himself on the stoop, surveying the crime scene. The area was crawling with police. The ambulance had just left with Miguel—dead. He hadn't had a chance. The shot hit him in the heart. From a distance like Carlos.

Liliana disengaged talking with Chief Winters and approached Cody. "Ready to check his house out? They're going to scour every inch of the park. See if they can discover where the shooter was."

Cody pointed toward the playground on the right side of the park near the line of trees. "It came from that direction. In an hour or so that place would have children playing on the equipment."

"That's what I told the chief. He's going to start there."

Having retrieved the set of keys from Salazar's pocket, Cody used them to let himself into the house. "Let's start with his bedroom."

"What are we looking for?"

"I wish I knew. We'll bag anything that might help us at all. When in doubt, take it."

Liliana sniffed the air. "Do you smell that?"

"He burned something." As he walked toward the hallway, he glanced back at her. "It's stronger over here."

Liliana slowed in front of the door to the kitchen to the right of Cody. "Nothing coming from here so it wasn't food." She continued toward him and trailed him into the largest bedroom out of two.

The top sheet on the bed laid in a wad at the bottom of it. Clothes were piled on a chair while a suitcase sat on the floor near it with a set of jeans in it. "He didn't tell us he was going somewhere."

"And where are his wife and child? Liliana inhaled a deep breath and moved closer to the door to the bathroom. "I think it's coming from here."

Cody went first into the bathroom, his gaze riveting to the bathtub, the shower curtain pulled back to reveal charred pieces of paper dampened with water. "We must have interrupted him. Maybe that's why his hair was wet. He was burning this when we came."

"Getting rid of evidence. This is not the act of an innocent man."

Cody knelt down and carefully investigated the pieces of paper, most burnt beyond recognition or already turned to ashes and littering the white porcelain, the water further making it impossible to tell what had been destroyed.

Liliana hovered behind him, pointing toward the back part of the tub. "That looks like part of a map." Leaning over the tub, she continued, "There's part of it intact that's lying against the side."

Cody sidled to where she pointed and, taking out a pair of tweezers, carefully extracted the evidence from the bathtub and put it in a bag. "A map to what? Why would he burn it?"

"I hope the state lab can do their magic and preserve this as much as possible so we can figure out what it's a map to. Then we might know why he went to the trouble of trying to burn it."

Cody waved his hand over the black ash in the rest of the tub. "Because this will be useless to us."

"Maybe there'll be something else he didn't have a chance to get rid of. I'll check the second bedroom while you finish up in here."

"We need to find his wife. She may know what Miguel was up to."

"Which could put her in danger."

Cody searched every place he could think someone would hide an item—in the toilet tank, in back of it, in all the drawers and cabinets, behind the one lone picture in the bedroom and the mirror over the dresser. He stripped the bedding off and inspected the mattress and all the parts of the bed. Nothing else.

Meeting Liliana in the hallway, he headed to the kitchen. Liliana opened the small refrigerator and freezer and went through all the packages and cartons. He did the same with the cabinets.

"It looks like Miguel ate better than his cousin." Liliana set what she had finished going through on the table in the center of the room.

"I saw a couple of expensive items in his bedroom that a person with his job shouldn't be able to afford. Two gold chains and a ring with a large diamond. I'm going to have them assessed to make sure they are real and how much they're worth. It looks like most of his wife's clothes are gone."

"The same with the baby's bedroom. Most of the child's clothes and toys were gone."

"Did she have family she could go to?"

"I don't know much about her, but I will by the end of the day." Liliana frowned. "In the baby's bedroom Miguel had a state-of-the-art computer system. If you ask me, a strange place to keep it unless you want to make sure no one knows you have it. We'll need to check it out thoroughly. I couldn't pull anything up on it. But I'm not very skilled in technology."

"I'll have the tech boys look at it. Even if he deleted files, they might be able to recover them."

Liliana knelt on the tile floor to check underneath the refrigerator. "So he's making good money somewhere and spending it. But I've never seen him wear a gold ring or chains. Neither has his wife worn any expensive jewelry, at least not to church where I've seen her."

"An investment?"

Liliana pulled out the tray under the refrigerator and wrapped in plastic was a lot of cash. "Or this is his bank and he took a withdrawal to buy his toys." Setting the tray with the large stash of money on the counter, she whistled. "The top one is a hundred dollar bill. If they all are, then Miguel was rich. He certainly could afford a house better than this five-room one."

"Let's finish and get back to the station and tear this guy's life apart. There's got to be something there we've overlooked that will help us."

"I hope so, because this is the fourth murder in less than two weeks. Was he killed to shut him up or is there another reason?"

"If we can figure out what he was into, then we might find the person behind his murder and maybe the others."

"So you think they may all be connected?"

"We have three possibilities. They are, they aren't, or a couple of them are."

Her chuckle floated to him. "We have one to four murderers to hunt down. I think we aren't gonna get much sleep in the days to come."

"Sometimes I do my best thinking while I'm asleep."

Liliana turned toward him, both eyebrows raised. "So do I. I can wake up in the morning with a solution to a problem that I had wrestled with the day before."

"A kindred spirit." When he said that, her eyes sparkled. Her reaction ignited his interest even more.

But before he could say anything else, movement out of the corner of his eye pulled his attention away. Chief Winters came into the kitchen.

"We couldn't find for sure where the shooter was. There wasn't a shell casing. But around the fort which is in the right location we found adult footprints—boots—in the sand. Now that could have been a parent watching his child or the killer. We followed the direction the person went. It was into the trees, but we couldn't find anything there either."

"He probably left when we ducked behind my car."

"We will process the fort and maybe come up with something. Taking a casting of the footprint." Chief Winters's gaze latched onto the stack of money in the tray.

"It doesn't look like Miguel is who he said he was." Liliana began putting the food back into the fridge.

"We also found where he was burning some papers in his bathtub."

"And we think he wiped his computer," Liliana added.

Chief Winters frowned. "That sounds like a guilty man. Guilty of what?"

"Killing his cousin?" She shut the refrigerator door.

"This is the first time in a week I feel I might have good news for the mayor. I'll be outside finishing up the search of the park just in case we are off base with the fort."

"When we get back to the station, I'd like to go through what we have and what we need to follow through. I'd like to be able to answer if these murders are connected or not. If so, we'll know we need to focus on Anna Medina. She started it all." Cody strode toward the living room. "I'll take the right side, you the left."

❧

A knock sounded at the door to the back room where Liliana had set up the white board and tacked up the photos of the crime scenes. One on each wall. "I hope that's Sean with our food. I didn't have breakfast this morning and it's three now. A late lunch or an early dinner." She opened the door to find the kid from the cafe across the street. The scent of hamburgers wafted from the sack in his hand. After taking the bag and the holder with two coffees in it, she said to Sean, "Let me get my purse. Wait right here," then to Cody. "You are gonna love these hamburgers. The best in town."

Liliana crossed the small room and placed the food on the table where papers and photos were scattered at one end. When she grabbed her purse and turned back to Sean, the young man's eyes grew round.

He stared at the crime scene pictures at Carlos's ranch, opening and closing his mouth. But no words came out.

Liliana scooted out into the hallway and shut the door quickly behind her. "I'm sorry. Those photos can be rough." Digging into her handbag, she withdrew some money to pay Sean.

"H—h—ow do—do you . . ." His face pale, he snapped his jaw together, his teeth clicking.

"Just forget it, Sean," she said, stuffing the dollar bills into his hand, then rummaging in her purse for more money for a larger tip. "Thank you." She started moving toward the end of the hallway, hoping that the young man would follow.

He didn't for a moment, then blinked and whirled around, hurrying past Liliana as though a rabid dog nipped at his heels.

She went back into the room she was using to lay out all the evidence on the cases. "I can remember the first set of crime scene photos I saw of a murder victim. I think I dreamed about them for months. I'm afraid Sean is going to do the same thing."

Cody glanced up from studying a report. "It's sad that we get used to seeing murder victims."

"If I had a reaction like I did the first time, I would never be able to function as a police officer."

"The same here. I wouldn't want Kyle to see any of these photos."

"What if he wants to be a police officer like you?"

"That's not gonna happen. He's never had any interest in what I do."

Liliana dug into the sack and pulled out the wrapped hamburgers then the two orders of fries. "We'd better eat before it gets cold. But I have to say their hamburgers aren't bad cold. Now the fries are a different story."

She sat at the table while Cody took the seat across from her. "So what do we know?"

"The man Maria saw had an evil eye, a tan cowboy hat, an old black pickup, and speaks Spanish."

"But we don't know what the child meant by an evil eye. We know two of the murders were done by someone who is a good shot from a distance. Sniper training?" Liliana popped a fry into her mouth, then another.

"Anna and Carlos were both here in the country illegally. Ruiz wasn't nor Miguel."

"Anna was pregnant. Was Carlos the father? Was she coming to be with him?" Liliana peered at the right wall that held the pictures of that crime scene. "Do you think we need to concentrate on Anna's killing? We have more evidence in that murder."

"If indeed it started all this, we need to know why. I'll call my contact and see when they're interviewing Anna's friends and coworkers. She came into this country illegally. That would take some money. We need to know where it came from. Or was she a mule carrying drugs across the border and that got her killed?" Cody gathered the trash from their meal and tossed it into the garbage can.

Liliana rolled her head and arched her back. "Until we get the forensics back on the evidence you sent to the lab today and we hear about Anna and Carlos from the Mexican authorities, we don't have much we can do other than find Miguel's wife."

"We need a break. We've been staring at this for hours, and I promised Kyle we would go back home tonight. Let's call it quits. It's nearly three and we've been putting in fifteen-hour days for the past week and a half."

Liliana rose and continued to stretch. "That sounds good. Might give us a different perspective if we take the rest of the day off and start back first thing in the morning."

"I need a day off. Maybe I'll think better. Especially with all that has been going on."

Maybe that was what she needed. She felt like the people with Moses, aimlessly wandering around in the desert. No direction. No purpose. "Maybe you should spend the whole day with your son. This move can't be easy for him."

He considered all the time he hadn't been able to spend with Kyle since moving to Durango. "When this is over with I intend to. I can't afford more than an afternoon away. What do you do for fun around here?"

"That's easy. Hike and take photographs."

"Let's spend the afternoon doing that. We can get a fresh perspective on these cases." He closed the folder before him.

Five minutes after Cody left, Liliana climbed into her car and started toward home. Halfway there, she made a U-turn and drove into Rancho Estates. Seeing the subdivision's sign a minute ago prompted her to pay the Martinez family a visit. She hadn't in a while. Maybe Mr. Martinez would change his mind about Maria talking to the police further. Liliana parked on the street and walked up their drive to the house.

Frowning, Mrs. Martinez answered the door. "We don't know anything," she said before Liliana could speak.

"I thought I would say hi to Maria and check to make sure she was doing all right. It's hard for an adult to witness what she did, let alone a child."

"She is not here. She hasn't remembered anything. Now if you would please leave, I have work to do." Mrs. Martinez started closing the door.

Liliana stuck her leg and shoulder into the opening. "If she remembers anything, please tell us. She may know something and not realize it."

"She doesn't know anything. Good day."

As she moved back, the door slammed in Liliana's face.

❧

"Mama! Mama!" Maria raced from the back of the house. "Is that Detective Rodriguez?"

Her mother nodded.

"I need to talk to her. I do remember something."

"What?

"He talked funny."

"What do you mean?"

Maria shrugged. "I don't know. Just funny. The lady laughed at him for doing it."

Her mama clasped her shoulder. "Baby, I want you to forget that whole day." She pulled Maria against her and hugged her. "You're having such bad dreams about what happened. I'm worried about you."

Maria could remember the dream last night—the one where the man yanked the cushion off the couch and dragged her out of her hiding place. Trembling, she drew even closer to Mama. "But Detective Rodriguez said she needed my help."

Her mother leaned back and stared down at her. "You have to take care of yourself, baby. She'll take care of catching the bad guy. I don't want you to think or talk about this again. Okay?"

Maria wanted to shake her head, but the worried look her mother gave her forced her to say, "Yes, Mama."

Maybe everything will be okay if I don't sleep. Then I won't dream.

12

"I'm glad you're game for riding a bike. We can go farther. There are some beautiful places I want to show you." Liliana removed her bike from the rack attached to her uncle's Jeep.

Cody studied his mountain bike before taking it down from the rack. "Are you sure we shouldn't go back to Durango and get some horses? I haven't ridden a bike in twenty-five years."

"Then consider this a challenge. If you can ride a horse, you can ride a bike."

"She says with laughter."

"I'm trying not to." She pressed her lips together to emphasize the point and handed Cody the helmet she'd borrowed for him.

He arched a brow, peered at it as if it were a strange object he'd never seen, but took it from her. "Personally I don't know how this is gonna protect my head if I crash. Wouldn't a football helmet be better protection?"

"I'm not going to ignore years of research that I'm sure went into the development of this helmet for bikers. And take it from me, I've fallen and it helps."

"I thought this was gonna be our afternoon of rest and relaxation, so we'll be refreshed to tackle the murder cases tomorrow. We're gonna be doing all the work. On a horse, the horse does."

She couldn't contain her laughter any longer. It burst forth, filling the air. "Okay, you're going to use different muscles today, but I assure you the scenery will be worth it."

"I hope so."

"This may not be a fact you're aware of, but this state park has some good bike trails. We're taking one. We'll go as far as time permits, but you should bring Kyle back here and camp out. I'll even loan you two bikes to use. My cousins won't mind." Liliana mounted her bike. "We'll go for about an hour and stop to eat a lunch I packed. I know a place that has a view."

"That means we're gonna pedal uphill?"

"That or walk your bike uphill. Whichever you prefer, but just so you know, I'm pedaling." After throwing down that challenge, she started down the trail.

It didn't take long for Cody to catch up with her, but he breathed hard as he went around her on the trail. "Eat my dust."

"But you don't know where you're going."

"It's a trail, isn't it? I can follow one of those."

"Wait, there's a . . ."

Before she could tell him about the gully wash, Cody went flying through the air and disappeared from her view. Liliana braked at the top while he scrambled to his feet, a cloud of dust rising up into the air from his tumble. He'd stopped only a foot from a large pickly pear cactus with its red fruit.

"Is that called crash and burn?" she asked as Cody righted his bike then looked up at her.

"I wanted to test how good the helmet was. I can reassure you it works well."

Liliana lowered her bike carefully over the two-foot incline and then clambered down it. "You don't have to go to all that trouble next time."

"I'll keep that in mind." He swept his arm across his body. "After you, ma'am."

"That's okay. I'll let you lead the way."

He grinned. "I was forgetting my manners. Ladies first."

The give and take between them set the mood for the ride. By the time Liliana stopped an hour later for lunch, she had laughed more with Cody in that time than she had in weeks.

Cody laid his bike down next to hers and covered the ground to the edge that overlooked a desert valley with wildflowers in full bloom. "Beautiful. Worth the ride uphill."

Liliana adjusted the focus on her camera and snapped some photos. "Yes, beautiful. This is one of my favorite places. I'm surprised there aren't more people on the trail."

"They're probably back home, enjoying their air-conditioning."

She glanced over her shoulder at him. "It's probably not even eighty-five."

"That's nearly Arctic temperatures. It just seemed so much hotter. Oh, wait, probably because I just biked uphill for the past twenty minutes."

She spun around, her hand on her waist. "Texas Ranger Cody Jackson, I do declare . . ."

The rest of her words were cut off when Cody stepped closer, hooked his arm around her and hauled her to him. Then he planted a fierce kiss on her mouth as though he were a settler laying claim to his property.

"What was that for?" she murmured when he pulled away slightly.

"Those lips are just so tempting, and it's my way of thanking you for inviting me. This has been fun. I haven't thought about work—"

Liliana placed her forefinger over his lips to still his words. "No talk about you-know-what. We have a right to one afternoon away from the job."

His mouth spread into a huge smile. "You're right."

He dragged her the few inches toward him and kissed her again—a gentle mating of their lips that was different from the other kiss but just as powerful. The sun bathed her face, his arms encased her in an embrace that made her feel desired, and the gentle wind blew the smells of the desert around her. That scent toyed with the lime-laced one wafting from Cody.

He broke away only long enough to lay his forehead against hers, then he cupped her face. "I needed to get away from everything."

Liliana wasn't sure what to say to him. This afternoon was changing their relationship. She dated when her job permitted, but nothing was ever serious. With Cody that could change, and she wasn't sure she was ready for anything like that.

"I don't know about you, but I'm starved." She stepped back several feet until Cody grabbed her arm and pulled her toward him.

"Another foot and you would have gone over."

He muddled her brain to the point she forgot where she was. She *definitely* didn't know if she should pursue anything with Cody. Not when she couldn't think straight around the man.

She didn't say anything to him but instead marched toward the backpack with the food. She reached for it. The rattling sound warned her she wasn't alone. She froze.

✑

"You did good today." Kyle took the weight from Serena and put it back on the rack.

"Are you sure you don't mind helping me? I could have done this alone if you had something better to do."

"I know you could have, but I made a promise to you I would get you into shape for your race."

"A promise?"

He turned toward the weight rack, shifting his gaze away from Serena whose face was flushed with her exertion. "I told you I would. That's a promise to me."

"It wasn't realistic to think I could be ready in three weeks. I only have a little over a week. The race is a week from Saturday. I'm not nearly where I need to be."

"Probably not for this one if your goal is to finish first. But maybe the next one or the race after that."

"Will you come watch me?"

"Go with you?" The idea appealed to him. It would give him a change of scenery. Maybe that was what he needed to get a better perspective on what was happening to him. "Yeah, I'd like to."

"It'll be a long day. San Antonio is three hours away. We'll leave about five in the morning and be back late at night." Serena wiped her face and neck with her towel.

"Who all is going?"

"Papa and Mama and my younger sister, but there'll be room for you." Her eyes gleamed with a brilliance that he didn't see in others. It made her glow as though an inner light shone outward from her.

"Why aren't you all staying overnight?"

"My younger sister has a school function the night before and Mama plays in the church band. She hates to miss."

"Do you miss going to regular school?"

She lowered her gaze, twining her fingers together in her lap. "Sometimes. But then I remember some of the kids that weren't nice and I don't. There was a group of guys that were particularly cruel."

"They hurt you?"

"They made threats but never did anything physically. I know Mama told me I should ignore what they say, but after a time it's hard to. Words can hurt, too."

"Who?"

"Aaron Taylor and his group." She lifted her head, and tears glistened in her eyes.

Seeing them twisted his gut.

"I know I won't ever walk again, but I'm not less of a person because of it. I still feel and hurt when someone says something mean to me. I miss my friends, but I don't miss the snickers or what some people said to me."

Her words yanked the knots in his stomach so tight pain shot through his body. In Houston, he'd been a part of a group that had done similar things at his school. What had he done? He remembered one boy moving to another school. Had he and his friends been responsible for that?

A tentative smile, the corners of her mouth quivering, pushed the hurt from her expression. "Hey, I don't want to think about them. They can't ruin my life anymore. That's what's important now."

"Then no more talk about them. Besides, we need to plan your exercise program for this next week. Eight more days you can work out before you leave on Saturday."

"When's your dad coming back?"

Kyle glanced at the clock on the wall of the workout room. "Probably not for a few hours."

"Good. I'm going to take a shower and change. Why don't you come over later and we can figure out what I need to do, and if you want, Mama said she'd like you to come to dinner tonight. Do you think you can?"

"Yeah, I'm sure I can. If Dad isn't home by that time, I can leave a note."

Serena swiveled her chair around and rolled toward the exit. "We eat early. Can you come at six?"

He hurried around her and opened the door. "Sure. It'll give me some time to finish a math assignment. Not my favorite subject. I'm having some trouble with Algebra II."

"Bring it with you. I love math. Maybe I can help you."

"You will? That's great. I had a friend back in Houston who helped me a lot."

"Then consider that you have a friend in Durango who can help you here. See you later." She wheeled herself toward her apartment at the opposite end of the same building as his.

He waited until she reached her front door before heading for the stairs to his apartment. Before she went inside, she glanced toward him and smiled. He felt a warmth suffuse through him. Even from a distance, he felt the radiance of her bright brown eyes when she looked at him.

He took the steps two at a time. He had someone to help him with math. This day was turning out to be a good one. This morning at breakfast he and his dad had a civil conversation for once. Maybe he should talk to him about Mom. He might understand what he was feeling. He was learning things weren't always what they appeared to be.

Inside he took a quick shower then went to the fridge for something to snack on. He grabbed the orange juice carton and drank several large swallows, then started for the table and his homework.

The bell rang. He tensed. He wasn't expecting anyone.

Cautiously he strode to the door and peered out the peep-hole. Aaron stood there with another guy behind him.

With a deep sigh, Kyle swung the door open. "Hi. What's going on?"

"We were driving around and thought you'd like to join us."

Kyle's gaze skipped from Aaron to the other guy. "Can't. I've got homework."

"Do it later. Durango High is playing in a baseball tourna-ment, and we thought we would go support some of our players on the team."

"Some?"

"Yeah, you know the white players. They're neglected some-times for people like Manny and Rafael. We thought we would drive around, get some dinner, then make the game."

He loved baseball, but the words to agree wouldn't form in his mind. "I can't. My dad is gone right now."

"Call him." Aaron's upper lip curled.

The look Aaron gave Kyle held a warning. "I can't. He's out of cell range."

"Fine. Just letting you know ahead of time, we're thinking of going to a border town next Saturday. Have us some fun. You need to go with us."

"I don't know if my dad will let me."

"Then lie to him. Tell him you're doing something else."

In Houston, he had. Now he wasn't so sure. So much was going on right now with the murders. Besides, he'd agreed to go with Serena. He wasn't going to back out now. That wasn't fair to her. "Sorry. I'm not going to do that."

"You're kidding!"

"No," Kyle said although it hadn't been a question.

A sneer marred Aaron's expression. "Does this have to do with Serena?"

"Serena?"

"Yeah, the girl I saw you talking to a while ago. I wasn't even gonna come up here to invite you to hang with us, but I thought you were one of us. You could have been saying anything to her. I was giving you the benefit of doubt. Now I don't think you were telling her to get lost. She ain't bad looking for one of *them,* but—"

Anger welled in Kyle. "I have homework I need to do now." He glanced from the other guy, a six-foot junior, to Aaron, then gripped the handle and slammed the door. Harder than he intended.

Aaron pounded against the wood. "You'll regret this."

His threat blared through the door, but surprisingly Kyle didn't care. He didn't need a friend like Aaron who was going to tell him who to like or not. That wasn't Aaron's call.

As he headed toward the kitchen table, a lightness to his step and spirit reinforced the feeling he'd done the right thing. The words of the preacher last Sunday still echoed through him. The preacher spoke about God being love and the energy it took to hate being so much more consuming than the energy to love.

❧

At the sight of the western diamondback rattler within striking distance of Liliana, coiled, its tongue flicking in and out, Cody went still. "Don't move, Liliana."

"I wasn't going to."

His gun was in his backpack under hers and wouldn't do him any good. He scoured the area, searching for anything to use as a weapon. His heart beat as fast as the snake rattling his tail. A few feet away he spied a long crooked stick. He kept his eye on the serpent and sidled toward the tree limb. With extra slow movements, he leaned over and grasped the makeshift weapon.

After a couple of minutes of the standoff between her and the snake, she said in a whisper, "And it isn't moving either."

"I know. Stubborn reptile. I'm going to come at it from another direction. Once it turns toward me get out of there."

"Be careful."

"I will. Don't worry about me. Just get away from it."

He sidestepped until he reached a place he could come toward the snake from the opposite side, then he strode forward, making a lot of racket and waving the stick at the rattler. With Liliana perfectly still and quiet, the reptile turned toward the new threat—him. As he did, she eased away from it. Out of the corner of his eye, he saw her grab a limb lying on the ground as she backed away.

Once she was out of the way, he began retreating, but kept the weapon between him and the snake that uncoiled and slithered toward some brush and a pile of rocks not far away. A minute later, the reptile disappeared from view.

Liliana crept forward again and snatched up both backpacks. "I think we'll eat at another location."

"A good idea." Moving toward his bike on the ground, he still didn't take his eye off where the snake had vanished.

Liliana passed his backpack to him, slung hers over her shoulders, and mounted her bike. "Race down the hill?"

"After the last time I went first, I don't know if I should accept that challenge."

"That's assuming you're in the lead." Liliana shot forward, pedaling for the trail that led down, her laughter drifting back to him.

He put all his energy into gaining on her. As he passed her, he slanted her a look and realized in spite of the snake he'd had a great time. He didn't even want to think about going back to Durango.

～☊～

Later Wednesday night, Cody heard the front door opening and called out, "I'm in the kitchen."

Kyle appeared around the corner and sat on the stool at the counter. "How was the ride?"

"Other than taking a tumble on the trail and fighting off a rattler, fine." Cody slathered mustard on his two pieces of bread. "Do you want a sandwich?"

"Nope. The dinner I had at Serena's was a feast. I'm stuffed."

Cody finished putting together his ham and Swiss sandwich and grabbed his glass of iced tea, then took a seat at the end of the counter. "Serena sounds like a nice girl."

"Yeah, she is. She asked me to go with her to the race in San Antonio next Saturday. It'll be a long day, but I would like to. She's been training hard. Her goal is to finish this first race. I want to cheer her across the finish line."

"That's great. You said she doesn't go to Durango High. Where is she going to school?"

"She's being homeschooled. She had problems at Durango High and decided learning at home would be better for her."

"What kind of problems?"

"Teasing."

"Because she's in a wheelchair?"

"Partly."

"What do you mean?" Cody bit into his dinner, watching the play of emotions flit across his son's face.

Kyle's expression settled into anger. "Some guys were making fun of her because she's in a wheelchair, but I think they were also motivated by her heritage."

"Do you know the guys?"

Kyle nodded. "Aaron Taylor is their leader."

"Your friend?"

"Not anymore. I see how he and his pals have made Serena feel. She left high school because of them."

"I'm sorry to hear that about Serena. Bullies are a problem in school but also other places. They lead people to do things they normally wouldn't. Like your friend not going to high school."

With his forefinger, Kyle drew a figure eight over and over on the countertop. "I never thought about how others would feel. I didn't stop to think about their feelings. When Serena talked about what happened to her, it made me sick for the times I ganged up on someone different. It made me realize how much words can hurt."

"Has Serena always been in a wheelchair?"

"No, she fell from a cliff when she was hiking with her family. Part of the edge gave way. She almost died, but she figured the Lord kept her alive for a reason. She was in the hospital for months when she was twelve." Kyle looked at him. "You know she's so upbeat considering all that has happened to her. She gives herself goals. She's determined she'll walk one day, and I think if anyone will, it'll be her."

"Sounds like you admire her."

Kyle cocked his head to the side. "You know I do. She's special. When she's working out, we talk about all kinds of stuff I've never shared with a girl. She makes me feel like I'm really helping her."

"Sounds like you're being a good friend." Cody ate some more of his sandwich, studying his son who continued to doodle on the counter. He might never have a better moment to talk with Kyle about Nate. The words formed in his mind but stuck in his throat. Lately, he'd faced a barrage of bullets striking all around him, and he wasn't as afraid as he was now. He didn't want to mess up with his son again.

"I guess I'd better go finish the rest of my homework. At least Serena helped me with my Algebra II assignment. She's good. She explains it better than my teacher."

Cody cleared his throat. "Stay a moment. I have something I need to tell you."

His son's eyebrows slashed downward. "What's wrong? I thought you got the guy who attacked you."

"Yes, we did and he's helping us with solving the smuggling ring case."

"He's in jail, isn't he?"

"Yes." Cody waited until Kyle sat back on the stool before saying, "This is about Nate and the reasons I took the Durango assignment." He coughed, trying to dislodge the lump in his throat. "I actually asked for the assignment when I heard about it."

Kyle's mouth dropped open. "But, I thought you had to come here."

"That's true. I did but not because someone made me. I came because I owed Al."

"I know that."

"But what you don't know is the other reason, the one that made it impossible for me not to take the job. Nate is under investigation for his activities with The Nation First Group, a white supremacist organization. They have been linked to a number of hate crimes. I didn't want you to be involved with him. I don't like what the man stands for."

"Like what?"

"One of their mottos is 'Violence Begets Change.' The group feels violence is the way to get their point across. I've seen more than my share of violence, and it isn't the answer."

"But Nate loves me. He's . . ." Kyle hopped down from the stool. "I've got work to do."

"Kyle," Cody called out, but his son disappeared down the hallway.

The slam of his door attested to the conflict Kyle was going through concerning Nate.

Cody hung his head. *I've messed up again. How do I fix this? I need help, Lord.*

❧

Kyle stared up at the ceiling in his bedroom, his dad's words concerning Nate rolling around in his brain. He wanted to deny what his father had said, but thinking back to some incidents he'd witnessed when he was with Nate, he couldn't. Nate belittling a Hispanic worker at a store, then reporting the man to the manager for something he hadn't really done. Nate openly laughing at a person of a different nationality when he stumbled and fell. More times poured into his mind, filling it with one episode after another until Kyle slapped his hand against his forehead.

"Stop!"

Nate loves me. He cares for me. He wants me to live with him.

A picture of the tears in Serena's eyes as she told him about the guys making fun of her at school took hold and wouldn't leave his thoughts. Whether it was because she was in a wheelchair or because of her heritage, she didn't deserve it.

But Nate loved Mom. He was good to her. She was happy.
I'd be betraying Mom and Nate. I can't just stop caring.

Nothing made any sense. Kyle snatched his iPod from the bedside table and stuck his earplugs into his ears. He turned the music up loud until he could hardly think.

13

Cody drove toward Cesar Álvarez's massive house, a sprawling two-story stone and glass structure that blended in with the terrain surrounding it. The recently painted black fences outlined the pastures with horses and cattle stretching as far as he could see. In the midst of an arid climate lay a lush green landscape.

A low whistle emitted from him. "This ranch is impressive."

Liliana shifted around from staring out the side window of his SUV. "I haven't been here much, but each time I'm stunned by the beauty of *Señor* Álvarez's ranch."

"What's your take on the man?"

"He's done a lot for the town."

"Where's his money come from?"

"He inherited a fair amount and over the years has grown the ranch and businesses he runs."

"What kind of businesses?"

"Banking and oil mostly."

Cody parked in front of Álvarez's house. "Do you think he's doing anything illegal? That he knows what happened on his property?"

"I'll tell you my opinion of the man after you meet him. I want you to form your own impression. Not be influenced by mine."

"Fair enough." He exited his vehicle and approached the ten-foot high entrance doors. The wooden doors were intricately carved and held beveled glass.

A short man with dark hair and eyes opened the door. "Ah, Detective Rodriguez, it's good to see you again." He swung his attention to Cody. "You must be the new Texas Ranger for this area. Come in."

Cody shook *Señor* Álvarez's hand. "Cody Jackson."

"I'll miss Al, but after what happened to him, I can certainly understand him retiring. Let's go into my office." Álvarez gestured toward a hallway that led to a large room with a beautiful view of the mountains and cliffs off in the distance. "Have a seat."

Cody folded his long length onto the brown leather couch while Liliana took the other end of the sofa. Álvarez, dressed in jeans, long sleeve white shirt, and boots, sat opposite them in a wingback chair.

"How can I help you? I want to fully cooperate with you in this investigation. I can't believe a smuggling ring was operating on my land."

"I want to show you some pictures of the men we caught in the cave transporting guns across the border. Let me know if you recognize any of them." Cody rose and passed the photo array across the coffee table to Álvarez then returned to his seat to watch for any kind of reaction in the man's expression as he flipped through the pictures.

When Álvarez finished studying each photo, he lifted his head. "No one looks familiar but I have to confess I don't have much to do with the running of the ranch. I have a capable foreman that I depend on for that. When Alfredo Flores retired a while back, Bart Collins who has been working here for the past six years, the last two assisting Alfredo in his job, took over as foreman."

"We'll need to talk with him and your other hands."

"Done. I'll call down to the barn and inform Bart of your visit."

"What is that land used for in the southwest part of your ranch? I didn't see any cattle out there."

Álvarez looked directly at Cody. "I've been thinking about giving part of that land to the state for a park. The land would be better utilized that way than lying dormant. I gave some of it to Alfredo when he retired. He'd always wanted a small ranch to run some cattle. When he asked to buy it, I gave it to him instead. Too bad his health has interfered with working his ranch. He'd worked for my father and had been with our family for thirty years."

"So you haven't gone out to those canyons recently?" Cody watched for any small change in his facial features.

The only thing was Álvarez chuckled and shook his head. "I wish I had the time to enjoy this ranch like my father did. I've just finished buying ten new banks. Don't have much time right now for anything but that."

"The caverns under the Rio Grande will be blocked off."

"Good. I offered to pay for that when I talked with the governor this morning. We can't have people smuggling guns into Mexico. That only helps the criminals, not the people—my family's people."

Cody stood. "Thank you for sparing us some time. If you'll let Mr. Collins know we're coming down to the barn to talk to him and the hands, we'll leave you to that work."

"Yes." Álvarez walked with them back to the front door. "Just a thought, I've been looking at my maps of the ranch and part of that cave system is on my neighbor's land. You might want to talk with him, too."

"We will. Thanks." Cody stepped out of the house.

Álvarez took Liliana's hand and smiled. "Tell your mama hello for me. I haven't seen her in months. The last time was when she accompanied Samuel and your sister to the Christmas party for the bank."

"I will."

Back in the SUV Liliana asked Cody, "What's your impression of *Señor* Álvarez?"

"Straightforward. When he was looking at the photos, there wasn't any indication he knew any of the men. Not a flicker or twitch. But that doesn't mean he might not be involved. He could be an incredibly gifted liar. I've encountered a few in my career." He slid his glance to Liliana. "It sounded like Álvarez knew your mother."

"They were elementary school sweethearts. But she wouldn't have anything to do with him once she met my father in junior high school. He married later and had one son who died of a rare blood disorder."

"Where's his wife?"

"After their son died, she moved away and lives in Dallas. They're still married, but I don't think they see each other much. I've always felt sad for him. It seemed like the light went out of him after that."

"How long ago?" Cody pulled up to the barn.

"Five years ago. *Señor* Álvarez used to be very involved in his ranch. Now he isn't. He threw his life into making more money."

A tall, rangy man with a brown cowboy hat appeared in the doorway of the barn. As Cody approached the man, he noticed blond, almost white hair stuck out from under the Stetson.

"*Señor* Álvarez said you needed my help." Bart Collins shook both his and Liliana's hand. "Not all the hired hands are here right now. But Slim is rounding up who he can find," he said in a deep, gravelly voice, slurring his words together as if he were talking with a couple of pebbles in his mouth.

"While we're waiting, I'd like you to take a look at these men and tell me if you have seen any of them around town or here." Cody passed the photos to Collins.

He pressed his lips together and flipped through the pictures, shaking his head as he progressed. "Nope. I haven't." He handed the photos back to Cody. "Sorry I couldn't be of any help. Maybe one of the others will recognize one of them."

But half an hour later, Cody and Liliana left with no leads. Not one of the ranch hands knew any of the men in the photo array. Gray hair and bowlegged, Slim paused on the picture of Dave Bond, frowned, then moved on. When Cody asked him about Bond, the older man had shrugged and said, "I thought I might have. In town a couple of weeks ago. Not at the ranch. Hard to tell. It was at a distance."

"That leaves talking with Álvarez's neighbor." Cody turned onto the highway that led to the ranch next to Álvarez's spread.

"I think we need to talk with Alfredo Flores again, too."

"I want to be back for the interview with Bond this afternoon once the lawyers work out the deal for him. The middleman might lead us to who hired Bond."

"I can interview Alfredo later today or tomorrow."

"Sounds like a plan. When I get the tape from Bond, I'm taking it to the lab. I want it processed as quickly as possible. Plus nudge them about the DNA."

Leaving the lunchroom, Kyle bumped into Manny. "Sorry. Wasn't looking where I was going." He'd been too busy rehashing the news his dad had told him the night before.

"It's okay. That happens." Manny started to walk past Kyle.

"I wanted to tell you congratulations on winning the baseball tournament. The team is really doing great. I hear you're one of the main reasons they are."

"Nah. It's a team effort."

"That's not what I'm hearing around school this morning. Your home run in the eighth inning cinched the game for us. I'm gonna have to come out and see your next game."

"You like baseball?"

"Used to play some in Houston. I was on my high school's team last year."

"If you stay around, you should try out for our team."

Kyle grinned. "I just might. I played shortstop."

"I'm going to get my lunch. Want to eat with us? Some of the guys from the team are sitting over there." Manny motioned toward a stone table in the courtyard where six teens sat or stood talking while chowing down on their food.

Kyle began to say no but stopped. He spied Aaron staring at him with a narrow-eyed look. "Sure. Why not." The cold shoulder Aaron and his pals had given him this morning in the hallway and class only reinforced his decision to stay far away from him.

~⊙~

Liliana stood at the two-way mirror and watched the interview with Dave Bond unfolding. Her mind saturated with so many clues and bits of information concerning what was happening in Durango. As though their town had split apart and evil infused every crevice—almost overnight.

The large man, shackled to the table, focused on Cody and said, "Miguel Salazar was the middleman who brokered the deal."

She closed her eyes and released a long sigh. Someone she'd known for years had helped bring this trouble to Durango. They still hadn't found his wife and child. Had he killed his cousin after all? Had Carlos been tied up in the smuggling ring? Or was this something else—tied to Anna and the baby she carried?

She massaged her temples and tried to ease the pounding behind her eyes. But it persisted.

"Where's the recording of *El Jefe?*" Cody asked.

"In a safety deposit box at Durango City Bank."

"We'll take a little trip for you to retrieve it." Cody rose and towered over the man.

"I'll accompany you." Chief Winters strode toward the door to the interview room and opened it.

Liliana headed out into the hall to catch Cody before he left. He hung back while the chief and Bond with Officer Vega made their way into the large room.

"While you're doing that, I'm going to interview Alfredo again. He is Miguel's wife's uncle and may know where she went."

"He could be involved. He's connected to Miguel."

"Yes. What if someone took Miguel's wife and child? We need to consider that, too."

"It's possible, but I think things were heating up in Durango and Miguel decided to get them out of town. Maybe with relatives in Mexico." He started forward. "I'll take the tape to San Antonio. I'll be back as soon as possible. *El Jefe* may be leaving town as we speak."

Liliana went to her desk and grabbed her purse, spying a new report placed on top of a pile of folders. When she picked it up, she noticed it was from the Mexican authorities where Anna had lived. The throbbing beat in her head increased as she read. There was a connection between Carlos and Anna. A couple of her relatives mentioned she was coming to the United States to be with him, the man who was the father of her baby.

She walked toward the back door, trying to put together the three murders a week before. Anna was killed first. Why? Who was the cowboy with the evil eye? Then Ruiz was murdered—tortured first. Why? Did he know something that the killer wanted? Was it Ruiz who brought Anna to the United States? Was Ruiz involved in the gun smuggling ring too? Then there was Carlos. Was he killed because of Anna or the smuggling ring?

Opening the door, she emerged from the police station attached to the Durango Courthouse and came to a stop. Juan, seated on a concrete block behind the building, stared off into space, tears shining in his eyes.

"What's wrong?" Liliana closed the distance to him.

"You don't have to ask Rafael to talk to José. My nephew has skipped town. He's supposed to go before the judge this week. I don't think he's coming back. He's going to be a fugitive."

She took the cinder block next to him and covered his hand on his knee. "I'm so sorry. I've been so busy with the smuggling ring and murder cases I hadn't heard."

"No one knows yet. He called my sister this morning and told her he was okay, but he wasn't coming back to—I can't repeat the words he used to describe Durango. It breaks my heart. I had such hope for José. But he's full of so much anger and doesn't know what to do with it except self-destruct. He wouldn't listen to me."

"He should have. You are a wise man."

Juan swiveled toward her. "You think I am?"

"I wouldn't have said it if I didn't. You've tried to cheer me up when I'm down. I wish I could do it for you."

He smiled, his eyes still shiny. "Just what you do helps me. So where are you off to this time?"

"To interview another person in connection with the smuggling ring."

"Gun smuggling is big business right now."

"And people aren't who you think."

He struggled to his feet. "So true. I'd better get to the courthouse. There's a restroom with plumbing problems. My work never ends."

"It's a big building plus the police station."

Liliana hurried to her car, deciding to empty her thoughts of all case-related information and take a fresh look at Durango as she drove to Alfredo Flores's sister's house. On the surface, everything seemed normal as it had been a month before. But she knew otherwise.

Fifteen minutes later she sat across from Alfredo, his complexion not as pasty as before. His dark eyes held a spark that hadn't been there when she'd interviewed him last week. "You must be feeling better."

"*Sí.* The doctor says it will take time and rest. I can be mighty impatient."

She leaned forward. "I'll tell you a secret. So can I."

His chuckles sprinkled the air, laced with a medicated scent. "I expect it from the young. I'm an old man. I should know better."

"You aren't that old."

"Ah, you must visit more often. But I know you didn't come to pass the time of day with me. You have to be busy with all that's going on."

"Yes and this is why I'm here again. Miguel Salazar has been linked to the smuggling ring."

Alfredo's eyes popped open wider. "Not my niece's husband? He can't be."

"Your niece is one of the reasons I came here. She and her child are gone. Do you have any idea where she would go? We've talked with friends and other relatives. No one knows anything."

A frown carved his facial lines deeper. "No." He shook his head as if he were trying to understand all that was happening. "Unless . . ."

"What?"

"It's probably nothing. Rita has lived here all her life. She has a few distant relatives in Mexico but most of her family is here. The same with her friends. Except there is one that moved away not long after high school. They were close as teens, but I don't know if she's kept up with Pamela Wilson."

"You wouldn't happen to know where Pamela moved to."

"Nope. Sorry. That was seven years ago."

The name vaguely sounded familiar, but Pamela would have been three or four years behind her in school. She knew others, though, who would have known Pamela. Maybe one of them knew where she went, and if she was still living there. "I appreciate anything you can remember." She passed him her card. "If you recall someone else Rita would visit, please let me know."

"Do you think something bad happened to Rita?"

"Miguel was murdered. It's a possibility, but I'm hoping not. I hope we can find her. So far she hasn't used any credit cards. We found her cell phone at the house so it isn't with her."

"It doesn't sound good." He laid his head on the back cushion and closed his eyes. "I'll think about this. Maybe something will come to me. My mind isn't what it used to be."

Liliana picked up the manila envelope with the photo array of the men caught in the cave system. "I have one more question for you."

He opened his eyes, the exhaustion she'd seen last week inching back into his expression. "If it will help Rita, anything."

"Do you know any of these men or have you seen them around, especially at Cesar Álvarez's ranch?"

"Who are they?" Alfredo examined each one, his eyes narrowing when they fell on the last photo.

"Have you seen him?"

He jerked his head up and after a long moment said, "Yes."

❧

The school bus dropped off Kyle at the corner, half a block away from his apartment complex. He'd told Serena he would meet her at the gym in fifteen minutes. He would just have time to get home and change—

"Hey, Jackson, where do you think you're going?" Aaron blocked Kyle's path on the sidewalk.

"Home." He stiffened as two of Aaron's pals stepped into view.

"You ain't meeting your little *girlfriend,* are you?"

The way Aaron said girlfriend curdled Kyle's blood. "It's none of your business."

Aaron's friends moved closer, one on Kyle's left, the other on the right. Kyle glanced over his shoulder to gauge his chances of escaping the way he'd come. Another guy, older and more muscular than the three, came down the sidewalk, his gaze drilling into Kyle as though intent on him. The new teen completed the cage Kyle was trapped in.

"We thought we'd teach you a lesson. No fraternizing with the enemy."

"What enemy?"

"People who don't belong in America."

Ice cold rage gushed to the surface. For a few seconds, he saw himself in Aaron and didn't like it. Hearing Aaron made Kyle regret all the previous slurs he'd said toward others different from him. He curled his hands into fists, preparing himself for what was to come. He wouldn't give up without a fight.

The first blow struck Kyle's back, nearly sending him to his knees.

Liliana came to look over Alfredo's shoulder at the picture of the man he said he knew. He was the wounded one in the tunnel who was still in the hospital. "How do you know him?"

"He came to the ranch a week before I retired and asked for a job. I was training Bart in the office near the barn about ordering feed. Can't remember the man's name, but I didn't hire him."

"Why not?"

"Didn't like the look of him and his references didn't add up. We hired only reliable people. Only the best for *Señor* Álvarez."

"References didn't add up?"

"He didn't count on me knowing most of the big spreads in south Texas and the people who run them."

"So he left and that was the last time you saw him?"

"Well," Alfredo kneaded his nape, "not exactly. About an hour later, I left the office to head to the barn and saw that man talking with Bart. He knew that Bart was taking over the following week so he was hitting him up for a job. I'd introduced them before Bart left to see about the feed delivery."

"That's what Bart said? That he was hitting him up for a job?" If so, why did he lie to them earlier about not knowing any of the men in the pictures?

"No, I just assumed that. Why else would Bart talk to him? I guess he could have told him of other job openings in the area."

"Yeah, you're probably right. Tell me about Bart Collins. What kind of foreman do you think he is?"

"He wasn't my first pick to replace me, but *Señor* Álvarez liked him better than the other candidate. I hear he's doing an adequate job."

"Adequate?"

"Yeah, that's the rumblings I've heard from some of the cowhands that come to visit me occasionally." He grinned. "He's not me they tell me."

"I understand Bart has been working for *Señor* Álvarez for about six years. Where did he work before there?"

"That's easy. He came from the ranch next to Álvarez's. He had been working for that spread for ten years until he had a falling out with the owner. I think that is why *Señor* Álvarez wanted to hire Bart."

"I gather the relationship between the two has never been a warm, fuzzy one."

Alfredo laughed, the deep belly kind. "By all means, no. Rivals for as long as I can remember."

Liliana flicked her hand toward the photo array. "Recognize anyone else?"

"Nope. But if they're new to town, I haven't gotten out much in the past six months to see people."

She took the pictures from Alfredo. "Thanks for the help. I'll let you know if I find Rita."

"I appreciate it." He rested his head again and closed his eyes.

Liliana left to go to the hospital. Roberto Cruz was the only suspect that hadn't been interviewed in depth. He'd been in surgery and had a complication. Earlier he was still in ICU. Maybe she could talk with him now, especially about what he and Bart had discussed.

༺

"Kyle, what happened to you? You're bleeding. Come in." Serena wheeled her chair backwards to give him room to come into her apartment.

So many parts of his body ached. With one eye swollen shut and the other filmy and hurting, he had a hard time maneuvering through the narrow hallway to the living room. The horror on Serena's face made him realize he should have told her over the phone he couldn't work with her today.

In the living room, he finally saw himself in the large oval mirror on the opposite wall. He flinched at the sight of himself. No wonder Serena looked so concerned. His face was a bloody pulp, his shirt torn in several places. What would Dad do? He peered down at himself and started to leave.

"Don't go. You need someone to take care of those cuts. You might need to go to the hospital. A few may need to be stitched." Serena positioned herself between him and the hallway. "What happened?"

"There were a couple of guys who didn't like my choice of friends. I just came to make sure you were okay."

"Sure. Why wouldn't I be?"

"One of them was Aaron Taylor, and he mentioned you."

"He's the one behind this?" She waved her hand at his face.

"Yes."

"Because of me?"

"Not really. I told him to get lost. I wasn't having anything to do with someone like him. He didn't take too kindly to that."

Serena wheeled herself toward the kitchen. "Come on. Let me help you clean up. See if you need to go to a doctor."

Kyle turned too fast and swayed, the room spinning before him. He sank onto a chair nearby.

"We need to call your dad."

❧

Liliana pulled into the parking lot at the hospital when her cell rang. Slowing to a crawl, she answered, "Are you in San Antonio yet?"

"I arrived half an hour ago, and on my way to the lab, I received a call from Kyle. I need your help. I can't get back to Durango for at least three hours."

"What's wrong?" she asked, hearing the tension and frustration in his voice.

"Kyle was beat up by four guys after school. They jumped him not far from the apartment. He insists he can wash himself up and will be fine after he puts some ice on his face. Serena, his friend at the apartment complex, has a different version. She thinks he might need stitches."

"I can take him to the ER if you want."

"Thank you," he said with a long drawn-out breath. "I'll be back as soon as I can get there."

"Don't worry. I'll take care of your son."

"Thanks, Liliana. I don't know what I would have done without you there."

"Called Al."

"He wasn't the first person I thought of."

The implication of his words warmed her. She cared about Ranger Cody Jackson. Too much. She needed to curb these feelings before she got in over her head. "See you later."

She hung up and headed toward the parking lot exit. Her interview with Roberto Cruz would have to wait.

ᏒᏋᏒ

Riding the elevator to the hospital's third floor, Liliana slid a glance toward Kyle, leaning against the wall with his arms crossed, his face bandaged in several places. Two cuts required stitches, and the ER doctor ran some tests to make sure the damage was external only. Other than the teen looked as though he'd gone through a meat grinder, he would be all right with time—at least physically.

Kyle peered at her with his one good eye, the other swollen shut and beginning to turn several shades of black and blue. His face reminded Liliana of her sister. Both victims of a bully.

"Thanks for bringing me here. Serena was really upset. I shouldn't have gone to see her. Just taken care of it myself."

"It was a good thing she was concerned. You needed to have yourself checked out. A couple of those cuts wouldn't have healed well without stitches."

His chest rose as he took in a deep inhalation, then winced. "It hurts more now than earlier."

"Your adrenaline is gone. That's when the pain really starts. But it will get better in time. You should press charges against the ones who did this."

"No!" His jaw set in a stubborn line.

"They ganged up on you."

"I know, but they won't next time. I got in a few good punches. It took four of them to bring me down."

"They will keep doing this to others they don't agree with if they aren't stopped."

The elevator doors swished open, and Kyle stepped out into the hallway. "I'll take care of my own problem." He looked up and down the corridor, then faced her. "What room is the patient in?"

"312. Up until a couple of hours ago he was in ICU so I'm not sure how much I'll get from him right now, but I need to try."

"Dad and you are really putting in a lot of hours in trying to solve the murders."

"Yep, sadly we have to. That can be hard on someone who has just moved to a town. I hope it won't be too long before we wrap up the smuggling ring case and find who killed those people. I know you could use your dad right now. He'll be here soon."

"I'm beginning to see what my dad does for others."

"Yeah, uncovering a smuggling ring is a big deal, but he won't take the credit. He gave our department the credit, but frankly we wouldn't have caught the smugglers if it hadn't been for his gut feeling." Liliana nodded to the county deputy who was helping by guarding the prisoner. "Kyle, I shouldn't be too long."

Liliana pushed into the hospital room. Roberto Cruz lay in bed, his eyes closed. She moved further inside, trying to decide whether to wake him or not when he looked at her. He scowled and averted his head.

"I have a few questions for you. If you cooperate, it will go easier on you. Right now the charges are piling up with help from one of your cohorts."

His gaze flared.

"Who hired you? Who is *El Jefe*?"

Silence.

"Is it Bart Collins?"

His eyes blinked several times. Other than that, there was no reaction to her question. His staunch expression remained in place.

"Why did you talk to Collins at the Álvarez Ranch after the foreman told you he wasn't going to hire you?"

In Spanish he answered, "I was asking for directions. At least he was friendly."

"Directions where?"

He lifted a shoulder in a shrug then winced at the movement.

"You don't remember, but you remember why you talked with Collins? I find that hard to believe."

He stared at a spot above her and to the right. "I asked him if it would be a waste of time to come back when he became foreman."

"What did he tell you."

"Yes. I didn't come back." Stabbing her with a slicing look, he fumbled for his call button and punched it. "I have nothing else to say to you."

"This conversation isn't over with. I'll be back. Is protecting *El Jefe* worth more years in prison?"

Liliana left the hospital room as the nurse approached. "Ready. I'll take you home, Kyle."

"How did the interview go?"

"I have a lead. Cruz didn't say anything, but his body language told me there's more to what he said." Liliana intended to look deeply into Bart Collins's life and finances.

"You don't have to stay with me. I'll be okay. Dad's on the way home." Kyle unlocked his front door and entered his apartment.

Liliana followed him inside. "I told your dad I would wait. I need to talk to him about the case. I'm not babysitting."

Kyle's face colored a faint shade of red. "I know that. I just didn't want you to feel you have to stay."

"It's okay to ask for help."

Kyle pivoted in the middle of the living room. "This isn't any concern of yours."

"Yes, it is. What those boys did was against the law."

"I appreciate you taking me to the ER, but I'm fine now. I have to call Serena and let her know I'm back." He walked toward the hallway to the bedrooms. "Make yourself at home."

While she waited for Cody, she called Chief Winters and told him her suspicions concerning Bart Collins. He would look into the man's background, but they didn't have enough for a warrant for his financial records. A hunch wouldn't work with the judge.

As she hung up, the front door opened and Cody came into the apartment. "Where's Kyle?"

"In his room talking with Serena. He wanted to let her know he's okay."

Cody tossed his keys on the table in the entry hall and strode into the living room. "Is he okay?"

"He's hurting and trying to act like he isn't, but he'll recover with no problems. Cuts and bruises."

"Did he tell you who did this?"

"No, and he knows. He doesn't want to press charges against them."

"We'll see about that."

Liliana touched his arm to halt him. "Give him some time with Serena. She might convince him otherwise. I think he feels that if he did, the problem would be worse, not better."

"Those guys are bullies and need to be stopped."

The word bullies raked down her spine in a chilling wave. Samuel was a bully. Her father had been. "Believe me. I know how you feel about bullies, but I also know from my brother if you force Kyle he'll shut down and not say anything. Serena was upset when I came to get him. She'll say something to him."

Cody opened and closed the hand that didn't hold a tape recorder. "Maybe I should teach him self-defense."

"From what I gathered, Kyle threw some good punches but was just outnumbered." She gestured toward the machine. "Is that the recording cleaned up?"

"Yes, the lab guy did a pretty good job. I think I know who it is, but I want your opinion."

"Okay."

Cody sat on the couch, put the recorder on the coffee table, and punched the button. "Get rid of the cattle. I don't want Carlos snooping around. If you have to, you can poison his whole herd. They won't stay where they should. I'll send Miguel out there to have a talk with his cousin. This arrangement isn't working out."

The distinctive gravelly voice grated against her nerves. "It's Bart Collins. This confirms what I discovered today. Right before he retired, Alfredo saw Collins and Cruz talking together at the ranch. Collins did know one of the guys in the pictures we showed him. When I talked with Cruz at the hospital, I got a reaction out of him, but he wouldn't say anything. I have the chief looking into Collins. This recording should be enough with what we have to get his financial records. We have a judge who is easy to work with."

"Like Miguel, there may not be much of a money trail. But maybe his phone records will help us. Have your chief see if he can get those records too. I got the lab guys to promise to run the DNA and have the results sent to me in the next day or so."

"It looks like you've had the kind of day I have. Long."

"Yeah, but I'm starting to feel like we're making headway for a change."

"Do you think Miguel killed Carlos? That *El Jefe* ordered him to?"

"Maybe. We'll bring Collins in tomorrow."

"I don't see him having the brain power to think of the elaborate plan he had going with the cave system. Maybe he is really a middleman like Miguel was."

Cody shoved to a standing position. "He would know Álvarez's ranch. From what I've heard from the Border Patrol and the Mexican authorities the pipeline had been open for a while. The person receiving the guns could be running it on both sides. Either way we'll figure it out. Put some pressure on our guests in jail tomorrow."

Liliana made her way toward the front door. "With that said, I'm going home and crashing."

Cody captured her hand and tugged her around toward him. "Not without me properly thanking you for helping me with Kyle."

"But you already did." His nearness triggered a reaction in her—the beating of her heart accelerating, her palms dampening.

"No, ma'am. Not nearly enough." He dropped her hand and cupped her face.

When his lips settled over hers, her knees went weak. She clutched his shoulders to keep herself upright. His arms wound around her and flattened her against him. She gave in to the heady sensations he created in her. Her emotional barriers crumbled some more.

Someone clearing his throat behind Cody ended the kiss. He broke away and glanced over his shoulder at the same time Liliana opened her eyes to find Kyle standing a few feet away, all expression wiped from his face.

"See you tomorrow," Liliana murmured and spun around to leave.

Kyle plowed ahead of her. "I'm going to Serena's. She needs to make sure I'm all right. Be back in a while."

Cody's son was out on the second floor landing and down the steps before Liliana moved forward. "Will he be okay?"

Cody watched Kyle stomp away. "I don't know. Which is my usual answer when it comes to my son."

The frustrated pain on his face enticed her to stay and comfort him. She couldn't. If she did, every obstacle she'd erected between herself and a man would vanish. It wouldn't take much with Cody. "Good night."

Out in the cool evening air, she paused at the railing, gripping it. *Remember Papa. Remember Samuel. I don't want to end up like Mama and Elena.* Yet, as she thought of her usual reason not to get serious with a man, she knew Cody wasn't anything like Papa or Samuel. Which scared her even more because her barriers, in place for years, were crumbling.

14

"Dad was kissing her!" Out on Serena's patio, Kyle paced from one end to the other. "How could he? Mom died three months ago."

When Serena didn't say anything, he halted and faced her. He couldn't read her expression, part of it hidden in the shadow where the patio light didn't reach.

"Can you believe that?" he asked her, needing a response from her.

"Didn't you tell me your father and mother were divorced for years?"

"Yes, but . . ." Kyle plopped into a lounge chair and at that level he got a better view of Serena's face, composure and calmness emanating from her. "He hasn't known her long. We've only been here two weeks. How could . . ." His rampage sputtered to a stop. "Say something."

"Is this the first time you've seen your dad with a woman?"

Kyle thought back to all the weekends he spent with his dad. "Yeah. When I stayed with him, the only thing that interfered with our time was an emergency at work. Otherwise, he had things planned for us."

"It sounds like he put his life on hold for you a lot of the time."

"Not all the time. He worked a lot."

"Crime doesn't occur between nine and five, weekdays only."

Kyle stared at her then a chuckle burst forward. "If only it would. It would be so much easier."

Serena laughed. "I don't think criminals want to make it easier. What are you going to do about Aaron and his friends?"

The question she'd asked, that he'd known she would, lingered in the cool air between them, taunting him to answer. "I don't know. Both Dad and Liliana want me to press charges against them. I can't."

"Why not?"

"Because I think all it would do is rile them. Not make a point or put them in their place. There's got to be something to do that will. They need to face what they're doing to others."

"Going before a judge would do that."

"I don't know if it would. I've got to think about this. I don't want them to get away with what they've been doing to me, to you, to others." His own guilt surfaced. He had been so wrong in Houston. How many had he hurt?

"The Lord wants us to turn the other cheek."

"I'm not ready to do that exactly. This beating hurt. But there's got to be something that will make them back off."

"Do unto others what you want them to do unto you."

"Hmm. You might have something there, Serena." In the back of his mind an idea began to bubble and form. "Did you work out today?"

"No, too worried about you."

He rose. "Then we can now. You've got a schedule to hold to. A race next Saturday. No time for slacking." Going behind her wheelchair, he took the handles and headed toward the sliding glass doors.

❧

Cody hung up from talking to a contact in the Border Patrol and giving the man the latest information gathered from his end. Cody suspected a Chihuahua cartel was the recipient of the guns being smuggled across the border. He gave him the names of the people they caught in the cavern for his counterpart to check in Mexico.

The sound of the front door opening directed his attention toward the hallway. Kyle came into the living room. He couldn't gauge his son's mood with his face so messed up. Seeing it sent a flash of anger through him that he fought to contain. But if the ones who were responsible had walked inside behind Kyle, he could have beaten them up without a second thought. Which would not have solved the situation his son was in with the bullies.

"We should talk, Kyle."

"I'm not telling you who did this."

"You don't have to deal with this by yourself. I'm here to help."

"Dad, there are some things a guy has to handle himself."

"But you aren't alone."

"I know. I promise I'll ask for help when I need it. This incident has made me think about some of the things I did in the past. I've done some things I'm not too proud of."

"We all do. It's what we learn from our mistakes that is important."

Kyle prowled the living room, his brows crunched. "Do you like Liliana?"

His son's question threw him off kilter. Where was Kyle going with this? How did he answer him when he was confused about the feelings he had for Liliana? "Yes, she's a good detective."

"That's not what I mean."

"I know. Not sure how to answer you."

"You two were kissing. That must mean something."

"It does. I'm attracted to her. She is an exceptional woman."

"Are you two dating?"

Cody moved further into the room, watching his son pace from the hallway to the window and back. "When have we had time?"

"Do you want to date her?"

For years, Cody had kept that part of his life private. He'd never had women to the house in Houston when Kyle was there nor have a date go on outings with him and his son. "Yes." After admitting it out loud, Cody held his breath, waiting for Kyle's reaction.

"I like her. She tells it like it is."

"Yes, that she does."

"I was just surprised earlier. I'd never seen you with a woman like that except Mom."

"Even though your mom and I were divorced, I cared about her and grieved when she died. I want you to know you can talk to me about her."

"But you don't like Nate."

"No."

"Because he's a bigot?"

Cody nodded. "I've seen how he's tried to mold you into a man like him."

Kyle stopped his prowling and plopped into the chair behind him, his shoulders hunched. "Why did you and Mom divorce?"

"Ultimately, it was because we grew apart. We wanted different things in life. We stopped talking to each other. I'm a cop. I've always wanted to be one. I was one when we married, but she couldn't accept that. She wanted me to change and I couldn't."

"She wanted you to quit the police force?"

"I thought about it and couldn't bring myself to do it because I would be denying a large part of me. It's not easy being a police officer, but it gives me a purpose. I'm helping to make this world a better place. Or, at least I'm trying to. Right now, I'm not so sure."

"How can you say that? Look what you've accomplished since coming to Durango."

"Still have a long way to go. We have a killer or killers out there that need to be caught."

"You'll find them."

Hearing his son say that gave Cody a rush. He might have a chance to repair their relationship. "Your mom was a special lady." He felt that, even though her choice of her second husband hadn't been what he wanted. "She loved you."

"I miss her every day. I still can't believe she's gone. There are some mornings I get up thinking about something I want to tell her. Then she's not there. I get so depressed. Will that ever change?"

"Time will help some. But I suspect there will always be a small part of you that will miss her. She was an important part of your life. Remember I'm here to listen when you need to talk."

Cody released a long breath and rose. "Thanks, Dad. I'm going to bed. Got school tomorrow and I won't miss it."

"You aren't going to do anything crazy?"

"I'm gonna make a statement with my appearance. Those guys can't keep me down. Good night." He shuffled toward the hall.

Hope grew in Cody's heart. For the first time in years he felt as though he'd reached Kyle and they had communicated as a father and son.

❧

"We didn't miss Bart Collins by more than an hour." Liliana entered the police station with Cody following behind her.

"Hopefully he won't get far with a BOLO out on him and his truck. I made sure to alert the Border Patrol in case he decides to cross into Mexico."

Liliana pulled out her bottom desk drawer and dropped her purse into it. "That might not be in his best interest since the last shipment was confiscated and the smuggling ring was caught. Whoever his client is could be unhappy with him."

"ATF is working with the Mexicans. With Roberto Cruz being an illegal alien, they're tracking down where he came from."

The front door to the police station opened, and Mrs. Martinez and Maria came inside. The child's mother saw Liliana and started back toward her. The chief's secretary stepped in her way to ask her what she wanted.

"Did you get her to come down here?" Cody whispered to Liliana.

"She's always told me no. I don't know why she's here, but I intend to find out." She covered the distance to the counter and said, "I'll take care of this, Nancy. Come this way." Liliana pushed open the half door to let Maria and Mrs. Martinez come back to her desk.

Mrs. Martinez panned the large room, her mouth turning down. "Can we talk in private?"

"Sure. We can use the same interview room we did before. Is it all right if Ranger Jackson joins us?" She didn't want to spook the woman and have Mrs. Martinez leave before she told them why she came into the station.

"Yes, but no one else."

Liliana signaled to Cody to follow them.

In the room, he hung back by the door while Liliana sat at the table across from Mrs. Martinez and Maria. Liliana smiled at the young girl. "How are you, Maria?"

The child threw a glance at her mother, who nodded. "Scared."

"Why?"

"I remember."

"Remember what?"

"About the man. He talked funny."

"How?"

"Funny."

Interviewing children was an art form. They told you things in their own time, in their frame of reference. "Can you describe why it was funny sounding to you?"

Maria lifted one shoulder. "I didn't think it was that funny. The lady did. She laughed at him."

"What did it sound like to you?"

"Like a character on one of Papa's shows he watched."

"Which show?"

"*Love Gone to the Dogs.*"

Not familiar with the show, Liliana looked from Cody who shook his head to Mrs. Martinez.

"At the end of the show a bunch of guys are sitting around a bar or at one of their houses, drinking beers and talking about what happened that day." Mrs. Martinez screwed her mouth up in a pinched expression. "They drink one too many beers sometimes."

"I see. Maria, did the man slur his words together?"

"I guess. I was scared. He was angry."

"Do you remember which hand he held the gun in?"

Maria squeezed her eyes closed for a minute. When they popped open again, she said, "Left," the little girl shook her head, "no, I'm not sure."

"That's okay. If you think about it later, let me know."

"Did that help you about the man talking funny?"

"Yes," Liliana shifted her attention to Mrs. Martinez. "If you think of anything else, please let us know."

The woman rose. "Maria, why don't you go with Ranger Jackson out into the main room?"

"But, Mama—"

"I'll be right there. I want to talk to Detective Rodriguez for a second. Okay?"

The child flounced out of the chair and stalked to the door, peering back at her mother before vanishing into the hallway.

Dressed in black as though she were going to a funeral, Mrs. Martinez folded her hands on the table and sat so straight, Liliana could imagine the tension running through the woman's body. "What did you need to talk about?"

"I'll let you know if Maria remembers anything else, but only if you don't say anything to my husband. He's against this, but my daughter's having nightmares over this. Also, we need to meet at my house when my husband is at work. I don't want anyone seeing us come to the police station anymore. I think she needs to have some kind of resolution to this murder so she can start sleeping better. Okay?"

"Agreed."

"Very well. I'll encourage Maria to talk about what happened that day. Unlike my husband, I think she does better when she does. Holding it in doesn't make it go away."

"I know a good children's counselor who might be able to help Maria."

Mrs. Martinez rose, her posture still stiff. "I don't know if my husband will agree to counseling. He thinks time will take care of this. If it doesn't, I'll get that name from you."

Liliana left the interview room behind Maria's mother and trailed her into the main part of the station. The little girl sat in a chair near the counter with Cody in one next to her, talking on his cell.

She jumped up when her mother appeared and rushed toward her. Throwing herself against her mom, Maria encircled her arms around her. "Let's go." Maria took her mother's hand and tugged her toward the front entrance.

She hoped Mrs. Martinez would get help for her daughter. When the child had told her about being scared, Liliana could remember the time when she would hide from her papa and hear him looking for her. Even today, the fear welled up inside her and nearly choked off her breath.

"Is everything all right?" Juan asked as he emptied the trash can at the desk nearby.

Liliana blinked and rotated toward the janitor. "Yes. How about you? And José?"

Juan grinned although his eyes were dull as if he hadn't gotten a good night's sleep for the past several days. "He called my sister last night. I think he'll come back in time for his court appearance."

"Did he tell her where he was?"

"No, but he said he would think about it. He isn't a stupid kid, just impulsive."

"Rafael says the team misses him."

"He's blown that chance for this year. Maybe next year." Juan moved to the next trashcan, dragging his left foot.

She, of all people, knew what worries concerning family could do to a person. Last night she probably didn't get more than a few hours sleep. Juan's physical problems always heightened when he was tired. And yet, he kept at his job until he was finished even if he had to stay longer than his normal workday.

Cody approached her, his eyes lit up. "Got a call from the highway patrol. Bart Collins was apprehended on a back road heading southeast. The officer is bringing him here. He should be here in an hour or so. Plus I talked with my ATF contact and they discovered that Roberto Cruz is the nephew of the head of one of the Chihuahua cartels."

"So he's more than he seems. Interesting. Do you think he's really *El Jefe*?"

"That or the liaison for the cartel. Either way, we're starting to put the people together."

Taking a seat at her desk chair, Liliana glanced around at the mess. She hadn't even had time to straighten up all the paperwork that was piling up. "What do you make of Maria's comment about the man talking like the people on *Love Gone to the Dogs*?"

"Drunk. That would fit in with the crime being one of passion. People who drink do things they wouldn't normally do."

"That's what I was thinking. But that doesn't narrow down our suspect pool much."

Liliana's cell rang. She quickly pulled it out of her pocket, noticing it was her sister's house number. "Hello."

"Daddy is gonna hurt Mama." Joanna sobbed. "Please come before—"

"Who are you talking to?" Samuel shouted in the background.

Then a slapping sound followed by the phone going dead flash-froze Liliana in place for a moment.

❧

"What happened to you?" Rafael Rodriguez stood behind Kyle in the lunch line.

"I had a disagreement with a couple of guys."

Manny joined them. "Do they look as bad as you?"

"Not quite. I had to spread the wealth around."

Rafael frowned. "How many?"

"Four."

Pursing his lips, Manny whistled. "Not exactly a fair fight."

"Don't think that's their style." Kyle grabbed a sandwich and chips and moved toward the cashier.

"Don't tell me. Aaron Taylor and his pals." Rafael pulled out his money to pay for his food.

Kyle nodded.

Manny chuckled. "So that's how Aaron got that cut on his jaw. Good for you. That group needs to be stopped. They're getting bolder, more vocal."

"I totally agree." Kyle headed out into the courtyard and found a table.

Rafael sat next to him, his fist striking his palm. "If you want to pay him back, let me know."

"You'd do that for me?"

Manny and a couple of other guys took a seat at the table. "Yeah."

"Thanks. But I've got an idea of another way to deal with them." Kyle bit into his chicken sandwich. "Tell me how baseball practice is going. Did you get your groove back?"

Manny launched into a discussion about what affects a person's batting.

As Kyle listened, he realized he'd missed playing the game. Next year he would have to go out for the team. He—his thoughts came to halt. He was planning what he would do as a junior at Durango High School.

Across the courtyard, Kyle noticed Aaron and two of his friends, one of them involved in the fight yesterday. Aaron strutted up to a table where two teenage boys sat. They looked like freshmen. One had dark hair and eyes and golden brown skin while the other was pale and blond. Aaron shoved the one of Hispanic descent until he almost fell off the bench. His companion began to rise when both of Aaron's friends crowded him, forcing him to sit back down.

Kyle shot to his feet and rushed toward the confrontation. This had to stop. Now.

As he approached, Aaron glanced his way, his eyes becoming slits. Then he returned his attention to the teen cowering in front of him.

"You don't belong here," Kyle heard Aaron say when he came to a halt a few feet from the bully.

"Why not, Aaron? He has just as much right to be sitting here as you do." Kyle moved in closer, positioning himself next to the dark-haired teen.

Aaron glared at him. "This is none of your business. You made that clear."

Stepping forward, his chest thrust out, Kyle said, "Yes, it is."

His two friends flanked Aaron, hands balled at their sides. "What are you gonna do about it?"

"Stop you."

Aaron straightened his slouching posture. "You and who else?"

"Just me." He didn't care if he got beat up again. *Enough is enough.*

"And me." Manny joined Kyle.

Rafael came up next to them. "Me, too."

Kyle scanned the crowd assembling. Several of the guys stepping forward from a tall, thin teenager with red hair to a short black student added, "Me, too."

Aaron's gaze swept around the group forming to defend the freshman. One of Aaron's friends backed away a couple of feet.

"Bullying won't be tolerated here any longer." Kyle got in Aaron's face. "Do I make myself clear?"

Aaron opened his mouth, but no words came out. Snapping his jaw closed, he whirled and hurried away. One friend followed. The other kept backing away from Aaron and the crowd.

When they were gone, Kyle stuck out his hand to the teen sitting at the table. "I'm Kyle Jackson. If anyone bothers you again, let me know. I meant what I said. Bullying has no place at Durango High School"

At first, a splattering of clapping sounded in the quiet of the courtyard, but before long many joined in. A cheer erupted through the crowd.

❧

Liliana screeched to a halt out in front of Elena's house, jumped from her car, and raced up to the porch, Cody right behind her. Her heart pounded so hard against her chest that she couldn't suck in a decent breath. Key ring clutched in her hand, she frantically searched for her sister's house key. When she found it, she inserted it and opened the front door, then pushed inside.

The sight of Cody withdrawing his weapon jolted her for a second, reinforcing in her mind that she was possibly entering a crime scene. The silence taunted her.

Where is Elena? Joanna?

Motioning to Cody to check the living room, she crept toward the hallway that led to the kitchen. Then she heard it.

A sob. Muted but growing louder as she neared the entrance.

Breath captured in her throat, she swung into the kitchen, her gaze sweeping across the floor. Empty—except for drops of blood on the tiles. Fear bombarded her from all sides. Where were Elena and her children? What did Samuel do?

Another cry sounded from the walk-in pantry.

Liliana hurried to the door and wrenched it open before she lost her nerve. Afraid of what she would find.

Elena lay curled in a fetal position on the floor in the dark, Joanna draped over her mother. Whimpers like a lost, wounded cat's filled the air with sorrows of heartbreak. Liliana flipped on the light switch, then knelt beside her niece and sister.

"Elena? Joanna?"

Her niece lifted her head to reveal an angry red handprint on the side of her face. Tears rolled down her cheeks as though bathing the welt rising on her skin. "He was hurting Mama."

Liliana peeled Joanna from Elena and hugged her. "I'm here, baby." *Please, Lord, let my sister be alive.*

"I had to do it."

"Do what?"

"I had to do it."

"The house is clear," Cody said behind her.

Liliana hadn't even heard him approaching, all her senses trained on her niece. Joanna's wide gaze took in Cody then fixed on Liliana. "Everything is okay. I'll take care of your mama."

Liliana scooted closer to her sister while Cody moved into the pantry. She wanted to hand Joanna to him so she could see to Elena, but Joanna clung to Liliana. Reaching out, she felt for a pulse at the side of her sister's neck.

When Elena's life force beat faintly beneath Liliana's fingertips, she sagged back against the wall taking her niece with her. She looked into Cody's worried gaze. "Call an ambulance and the police."

Even before the words were out of her mouth, Cody had his cell in hand and backed away to notify the necessary people.

"Joanna, look at me."

Her niece, her face buried in the crook of Liliana's arm, tightened her hold on Liliana even more. "He was hurting her. I had to."

"Baby, had to what?"

"Hurt Daddy." Joanna pointed toward the bottom shelf behind her.

Liliana inspected the area and saw the hilt of a knife sticking out from under it. Her earlier fear multiplied tenfold.

❦

When Serena answered the door to her apartment, Kyle stared at her for a long moment before saying, "Ready to go to the gym?"

"What happened?"

"Why do you think anything happened?"

"You have a silly grin on your face."

"I'm glad to see you."

Serena's expression transformed from a concerned look to one of joy. "I'm glad to see you, too."

"Now that we have that established, it's time for your workout. We have less than a week to get you ready for your big race." Kyle stood to the side so Serena could roll her wheelchair out the front door.

A few feet away, she peered back at him. "You still haven't answered me. What happened at school? You're different."

"That's because I did something about Aaron and his buddies today."

She stopped and maneuvered her wheelchair around. "I don't see any more injuries."

"I think I'm insulted. Why would you think there would be more injuries?"

"Aaron and his friends," she held up four fingers, "on one side and you on the other doesn't make for even odds." Her other hand indicated the number one.

"It was a peaceful resolution, at least today. I'll tell you all about lunch if you'll work extra hard today on your exercises. A deal?"

Her laughter made him smile even more. He liked hearing that. He liked her. Durango might not be such a bad place after all.

Cody followed the trail of blood drops from the back door of the house while Liliana calmed Joanna down. The path led across the stone tiles around the pool to the cabana. The door was ajar. Gun in hand, he nudged it open wider. Samuel sat in a chair pressing a red drenched cloth against his upper arm. His face pale, he swiveled around and glared at Cody.

"My wife tried to kill me."

15

"Mama's gonna be okay?" Joanna yanked away from Liliana and plastered herself against her mother.

Liliana tried to pull her niece away from Elena. "Help is on the way. Why don't ya let me take a look at her?"

"No, no. Must protect her."

The frantic ring to Joanna's voice frightened Liliana. She gently pried one of her niece's hands from Elena then moved in closer so she could assess the injuries better.

But Joanna wailed, fighting to get back to her mother. "Gotta help. Gotta help."

Liliana's heart broke into hundreds of pieces—at least it felt that way as she again wedged herself between her niece and her sister. She folded her arms around Joanna and inched her away from Elena. "Baby, I need to help your mama. Okay?"

Joanna clung to Liliana so tightly it cut off her next breath. "Mama can't die."

As sirens in the distance sounded, Liliana managed to loosen her niece's hold enough so she could drag air into her lungs. "See help is coming. Let's get out of here so they'll be able to help your mama." Out of the corner of her eye, she noticed Elena shifting slightly on the floor. That was when she saw the blood oozing from the gash on the side of Elena's temple. Some had pooled on the tiles beneath her sister.

Joanna turned and glimpsed her mother moving. She jerked away from Liliana and nearly fell on her mother if Liliana hadn't stopped her. "Mama!"

"Baby, give her room. We need to stay back some." Her words didn't seem to register with her niece.

Joanna struggled to get closer to Elena. The child's strength grew each second until it took all of Liliana's might to keep the little girl from hurting her own mother unintentionally.

"Mama! Mama!"

Elena's eyes fluttered open. For seconds, no recognition dawned in her gaze.

"Mama!" One last wrench from Joanna, and she flung herself against her mother.

Elena blinked, locked looks with Liliana and whispered, "I'm okay." She tried to lift her arm to touch her daughter, but it slumped back to the floor.

The sirens came closer, the ambulance probably at the end of the long block. Again Liliana tried to drag her niece off Elena, but the child clamped her small hands around her mama and wouldn't let go. Tears flowed down her sister's and niece's cheeks.

"I'm sorry. Sorry, Mama."

"Shh. I'm okay," Elena murmured, then her eyes fluttered closed.

⌘

"Did you hear me? My wife tried to kill me. Look what she did." Samuel lifted his hand briefly from the wound, a slice into his upper arm, then pressed the cloth back down to stem the flow of blood.

"I heard you just fine." After a survey of the cabana, Cody holstered his gun.

"Get me help before I bleed to death."

"You aren't going to do that. Help is on the way."

The blare of sirens grew closer. As much as Cody wanted to check on Liliana, Elena, and Joanna, he wouldn't go anywhere until backup arrived. He didn't trust this man to stay put even though he looked pale. Samuel had lost some blood but not enough to kill him.

"I want to press charges against my wife. She can't get away with this."

Samuel's gravelly words aroused Cody's ire. "The person responsible won't."

Liliana's brother-in-law rolled to the side and reached toward his pocket.

"Don't move."

The man glanced up at him, contempt in his expression. "Why can't I? I haven't done anything wrong. I need to make a call. My cell's in my pocket."

"Best make it to your lawyer then."

"My lawyer! I'm the one hurt!"

"Doesn't mean much to me right now other than it will require a ride to the hospital to get your arm patched up before heading to the police station."

Samuel's eyes rounded then narrowed. "You can't believe a word that woman says."

"Who?"

"My wife."

"She didn't say a word. It's your daughter."

"She's lying, too." Samuel continued to reach toward his pocket.

"Slow and easy."

"You don't know who you're speaking to. I have the mayor on speed dial."

The wail of the sirens came to a stop.

"You might, but that doesn't concern me one bit. You can make your call from the hospital."

～❧～

The past couple of weeks dragged Liliana into a dark abyss. Memories of her childhood swamped her, bringing to the foreground the mind-numbing exhaustion she tried to keep at bay. She couldn't give into it—too many people depended on her to be the strong one.

Liliana's mama scurried into the ER waiting room, a second time in a week. *Will Elena do what she needs to stay safe now?* Liliana would do all she could to make sure she did, and she'd use Joanna and Sammy as a means to convince her sister to press charges against her husband. This time she had photos to show Elena if she wavered. No matter what she wouldn't let Elena go back to that house as long as Samuel was around.

Lord, I can't do it without you. You can make anything possible. Please help Elena and her children.

While Joanna slept on the couch from emotional exhaustion, Liliana rose and went into her mother's open arms. "Mama, next time he'll kill her."

"I did this. I did this." Her mother burst into sobs.

Liliana held her, rubbing her back. "Shh. Samuel did this. We'll make this right. I'll need your help."

Her mama pulled back, wet tracks down her cheeks. "Anything. I've got Sammy at my next door neighbor's. Good thing he was at my house when all this happened. I wish Joanna hadn't been there."

"Joanna saved Elena's life."

"Where is Samuel? The police station?"

"Here."

"Not with Elena?" Fear marked each word from her mama.

"No," Liliana glanced down at her niece to make sure she was still sleeping, "Joanna knifed her dad when he went after Elena. I'm not sure how she managed to drag her mama into the pantry, but she did."

"Samuel didn't come after them?"

"No, Mama. Which surprised me."

Her mother crossed herself. "The Lord was looking out for them."

"Now we've got to help her."

"*Sí. Sí.* We will pray for Elena, then you go make sure *he* can't touch her again." A quiet fierceness entered her mama's voice and bearing—something Liliana had never seen or heard before.

Her mama sat, took hold of Liliana's hands, and bowed her head, murmuring over and over, "Please, dear heavenly Father, take care of my baby. Protect her from the evil that has befallen her."

Listening to her mother's prayer, Liliana thought back to the first time she'd met Samuel. Smooth talking. Full of flattery. Flashy smile. At odd times from the beginning, she'd noticed a calculating glint possessed his eyes whenever he looked at Elena.

Joanna stirred and lifted her head. Her gaze latched onto her grandmother, and she launched herself from the couch into the older woman's arms. "I didn't mean to. I'm sorry." She buried her face into the crook of Grandmama's arm.

"Shh, baby. Everything will be all right. I'll make sure it is." Her mother snagged Liliana's attention, her eyes sparking with ferocity. "You are safe now."

Liliana stroked her niece's back, the trembling beneath her palm fueling her anger. "Your mama will be okay, Joanna. The doctor is fixing her up." Physically her sister would recover, but emotionally the scars ran deep—slashed open as a child and left to fester as an adult.

As Joanna clung tighter to her grandmother, Cody came into the waiting room and paused by the entrance, his gaze seeking Liliana's. She rose and followed him into the hallway. The look on his face unnerved her. A troubled look.

"What's wrong?" she asked, a tic in his jawline jerking.

"Samuel is pressing charges against your sister for attempted murder. The chief is taking his statement right now."

∽≈∾

"Samuel's lying, Chief." Liliana stood in her boss's office early the next morning, shaking with such anger that she crossed her arms over her chest.

"But your sister has confessed she did it."

"She doesn't know what she's saying. Did you get a look at her?" Liliana didn't know what to do. Had Elena defended herself or had Joanna tried to protect her mother? Early this morning at the hospital, she couldn't get a straight answer out of her sister and Joanna had retreated into herself, quiet, not saying much at all.

"That's what I have down here. But it won't take long for him to be out on bail because he was injured, too."

"If Elena did it and I'm not saying she did, she was only defending herself. That's why he is injured. A few cuts on his arm isn't the same as what Elena has gone through with that man." Liliana leaned into the desk, gripping its edge to keep from swaying too much. Her mind spun.

"Go home. Get some sleep."

"I can't do that. What if Samuel gets to Elena?"

"I've got Officer Vega with her at the hospital. She is safe until we can figure it all out. You won't be able to help her if you don't get some sleep. You've had to deal with a lot these past couple of weeks. I don't want to see you back here until you've rested. Understood?"

"What about the smuggling case? Isn't Bart Collins being transported back here from Laredo?" She was afraid if she slept she would not wake for the next two days.

"Ranger Jackson will interview him along with an ATF agent."

"Fine." Then she would go home, take a shower, and go back to the hospital. Her mama needed to be relieved so she could be with Joanna and Sammy. Rest, no matter what the chief said, wouldn't happen until Samuel was behind bars permanently. She headed for the office door.

When she stepped out into the main room, it was empty except for the chief's secretary. Juan shuffled into the area from the back hallway. His gaze captured hers. Support poured from him, silently conveyed. He had started toward her when Cody entered the station. He spied her and came toward her. Exhaustion marked deep lines on his face from his own long hours on the job.

"Wanna talk?" Cody's expression wrapped her in comfort.

It threatened her composure, and there was no way she wanted to break down in the middle of the police station. "Yes . . ." No other words would come out.

At that moment, Officer Hudson escorted Samuel into the main room. Her brother-in-law snared her with a pinpoint look—arrogant, intense, full of malice. One corner of his mouth tilted up in a smirk that went right through her. She fought the tears clogging her throat, the words of anger cramming her mind all at once. Her hands balling at her sides, she took a step toward him.

Cody grasped her arm and halted her forward progress. "Don't give him the satisfaction. Let's talk in the back."

She glanced at his hand on her then back up into his eyes. Again, comfort blanketed her, and for a few seconds she forgot that Samuel was in the room, striding toward the exit. Toward freedom.

Cody tugged on her arm. She turned toward him and allowed him to lead her to the break room in back. The sound of the front door slamming closed reinforced the injustice occurring with Samuel's release as if he was the victim, not Elena.

Seated on the old leather couch in the break room, Liliana couldn't stop the trembling that moved from her hands through her whole body, anger propelling it at an alarming speed. Taking possession of her.

Cody cupped her quivering hands and held them tightly as though his strength could flow into her to calm the fury assailing her from all sides. "I heard what Elena told the chief."

"I was there and couldn't stop it. I tried, but she insisted she knifed Samuel. This was after she talked with Joanna alone. I'd gone to bring some items she wanted from her house. That was a ruse to get me out of the room. When I came back, Joanna wouldn't say anything one way or another about what happened and Elena confessed to hurting Samuel. When I tried to talk to her, she asked me to leave. She started crying and the doctor had to sedate her. I came down here to convince the chief she was protecting Joanna."

"Probably, but her fingerprints were on the knife from when she'd taken it from Joanna."

"Or Elena could have used it earlier. There were other fingerprints that were smeared. Those could be Joanna's when she defended her mother. Why would Joanna say she did it, if she didn't?"

"To protect her mother."

Liliana shook her head. "I was with Joanna in the kitchen. She wasn't lying about that." The tears she'd suppressed welled up and jammed her throat. She swallowed hard but couldn't dislodge them. They filled her eyes and spilled out. "This is all a mess. All I want is for my sister to be safe and happy. She is neither of those." She pulled a hand free and wiped it across her cheeks, but nothing stopped the sorrow she felt deep in her bones.

Cody pulled her against him. "Somehow we'll work this out. Elena is *not* going to suffer any longer at the hands of her husband. It just happened less than twenty-four hours ago, and she isn't thinking straight."

Biting down on her lower lip to keep the sobs inside, Liliana listened to the beat of his heart beneath her ear, his declaration, and wished it was true. "You can't guarantee that. Samuel is wealthy and has power in this town. He can persuade people to his way of thinking. I've seen it. With Elena. With others."

"I've dealt with his kind before. They aren't invincible."

Liliana drew away. "He thrives on lording himself over others, and he has the money to back it up."

Cody cradled her face and looked deep into her eyes. "He won't do anything to Elena. Now that the accusation has been made, he won't draw attention to himself."

"No, he'll bide his time until people forget. He'll find a way to get to Elena. He's a bully. Like the ones your son dealt with. They feed off others' fear. It makes them feel superior. I lived with a father like that. I made a change. Elena didn't. That's all she knows."

The realization chilled Liliana, but she focused on the heat from Cody's palms on her cheeks and it warmed her. In that moment, the emotional connection between them strengthened. This man in a short time had become important to her. He wasn't like other men she'd dated. She'd shared a part of herself she didn't with others—her childhood, and he'd given her a part of himself.

"Every time I try to control my life it seems to backfire."

The rough pads of his thumbs caressed her face. "That's because we can't control our life totally. The only one who is really in control is God. Once we realize that, we can give it over to him and not fight life so much." His mouth quirked up. "I'm not quite there. I'm still learning how to do that."

He tugged her toward him and laid his lips on her forehead, nothing but support in the brief kiss, meant to reassure her she wasn't alone. When he leaned back and seized her full attention, she realized she was falling in love with this Texas Ranger—the feeling both scary and heady at the same time.

The sound of footsteps echoed down the hallway outside the door. Cody's hands slipped away from her face, and she sat back in her chair as Officer Hudson poked his head into the room.

"Bart Collins is here."

"I'll be there. Let him stew in the interview room for a while." As Hudson left, Cody peered back at Liliana. "Ready to talk with Collins?"

"I've been ordered to go home and rest by the chief."

"A good suggestion." His thumb caressed across the damp skin under her eye. "Things will be clearer when you do. I'll let you know what Collins says."

"I appreciate that." She decided not to tell him she wasn't going to stay at her house. Cody would be on the chief's side. She couldn't rest until she made Elena see what she was doing to herself and her family.

He stood and offered her his hand then pulled her to her feet. "I'll call later. Try to get some sleep."

"Sure."

"I know it won't be easy but it'll help you when dealing with your sister. C'mon. I'll walk you to your car."

"No, go on and talk with Collins. We need to settle that case. We still have the murders to solve. I don't think he was behind them."

"Neither do I, especially since I talked to some of the ranch hands and he has an alibi for the first and fourth one. Your sister has an officer outside her room at the hospital, the doctor is keeping her sedated and letting her injuries heal, and your mother has just taken your niece and nephew to Al's place. That's where I've been, getting them to Al's. He'll watch out for them," Cody said as he walked toward the hall.

"Thanks. I know the chief is making sure everything that can be done is being done."

He squeezed her hand then released it and turned toward the interview room. Liliana made her way toward her desk to get her purse. A shower and a clean set of clothes would have to suffice. She would go see Joanna and Sammy then stay with Elena until she could persuade her to tell the truth.

❧

"Are you *El Jefe?*" Cody finally asked as Bart Collins danced around every question he'd asked so far.

"I may be the boss at the ranch, but that's all." The chain rattled as Bart moved his arm. "I'm an innocent man. I want these cuffs off me."

"Not gonna happen. You ran. Why?" Cody wasn't convinced Collins was El Jefe as Dave Bond implied. The man wasn't smart enough to run the whole operation.

"I decided to take a little vacation. There's no law against that."

"I don't need you to confess. I have three guys ready to testify against you. You were part of the gun smuggling ring. We found the gun you used to shoot Ranger Garcia in your house at the ranch. Your prints are on it. We do check out crawl spaces."

Collins flinched and studied his clasped hands. "I don't know how it got there. Nor my prints on it."

"Keep it up. Your digging yourself in deeper. Personally I'm fine with that. You tried to kill a friend of mine. We're really after the boss, but since you don't want to cooperate . . ." Cody rose.

Collins lifted his head. "What kind of deal will you give me if I tell you?"

"A reduced sentence. You'll still do time just not as long as you deserve." The words tasted sour in Cody's mouth, but he wanted the person behind the gun smuggling ring. They knew the weapons and ammunition were going to the Chihuahua cartel, but who brought Roberto Cruz into this country? Who was the brains behind the operation? He was even more convinced it wasn't Collins.

Álvarez's foreman stared at Cody for a long moment. "Okay. You've got a deal. Alfredo Flores."

The man who had helped them, leading to Miguel's part in the whole operation. "Do you have any proof?"

"He keeps records. You'll have to find them. They're at his house somewhere." He shook the chains again. "Now can I get these cuffs off?"

Cody nodded toward Officer Robertson. "Sure. This officer will take them off you after you're back in your cell."

Cody left the interview room and went to the chief's office to tell him the news and coordinate paying Flores a little visit before the man realized Bart Collins had been captured. As Chief Winters was obtaining a search warrant for the former foreman's house, he glanced at the wall clock in the main room and noticed the interrogation with Collins had lasted longer than he thought. Not wanting to disturb Liliana, he'd wait to call her until the chief got the search warrant and they made their move on Flores. Knowing Liliana, she wasn't sleeping, but maybe she was taking time to regroup.

Knowing her. In these past two weeks he had gotten to know her. And care for her. But he was wary of that feeling. He'd known his wife—or at least he'd thought he had. He'd thought she'd known him and accepted what he was—a law enforcement officer whether a highway patrolman or a Texas Ranger. She never did.

Liliana is different.

Yeah, she was. He didn't want to be hurt again, though.

The front door swung open and Mrs. Martinez came into the station. The urgent look on the woman's face alerted Cody. He detoured and headed toward her.

"Is something wrong, Mrs. Martinez?" Cody asked before Officer Hudson said anything.

"Maria remembers more. She woke up this morning screaming. When I went into her bedroom, she sobbed and threw herself at me. When I could calm her down, she told me she dreamed about the man coming to get her. She kept saying she heard a dragging sound coming toward her. She thought she would die, too."

"Where is Maria? I'd like to talk to her."

"I left her at home with my husband. He didn't want me to come here. But I told him this has to end. Our daughter is scared."

"Anything else?"

"Yes, she remembered because the man here was dragging his foot across the floor yesterday."

"Which man?"

"I don't know. She wouldn't say anything else. But if you talk with Maria, please do it at the house. My husband won't let me bring her down here again. He was livid I did yesterday."

"Go home. I'm going to do some checking with the chief then someone, probably me, will come to interview Maria again at your house."

Mrs. Martinez glanced around her. "Please keep this quiet."

"No one outside the officers will know."

After another quick sweep of the station, Mrs. Martinez hurried outside and collided with Sean coming inside with a snack of food from the restaurant across the street. As the young man moved into the station, he still limped slightly, his booted foot scraping against the tile floor. Had Sean been here yesterday when Maria was here? Was that the sound she heard that reminded her of the killer?

Sean took a container from the sack and placed it on the secretary's desk. She smiled at him and also took the chief's breakfast then paid Sean.

Cody cut a path across the room and blocked the man's way. "You often bring breakfast and lunch over here, don't you?"

Sean nodded, his eyebrows slanting down.

"What time did you come yesterday?"

The wrinkles on Sean's forehead deepened. "I—I—dooon't—know." He stared at the floor a minute then murmured, "Noo—n."

"That's the only time yesterday?"

He bobbed his head once, then stepped around Cody and strode toward the exit.

The sound his left foot made coupled with his speech patterns caused Cody to ask, "Sean, where were you Friday two weeks ago around ten in the morning."

Sean peered over his shoulder. "W—work."

When the young man left, Cody got the number of the restaurant from the secretary then called Sean's employer.

❧

Parked around the corner from the car Samuel borrowed at the bank, I watch him watch Liliana's house. She's inside. What's he going to do? I can't let this monster do anything. I fumble behind my seat under some blankets for my rifle and clasp the stock.

A movement out of the corner of my eye catches my attention. Liliana is leaving her place and walking to her car. As she backs out of her driveway, Samuel starts his car and follows her. I drop the rifle back under the covers and crank my engine.

Samuel is up to no good. I need to protect Liliana from that man. Rid the world of him.

❧

Cody hung up from talking to the owner of the restaurant across the street. Sean couldn't be the killer. He had been working when three of the people had been murdered. The only time he hadn't been on the job was when the coyote, Victor Ruiz, was killed. He wasn't the man Maria was describing.

Then who was it? Cody suddenly surveyed the large room. Officer Hudson came out of the chief's office. The secretary was at her desk eating her breakfast. Juan was here earlier. Juan dragged his foot because of his cerebral palsy. He slurred his words. He was always in and out of here and probably was yesterday. He was around a lot, so often he went unnoticed.

Cody surged to his feet and covered the distance to the secretary. "Where is Juan?"

"He left a while ago. Wasn't feeling well. Most probably because of all his worry over his nephew. Do you need him? He's home by now."

"No. Thanks." Cody rushed toward the door, digging his cell out of his front pocket.

Liliana knew Juan well. Before he did anything, he wanted to talk with her. He called her house. No answer. Then he punched in her cell number.

Pick up, Liliana.

❧

"How are Joanna and Sammy?" Liliana asked as she stepped into Al's house.

"Quiet. Too quiet. They're watching TV. Your mama has been holding Sammy while Joanna sits right next to her, sucking her thumb. Joanna may be in front of the TV, but she isn't seeing what's on it."

"I'll talk with her." She headed toward the sound of the television coming from the back room.

Halfway there her cell rang. She stopped and answered it.

"I think the guy we're after is Juan."

"Juan Castillo? He wouldn't hurt anyone. He's kind. He's—it can't be him."

"Where are you? I called you at home."

"Al's. I thought I would talk with Joanna before going to the hospital." She spoke low into the phone so the kids and her mother wouldn't hear.

"Why does that not surprise me?"

"Because you know I can't rest until this is settled one way or another."

"I'm heading to Al's. We need to talk. I still think it's Juan. Mrs. Martinez came into the station. Maria remembered the killer dragged a foot. Juan does."

"So do others in town. Al does."

"I hope I'm wrong. I like Juan."

"Anna was killed during the day. He works during the day—Carlos and Miguel, too. He rarely misses work. He prides himself on his job and his attendance."

"He left this morning. He goes between the police station and the courthouse. Who keeps track of his whereabouts?"

"No one. The job is always done."

"Remember Ruiz's ledger? He put Crip $5000. Crip could mean cripple."

"I don't see Juan having that kind of money."

"I'm ten minutes away. We'll talk then."

༄

What's he doing? Samuel is parking his borrowed car on the shoulder of the highway and climbing out. I turn into a drive overgrown with bushes down the road from Al Garcia's place and grab my rifle.

Samuel disappears over the ridge, heading toward Garcia's house. Is that a gun in his hand? I hurry. I have to stop him before he gets to Liliana and the children. I run through the small grove as fast as I can.

༄

Instead of entering the den, Liliana motioned to Al to come into the kitchen with her. "That was Cody. He thinks Juan Castillo is involved in the murders in Durango based on the description Maria Martinez has slowly been giving us. Talks funny. Drags his foot. I suppose his drooping eyelid could be referred to as an evil eye, but I don't see Juan as a murderer, especially the brutal ways perpetrated on Ruiz and Carlos."

"More than one killer?"

"We think more and more there was only one committing the murders. The four people are linked together. You know Juan. What do you think?"

"Actually, I really don't know him. Yes, I've been around him a lot through the years he's worked at your station, but he's a very private man. There are times I don't even realize he's around. Is he capable of murdering? Anyone is under the right circumstances. You'll need to follow the evidence."

Liliana released a long breath. "I know. I'm going outside to wait for Cody on the porch. I don't want Mama and the kids to overhear us talking about the murders. Enough has happened to my family. I don't want them upset any more than they are. Mama and Juan are friends. My little brother is a friend to Juan's nephew. Besides, I'm hoping Cody is wrong."

"So am I. If your mother says anything, I'll tell her you'll be back in a while."

"Thanks. I still need to talk with Joanna. I won't let Samuel ruin my sister's life."

Liliana stepped outside, shutting the front door behind her. Her thoughts swirled with the conversations she'd had with Juan over the past couple of weeks. Was there anything in them that indicated he was capable of killing a woman with child? That murder started the spree. Anna was carrying Carlos's baby. Why would Juan care?

A sound disturbed her thinking. A prickling along her neck caused her to whirl around. Samuel stood flattened against the wall of the porch between the door and the living room window, his right hand on the handle of a gun stuck in his belt. His left arm hung at his side, bandaged.

"Where are my children? Here?"

"I'm not letting you near them."

"You can't stop me." He pulled his weapon free and pointed it at her. "You have kidnapped my children. You have no right."

"Yes, I do. Someone has to protect them and Elena."

"You just don't get it. This is none of your business. I have tried to make you understand it. You aren't taking any of my hints."

"Like slashing my tires."

"You're lucky it was just your tires." The gun wavered in the air only a foot from Liliana's face. "I'm their father."

Her heart pounded in her chest. "Who abuses his wife and children."

"I haven't laid a hand on them," he said in a shaky voice that rose in volume.

"Yes, you did. You slapped Joanna yesterday. Your hand-print was still on her face when I saw her. What else have you done I don't know about?"

He brandished the gun. "Tell me where they are, or I will call in favors to take care of this problem. I know influential people who won't care you're a police officer."

16

Samuel is waving the gun at Liliana. He deserves to die.

I move closer to get a better shot because Liliana is blocking my view. I don't want to hurt her. She's always been kind to me. Freeing her from Samuel is something I can do for her.

Positioning myself on the side of the stable, I lift the rifle and use a railing to steady it on my shoulder then sight Samuel in my scope. One less bully in this world.

⁂

Liliana straightened, trying to remain calm, but seeing the frantic look in Samuel's eyes underscored what was at stake here. "You won't get away with pulling a gun on me."

"It's your word against mine. I can accuse you of framing me."

The thumping of her heartbeat against her ribcage and thundering through her head drowned out his words. She saw his mouth move, the gun raised higher.

Where is Cody?

The crack of a gunshot reverberated through the air at the same time a bullet went through Samuel's heart. He remained standing for a few seconds then toppled over.

Cody?

Liliana swung around, drawing her gun. The shot came from the stable area, but if it had been Cody, she'd see him. That awareness motivated her to drop down behind the porch post, the only place to partially hide. The door opened behind her.

She glanced over her shoulder and spied Al, a weapon in his hand. "Samuel was killed. Call the station and protect Mama and the children."

"I'll cover you. Get back in here before you're shot."

"I think the shot come from near the stable."

Al protected himself while pointing his rifle out the door toward the area. "Now."

Liliana took a composing breath and dove toward the entrance.

❧

Cody sped toward Al's place. As he passed the deserted property next door to his friend's, he glimpsed a dark green truck pulled off the road, partly hidden in some overgrown bushes. A little further down the highway, a car was parked along the shoulder. Not Samuel's. Juan's? Whose?

The sound of a gunshot reached Cody as he turned into the gravel drive that led to Al's house. He pressed his foot on the accelerator and after he crossed the bridge over the gully, he swerved to the side to block anyone leaving Al's in a vehicle. Then he shoved his door open and hit the ground running, withdrawing his Wilson from its holster.

As he neared the bend in the gravel road that opened up onto the yard just before Al's house and stable, he suddenly remembered where he'd seen a dark green truck like the one parked in the bushes. In the lot behind the police station. Juan?

The blast of another weapon going off spurred him even faster.

⇜⇝

Al released the trigger, the shot deafening Liliana as she threw herself through the opening and landed on the floor in the entry hall. She peered up to find her mother standing in the hallway that led to the den, her eyes wide. The front door slammed shut behind her. With a bum leg, Al hobbled as fast as he could into the living room and posted himself at the window to watch outside.

"What's going on?" Her face pale, her mama wrung her hands together in front of her.

Liliana rose, ignoring the pain emanating from her elbow where she hit the tiles. She hurried to her mother and bent toward her ear. "Samuel was killed on the porch."

"By you?"

"No. By someone else."

"Who?"

"Don't know for sure."

With his gaze trained on the front of his house, Al said, "Keep your grandchildren and yourself in the bathroom near the den. There are no windows. You'll be safe in there."

Still twisting her hands together, her mama nodded. "What are you going to do?"

"Go out the back and hopefully find the person who killed Samuel." Liliana started around her mother.

"Don't. Please." Her eyes shiny, her mama grasped Liliana's arm, her fingers digging into her to keep her from moving.

"It's my job, Mama." From behind her mother, Liliana glimpsed Joanna peeking out of the den. "Take care of Joanna and Sammy." She tugged her arm to her side and started for the kitchen.

Joanna rushed forward. "Don't go, Aunt Liliana. Don't leave me."

"You'll be all right. Grandmama will be with you."

"No." The child latched onto Liliana's leg.

She didn't know what to do. Pausing, Liliana settled her hands on Joanna's shoulders and kissed the top of her head. "I have to do this. I'll be okay, honey. You have to be brave for Sammy."

Her nephew came out of the den rubbing his eyes, fear behind his expression when he saw his sister. "What's wrong?"

"I'll be back and we'll talk, Joanna." Liliana threw a look at her mama who scurried toward them and took her grandchildren.

"Joanna and Sammy, I've got a game we can play in the bathroom . . ." Her voice faded as she escorted the children into the room and shut the door.

Liliana raced for the back door before her niece came after her.

⁂

I keep the stable between me and the house and run toward the slight rise not far from me. I can't be caught. I have too much work ahead of me. Too many bad people who need to be taken care of.

But not Liliana. And if I know her, she will come after the shooter. I don't want to be forced to kill her. I can remember the tired, angry look on her face this morning. Killing Samuel will wipe that expression from her.

As I mount the incline, I see the Texas Ranger coming down the road toward Al's. I don't want to kill him either, but I'll do what I have to in order to get away. To continue what I've started.

⤳

Liliana spotted Juan scrambling up a rise then suddenly flatten himself on the ground. He peeked over the incline, his rifle clutched in his hand. Ducking behind the front of the stable, she withdrew her cell and called Cody. It could be him, and she didn't want him ambushed by Juan.

"Liliana, what's happening? I heard gunshots."

"Get off the road. I think Juan has seen you."

The janitor lifted up and positioned his weapon to shoot. "Now."

Liliana rushed from her protective cover, raising her gun at Juan about a hundred feet away. Before she could pull her trigger, Juan got off a shot, shattering the silence.

Liliana's heart plummeted. "Drop your rifle." She came to a stop sixty feet away, planted herself, and aimed her weapon at Juan. "I'll shoot if I have to. Drop your rifle, Juan."

He swung around, his restrictive movement in his left arm causing him to fumble with his gun.

"Don't even think it."

Is Cody dead? Please, Lord, don't let him be. I beg You.

Juan made eye contact with Liliana and let his rifle fall to the ground.

She moved in fast, desperately needing to see Cody alive. "Get down," she yelled at Juan when she was ten feet from him.

As she came over the rise to inspect the road below, she saw Cody halfway up the small hill. Relief momentarily pulled her focus from Juan. But when he started to roll toward his dropped rifle, she surged the last few feet and kicked it away. Then standing over the man she had considered a friend, she pointed her gun at him.

"Hands behind your back." She removed her cuffs and snapped them on Juan.

Cody crested the incline. The most wonderful sight she'd seen.

༺

Cody sat across from Juan in the interview room while Liliana leaned against the wall with her arms folded across her chest. She didn't know what to think. Relief. Anger. Sadness.

Conflicting emotions bombarded her from different sides. She still had a hard time believing Juan's confession to all five murders. A man she had talked to, cared about for years.

She knew one thing—she couldn't keep fighting the Lord over control of her life. It hadn't worked in the past. Something always came along to mess up her plans. She was going to try to give control to God. It wouldn't be easy, but she needed the peace.

Ramrod straight in his chair, his arms cuffed to the table, Juan raised his chin. "I was doing your job. Cleaning up this town. Victor Ruiz. Miguel Salazar. Samuel Thomas. All evil men."

Cody's eyebrow rose. "You don't think you're evil?"

"I'm dedicated to helping others."

"What was Anna Medina's crime?"

"She played me for a fool. I paid for her to come to this country and marry me. That's like stealing five thousand dollars from me. She had no intention of fulfilling her obligation to me. I'm not going to be used anymore."

Liliana listened to the haughty tone in Juan's voice and couldn't believe the transformation of this man she'd called a friend. She wanted to grasp onto her fury and hold it against him. She couldn't. It took too much of her energy. She was just glad everything was over.

"And Carlos? What did he do?" Cody closed the folder in front of him.

"He took Anna away from me. I deserved better. All my life, people have ignored me and belittled me. Not anymore. They know now I won't take it."

Finally, sadness mantled Liliana's shoulder. "I feel sorry for you. You had much to offer others."

Juan looked at her, his eyes hardening. "No one will mess with me again. Now they know I can take care of myself. I practiced years to learn to shoot like I do. I can—"

"That won't make any difference in prison." Liliana pushed from the wall and grasped the door handle. "You won't have a moment's peace from now on. I never wished that for you. May God forgive you." She left the room, passing Alfredo Flores being escorted into the other interview room.

Chief Winters paused outside that door. "Go home now. There's nothing else to solve here. You've done good. You deserve the rest."

Liliana kept going down the hall. The word *deserve* replayed in her mind, remembering what had driven Juan over the edge. Bullies. This had all boiled down to people exploiting others. Using fear, their position, and their perceived superiority. First, her father with her mama, Elena, and her. Then there was Samuel continuing that legacy with her older sister. Even Kyle had to deal with bullies at school.

Somehow, Liliana arrived at her house fifteen minutes later. Numb to her surroundings. So exhausted she wanted to fall into bed. But she needed to see Elena at the hospital, then rest.

After taking another shower, hoping to revive herself, she gathered up her purse and keys and started for the door. The bell rang. Checking her peephole, she spied Cody on her porch. She let him inside.

"You didn't want to interview Alfredo Flores?" She shut the door.

"Nope. The chief is perfectly capable. We have his records. He isn't going to be able to get out of the charges. Alfredo's sister did tell us that Rita is fine and with a cousin in Santa Fe."

"That's good. I wonder if she knew about what was going on."

"Who? Rita or Alfredo's sister?"

"Both."

"Only time will tell, but from what we've learned no. Alfredo thought a woman's role was to run the house and it looked like Miguel felt the same way. It appears he went to great lengths to keep his wife in the dark."

"Did Juan say—no don't tell me. I'm going to remember Juan the way he was before—he snapped. I don't have any other way to explain what happened."

Cody gestured toward her purse and keys. "Where are you going?"

"To tell Elena what happened to Samuel then speak with Mrs. Martinez. I want Maria to get the help she needs, but hopefully with the murders solved she will have some closure."

"I'll go with you. Drive you."

"You don't have to."

He stepped closer. "Yes, I do. I can't let you go through this without me by your side."

"Aren't you as tired as I am? We've both been working this case almost nonstop."

"I know, but I want to be with you."

"Why?"

"Because I'm falling in love with you and that means I need to be here for you."

She heard what he said but for a few seconds his meaning didn't register on her mind. Then it did. "You care?"

His hands framed her face. His gaze linked with hers. "Yes. I know we need time to get to know each other better, but these past two weeks we've gone through a lot together and I love what I've gotten to know about you. I want us to have a future together. Go out on dates like a normal couple."

"Does that mean you're staying in Durango?"

Cody nodded. "It was actually my son's suggestion. He's going out for the baseball team on Monday. It seems the Durango High School team is in need of a good shortstop since José left and that just happens to be the position Kyle has played."

She wound her arms around Cody. "We can go to their games together."

He settled his mouth over hers and drew her close. Her kiss expressed what she hadn't told him yet—that she was falling in love with him, too. But mostly she trusted him with her heart—something she'd never given to another.

When he pulled back, he laced his fingers through hers and started for the door. "C'mon. I don't want you to tell your sister about Samuel by yourself. I'll be with you. Just like you'll be here for Elena. That's what family is all about."

"She'll need a lot of help."

"I know. But she has you."

"And God. He has been with her the whole time. She's alive and has her two children."

Outside Cody placed his arm along her back and pressed her along his side. "Maybe your friend at Grace House will help Elena deal with what happened to her."

"Jackie's great. If anyone can, she's that person. Not only does she have a counseling degree, but she has gone through what Elena has."

On the porch Liliana paused and faced Cody. The soft expression in his eyes, totally focused on her, nearly undid her. She couldn't remember a man ever looking at her like that—as though she were his world. She cupped his face to memorize every inch of the—love—yes, that was it. Love in his eyes. Her own swelled to the surface.

"I thought Juan had shot you earlier. I never want to experience that again." She stood on tiptoes and kissed him.

He smiled against her lips. "If I have anything to say about it, you won't."

Discussion Questions

1. The theme of *Shattered Silence* is bullying (in various forms in the story). What are some examples of bullying in the book? Have you ever been bullied? If so, how did you handle it? Would you have done anything different in hindsight? What?

2. The hero's son, Kyle Jackson, became the object of bullying at the new school he attended. At his old school in Houston, he was a bully. Seeing aggression from a victim's point view makes him realize the harm he has done before. He refused to let his dad handle the problem by pressing charges against the boys who beat him up. Instead, he took care of the problem. Do you agree with how Kyle dealt with the situation? Would you have done something different? What?

3. Elena, the heroine's sister, was being abused by her husband. She thought if she did everything perfectly that he wouldn't belittle her or hit her. Have you been in an abusive situation? If so, why did you think you were being abused? Some people in an abusive situation think they are the cause of the abuse. How can a family member or friend help change the self-blame of the person who is being abused?

4. Why do people feel they can bully others? As observers, what can we do to stop this? As victims, is there anything we can do? What?

5. Who is your favorite character? Why?

6. Kyle said some unflattering things about people who are different from him. He learned this prejudice from his stepfather and the people he hung out with in Houston. Have you ever faced a person who was prejudiced against you because of race, gender, or some other reason? How did you deal with it?

7. What causes a person to be prejudiced against another? How can we change this as a society?

8. Liliana was angry about how her father abused her mother, her sister, and her. She had a hard time forgiving him for what he did—even though he was dead. She couldn't move on in her life because of her feelings. Do you have trouble forgiving someone, and it affects your life? How can you change that?

9. What is your favorite scene? Why?

10. Cody Jackson wasn't sure how to relate to his son. He usually only saw him every other weekend, and after Kyle's mother died, Cody had full custody of Kyle. He was a full-time father and struggling to do the right thing. What advice would you give Cody about being a parent?

Be sure to visit Margaret Daley online!

www.margaretdaley.com